Safe Haven
George Timmons

MELROSE
BOOKS

Published by

**MELROSE
BOOKS**

An Imprint of Melrose Press Limited
St Thomas Place, Ely
Cambridgeshire
CB7 4GG, UK
www.melrosebooks.com

FIRST EDITION

Copyright © George Timmons 2010

The Author asserts his moral right to
be identified as the author of this work

Cover designed by Jeremy Kay

ISBN: 978-1-907040-04-7

Printed and bound in Great Britain by:
The Good News Press. Ongar, Essex

Peter McFall
May 4th 2010

T HIS BOOK IS DEDICATED to the memory of my mother, Ann Elizabeth Timmons (1900–1999), who died five days before her ninety-ninth birthday, and to Albert Timothy Lowry (1935–1999), my Best Man, who kept the Faith.

Chapter I

HE WASN'T EVEN SURE he could hear the drone of the aeroplanes, but already he had begun to feel the first signs of the fear that later would become terror. He was standing on a chair so that he could look out from the basement window, across the little square garden, to the dark street, which from this vantage point was at eye-level. He stepped down on to the floor. Perhaps they would not come; there were times when they did not. Briefly his fear eased: he felt he could control it. But the drone was really there and the unease began to grow again, and with it the almost irresistible need to find safety. He began to run to the kitchen, but slowed to a walk as he went along the passage. He wanted to be with his mother but didn't want her to feel his panic – not yet, at least. She was at the sink and he stood next to her, his head by her hip. She didn't touch him because her hands were soapy, but she said softly, "What's the matter, Pan-shine?"

This was an expression she usually used when she joked with him or gently teased him, but this evening it was meant to calm him; to make everything seem ordinary. However, the very softness of her voice meant that she knew that he was beginning to be afraid. He pushed his head into her hip, just as he had on the day the flowers came. Again, his fear eased as he remembered the excitement they both had felt when, about a week ago, the postman had knocked.

"It must be a parcel," she had said. And they had rushed upstairs into the lobby and opened the door to be presented with a shoebox done in brown paper and string. She recognised the handwriting.

"It's from them."

They had run down to the living room and opened it up to reveal, only a little bit faded here and there, violets and primroses and daisies and flowers they'd never seen before, all surrounded with leaves and greenery. It was from his brother and sisters, who had been away since the very first day of the War. His mother began to read the letter from Jane, the eldest of them.

"Dear Mam and Jimmy,
We've all been taking flowers into school. Our teacher gives a little prize for first-finds. We thought you would like some too, so..."

She couldn't read any further and, try as she might, she couldn't choke back the tears and her body shook with the big sobs that overwhelmed her. That was when he had pressed himself to her, as he did now. At that time, he had felt confused: why was his mam crying when they had just got such a lovely present? Why was it that just when everything seemed happy it could all turn sad? He remembered his fear again. His mother had dried her hands. She picked him up and even though he thought he was too big for this, he let himself be hugged.

"Let's go to Grandma's," she whispered.

Perhaps she could hear the drone too, because going to Grandma's meant going into the Anderson shelter and giving way completely to the terror, as he had done so often before. The siren sounded. It was not only the shattering manifestations of the air raid that made the shelter such a hateful place: its damp earth floor made it smell mouldy; the condensation from the frightened breathing of too many people ran in rivulets down channels in the corrugated iron; and the great aunts with their incessant praying added to the air of impending catastrophe. And the praying was like a barometer of the danger level. If the bangs and vibrations from the bombs were slight and far away the praying was in monotone, but as they got nearer the level of anxiety in the voices rose. If an explosion was very close and sudden, the old ladies came off their chairs and on to their knees, and the sacred ejaculations of years sprang uncontrollably from their lips.

"Jesus, Mary and St Joseph!"

"God in Heaven, help us, help us!"

"Lord, have mercy on us!"

And that was when he felt himself give way completely to the terror and pressed himself into his mam for her to take it all away and make the raid stop. Yet, he hadn't wanted to communicate this to her for he in turn could feel the helplessness that flooded over her: three of her children miles away and the other consumed with fear. We can't stay here. But they did, though there were worse terrors to come.

The first came unexpectedly. It was not even teatime on a sunny afternoon and all the children who had not been sent away were playing in the street. One group, hot and sticky from skipping with a long rope, had become a band of Red Indians and were tying a giggling girl from another tribe to a stone gatepost, which had become a totem pole. He was sitting on the kerb with Wally, a lad of about four like him, their game of mad horses having subsided into half-hearted pawing at each other. Nobody heard the approaching planes. There was no siren. Suddenly there they were, black against the bright blue sky. Children who were aware of them thought they were 'ours,' until a little girl screamed and pointed. As they all turned to look, they saw the bombs tumbling nose over tail as they do in the first part of their deadly descent. And they seemed so very near because they were bombing the docks, which were at a much lower level than Everton, and so the flight path seemed only just above the roofs of their street. Everyone began to scream and shout. They ran in all directions, mostly towards their own homes. Jimmy ran to his house; up the path, up the steps, and kicked frantically at the weather-board on the front door. Nobody came. He turned and ran out again and down the street to Grandma's to kick her door in the same way, but nobody came. Back up the street. Kick. Kick. Kick. Back down the street, until the noise of the bombs and the scream of the planes became unbearable and then no more until he woke in the arms of his mother in the shelter, when the worst of the raid was over. The others had heard him kicking but each time someone had opened a door, he had disappeared. Uncle

Tommy, hurrying down the street from his early shift, had found him halfway under the privet hedge next door to Grandma's. He had carried him into the shelter and then had gone back out to untie an equally senseless girl from a gatepost.

After this, Jimmy became very sick. His large cot was brought into Grandma's cellar-kitchen and there he stayed for several weeks, next to the pantry into which the cot could be trundled if there was an air raid. Everyone knew that, after the shelter, the safest place to be was the pantry in the basement, because it was situated under several flights of stairs. So, during his illness, when the sirens went, he and Grandma were put in the pantry and the rest of the family ran out to the shelter. He did not feel so afraid in there, even though it was pitch-black: the noise of the bombing was muted and Grandma seemed unperturbed by what was going on outside, perhaps because she was deaf. Though she prayed earnestly, she prayed quietly and calmly, in a way that made him feel safe. He always knew where to find her hand in the dark and sometimes he could even fall asleep, though not on those occasions when he knew his mother was still out at work in the hospital.

Then came cataclysm. Jimmy had heard adults say that you never hear the bomb that gets you, and this he found was true. There was a raid one night when his mother was at work in the hospital. The crumps and shakes had been getting nearer, but they did not seem really threatening. However, suddenly he and his cot and Grandma seemed to be lifted into the air and then rammed down again very hard, to be hit by a deluge of crockery falling from the shelves. For a moment he felt nothing, then began to choke. He screamed but that made it worse because it was followed by an even bigger intake of dust into his lungs. He coughed violently and then was able to shout, "Grandma!"

He could hear no reply over the horrifying rumble, which seemed to be going on forever. Then it stopped suddenly, as though the whole house had settled down again. Momentarily there was a silence, followed by the muffled sound of people shouting. He was overtaken by another bout of coughing, but it was not as bad as before. When it ended, the terror that he felt exploded into another scream of, "Grandma!"

This time she did respond but only with a spate of coughing, followed by a huge gasp of breath and more coughing. By now he was standing in his cot with his hands waving in the blackness as he searched for her, all the time screeching, "Grandma! Grandma!"

At last she seemed to calm down and her hands met his. She too stood up and they clung to each other with the bars of the cot caught between them. She kept saying, "Never mind, son. Grandma's got you. It'll be all right soon."

The dust seemed to have cleared a little and they could breathe more easily. His terror subsided too. After a while Grandma said, "I'll have to sit down," and immediately the fear returned as he felt her relax her hold on him, but she continued, "Let me lift you out, and you can sit on my knee".

Once they were settled he pushed his head into her and she held him tight and rocked gently to and fro. Gradually he relaxed and the warmth of her body made him feel safe. Time passed slowly. Grandma said, "I'll try the door but you'll have to go back in the cot for a minute".

He clung to her, crying, "No, Grandma. No!"

But gently she said, "Now be a brave boy and let me try the door". She put him in the cot and loosened his hands from her. He gripped the cot tightly and shivered, whimpering, "Grandma, Grandma."

She tried to move the door but it would open only a little. He sensed her panic in the dark and howled, "Oh! Grandma!"

She lifted him out of the cot again and sat down with him tightly in her arms saying, "Never mind, never mind. Granddad will come soon. Never mind."

But it was a long time before they heard anything but the muffled cries from next door – and even they ceased after a time.

Jimmy and Grandma began to feel cold. He let her put him down briefly while she got blankets from the cot to wrap around them both. She rocked and rocked. After a while, they could hear noises that sounded like bricks being moved. Next there were voices – indistinct at first and then Uncle Tommy shouting,

"Mam, Mam, are you all right? Jimmy, can you hear me?"

They both shouted, "We're here. We're here!" and Jimmy started to cry and so did Grandma.

Somebody was trying to pull the door open and they could hear someone say, "Shine that torch over here. Get them bloody bricks shifted."

Soon they were both out into the wreck of Grandma's kitchen and lifted bodily over the rubble, into the back kitchen and out of the back door. The dreaded Anderson shelter was the nearest place of safety. It was unscathed, but Jimmy cried all the time he had to stay in it. The raid was over. Jimmy's mother, in a highly nervous state and holding Jimmy in a blanket, ushered every-body into her house.

Once it was light, it became clear that the house next door to Grandma's had taken the full blast and one side of Grandma's house had collapsed in on it. The family there had been shelter-ing in the pantry, just like Jimmy and Grandma. However, the rescuers had got to them too late and they had all suffocated.

The next few days were dreamlike for Jimmy, but his mother did not go to work because she was very worried about him. He did not notice that the house seemed crowded, with Grandma, Granddad, Tommy and the two younger daughters living there. The men spent most of the time salvaging what they could from the bombed house. Granddad also began the search for another house, but Grandma was very ill: she seemed to have swallowed more dust than Jimmy.

Though the cleaning job in the hospital was the first Jimmy's mother had had since before the death of his father, and though they sorely needed the money, it was decided that they could no longer stay in the city: she wanted the family to be together. As soon as Jimmy was well enough to travel, they set off for Shropshire, but they could not stay in the same billet as his brother and sisters, at least not immediately. As soon as she could, however, his mother rented a tiny cottage, and even got a job – incredibly, making bombs. They were to be joined later by Grandma and the daughters.

All seemed well. They began to get used to each other again, and learned new ways of doing things in this very strange situation. The rituals of family life had to be different in this tiny, overcrowded house with no water, no toilet, and only a gas-ring, along with a coal fire, for cooking. Water had to be fetched in a bucket and usually by two children, because it was so heavy. Kindling was gathered from the woods behind the house, just beyond the earth toilet, and usually an expedition was organized for this.

It was on such an occasion that Jimmy discovered that nowhere was completely safe. The children had gone off together with old sacks to collect firewood and any larger logs they could carry to augment the meagre coal supply. It was a jolly occasion: the work was not difficult. Just like the others, he was able to break the branches which had fallen and lay rotting on the floor of the wood, but he was surprised at how full of praise the older ones were for what he achieved. They seemed to make too much fuss of him. After a while, the work seemed to become more onerous and they stopped and went and lay on a patch of grass in a clearing from which there was a view back up the valley.

He heard aeroplanes and felt a mounting panic, while his brother and sisters went on chattering. The noise grew louder: they heard it too and stood up. He ran to Jane. Then they all shouted and pointed to a bomber being chased by a spitfire. They cheered but he ran. Down through the trees he went, through the nettles, with the brambles snagging at him, down to the house, the mounting terror made worse by the crump of explosions. The house was locked. Where to go? Where to go? He pushed on the coalplace door; it was locked. Oh, where to go? He pushed on the washhouse door and it crashed open. He slammed it shut behind him, climbed in behind the mangle and crouched down with his eyes shut tight and his hands over his ears. The suffocating fear he had felt in the pantry shook him and he almost screamed, "Grandma!" But it was only in his head.

After a while, he realized that all was quiet, but he felt so anxious he could not move. Then, gradually, his fear subsided and he began to feel silly. He listened carefully, but could hear nothing except the singing of the birds and that made him feel calm enough to come out into the yard, so that when the others at last arrived he was sitting on the front wall. They were laughing and talking excitedly about what to them was simply an incident, even if an extraordinary one, the hunted plane having dropped its bombs. One of ours had got one of theirs.

"What was the matter with you?" they said.

"It was not an air raid, silly, it was only a dogfight," said his brother, Alan.

"Were you scared? We weren't, were we?" said Alice, the younger of his sisters.

"You are funny," and so on.

They didn't seem to understand.

For the rest of the War, he never heard an enemy plane. He got used to the sound of ours, so that later he hardly noticed them, unless they were Lockheed Lightnings, whose twin bodies were futuristic, and he drew pictures of them in school. At the time of the doodlebugs, other evacuees came from London and a little four-year-old among them spent the whole of the first week there making a dug-out; it was a shallow trench covered by a sheet of rusty corrugated iron. Everyone but Jimmy found this amusing, but by then he had discovered other things to fear.

Chapter II

Living in the countryside during the Second World War, away from the danger, could be idyllic for a child. The summers were good and long afternoons could be spent in and by the river. Jimmy learned to swim, in a leisurely way, by easy stages. For a long time he swam with one foot touching the bottom and nobody knew or cared. He spent hours trying to catch minnows, with a bent pin for a hook and bread and spit for bait. In one particular pool in a backwater he watched the minnows eat their way through a very large lump of this dough without ever once touching the point of the pin. He learned to catch them with his hands instead: it was merely a question of manoeuvring them into the shallow water. Jack-sharps, or sticklebacks as they were known elsewhere, presented a different set of problems, because they lay tantalisingly still until the very split second before you moved to grab them, then they flashed away as fast as flies. But he found a way to catch them too without a net. When you saw one in an accessible place on the bottom, you slowly put your jam jar about six inches to its front. Boldly, the fish would remain where it was. Very, very gently you brought your other hand up behind it. Just before you touched its tail, it would dart away and into the jar, which you snatched up out of the water with the fish still spinning, confused, round the bottom.

He spent much of his time simply wandering about. In this part of the valley there were few cultivated fields, though there was some pasture: you could go almost anywhere you pleased. He was not unhappy by himself, and there was so much to look at and so many places to investigate, and not only woods and overgrown paths; there were also old buildings which, hidden away, took you by surprise. There had been brick-kilns, potteries, and even blast furnaces all about. There ought to have been an industrial city here, but by the 1940s many old places were disappearing under a tangle of vegetation. He discovered a patch of wild strawberries by the railway line, and raspberries by the river, in what must have been a garden in the distant past. There were hazelnuts in the overgrown coppie (as the local people called the woods behind his house), and blackberries everywhere. Yet the War was a pervading influence.

Rationing did not make life any easier because, although everyone had enough to eat and a balanced diet, it caused problems. If the oven, which was heated by the coal fire, was too hot or not hot enough, the meat, which was in limited supply, could be spoilt. The butcher called twice a week; at the weekend when he usually brought a joint, and mid-week when he might bring sausages or perhaps liver. One Wednesday afternoon, when they were all at work or school, the butcher left his package on the shelf behind the mangle in the washhouse. When Jimmy and Alice were nearly home they saw a dog coming out of their front fold with something in its mouth, so they ran after it and discovered to their chagrin that it was a string of sausages. They chased him and managed to catch him, but getting the sausages off him was not easy. They wondered afterwards if it was worth it; not only were they partly chewed, they were also full of grit from the cinder-track that served as a road. Nevertheless, they washed them and cut off the worst bits and then waited in some trepidation for Mum (which his sisters now insisted on calling her) to come home from work. She was not pleased, but even so she cooked the sausages and nobody refused to eat them.

Milk was another problem. Half the family was registered with one milkman and the other with another because originally they had been in separate billets. Nobody could explain why this situation could not be changed but it meant that someone had to go to Ironbridge every day to fetch three pints of milk. More often than not, in the arguments over who should go, Jimmy lost out and had to make the trek to the Hygienic Dairy and back. This was not as awful as it seems because you could dawdle, or sometimes you could borrow a bike, and there were always things to do

on the way. One hot summer afternoon he sat by the river thinking about how, later on, he could join all the other kids swimming down by the sand hole, when it struck him that there was
nothing to stop him from swimming there and then. He did hesi-
tate because nobody swam in that part of the river, it being difficult to get in, and he had no bathing costume. But it was shallow,
and so, although it ran fairly fast, in he went naked to find the
experience much more pleasurable than was usual as the water
washed around areas unaccustomed to such sensations. And, as
he felt lighter, he thought he must be swimming faster. He swam
only across the river and back because the weeds dragged at him
and he thought he might become entangled in their long tendrils.

Alongside the road were huge lumps of foundry ash,
which seemed to be made of egg-sized pellets of black glass
all compressed together, and which he supposed had been put
there to stop cars from falling into the river. You could run along
their tops, which were flat, and easily jump from one to the next.
He felt very confident doing this until, one day, he slipped, and
though none of the three bottles smashed, the top came off one
of them and something like a third of the milk was lost before he
could put the bottle upright in the bag. He was worried by this
because his mother would find out he had been running along
the blocks. He met another boy, who asked him why he looked so
glum and who suggested filling the bottle with water. There was
a tap on the way home.

Unfortunately, that was the evening his aunt decided to have
a drink of milk instead of tea. No one believed him when he told
the truth: they were all convinced he had been drinking the milk
on the way home. The thought of being blamed for something
he had not done was more than merely irksome, because there
seemed no way out of the cage he felt trapped in. Adults were all-
powerful, children helpless. But there was more to it than this: he
would do almost anything to avoid blame. He still had an image
of himself as good, someone who did not steal, or tell lies; someone who was not rude, who was never disobedient. To be disobedient was dangerous.

He had been warned several times that if he went out to play in the evening he should be home by nine o'clock, which seems late, but in the era of double summertime it was still light even at eleven o'clock. It was very difficult for a seven-year-old to realize time was passing, especially if engaged in an absorbing activity such as constructing a complex town in the sand hole with houses, factories, roads, bridges and canals. Nobody else's parents seemed to be bothered. He called to a man going by on the road and was aghast to discover it was ten past nine. He took off up the road, feeling the old fear gripping at him again, even though he was running home to his mother, his usual source of protection. He thought about what she might do: he knew she could smack hard, because it had happened before, if only in the form of one slap. He had also seen her very angry with his elder brother. He imagined her slapping his legs over and over again, or maybe hitting him with a stick, though there was no real reason why he should think this. He felt his flesh creep, he was so afraid of pain. He was already crying with apprehension when he got in.

"What did I tell you?"

"Mam, I forgot the time," he said with a whimper.

"I said, what did I tell you?"

"To be in by nine o'clock."

"And what time is it now?"

This was almost as bad as being hit. The apprehension mounted. You did not know what was coming next.

"What time is it, I said."

"I don't know."

"Yes, you do. It's twenty past nine... and what did I say?"

She advanced across the room, looking very annoyed. What would she do? Before he could answer the last question she pounced, took him by the shoulder and slapped him hard on each leg. He tried to pull away and began to cry loudly.

"Mam, Mam, I'm sorry, I won't do it again."

She almost threw him towards the stairs and shouted, "Get to bed. Go on and quick."

And as he set off up the narrow staircase, she hit him again. He scrambled up to the back room and, crying and sobbing, he got undressed. He saw that his hands were grubby, especially his bitten fingernails, as they contrasted with his clean pyjamas. Should he ask if he could go back down to wash his hands and face? That might risk another smack. But in the morning, if she saw his hands were dirty, he might still be in trouble. His scabby knees were also filthy. He put his hands under the bedclothes and turned towards the wall. When he had stopped crying and sniffing he thought about how strange it was that one minute you could be happily engaged in doing something you liked, and the next you could be plunged into disaster. He consoled himself that it would not last and happy times would come back. He went to sleep. Later his mother woke him to give him a jam butty and a cup of cocoa.

Being caught out seemed to be the real problem, and it was worse if you had no excuses; if there were no way to deflect your mother, or your teacher, or some other accusing adult, from knowing the truth, from discovering that you had done something you shouldn't have, or not done something you should. From this kind of predicament he learned something about himself.

He had a new mac. He was walking home from school, but this time on the other side of the river away from the blocks. He came to the Black Swan, where a wall ran alongside the road. He had been told not to climb this wall to run along the top, because it had rounded coping stones and you could easily slip. Also, it got higher as it went from the pub towards the level crossing, though this did not worry him because at the far end you could climb down the railway fence. Despite the warnings he could not resist the temptation, but what he did not notice as he climbed up was that the part of the wall by the pub had been newly whitewashed and it was only when he was on the top and looked down to see where his feet were that he realized that his new coat was covered in white. His unthinking attempts to brush it off with his hands only smeared it more: it was still wet.

He got off the wall and tried rubbing it with grass but it got worse. He began to search for excuses, for explanations that he might give to hide his disobedience. There weren't any, and as his mother also came this way home from work, she would know that the wall had been whitewashed. There was no way out. He was responsible for what had happened. A strange sensation passed over him. He did not know at first what it was or what it meant. It was only after it had happened on other occasions that he began to realize it came when he felt separate from everything, from everybody else. He was Jimmy and nobody else was Jimmy and he was responsible for what Jimmy did and there was no way out. Nobody else and nothing else could be blamed for what he did. Though it was a frightening, or at least a very disturbing, sensation, it was also thrilling and he felt it all over his body. Sometimes he tried to make it come on, but couldn't. When it did come, it always took him by surprise. It was worrying: he felt different from everybody else, or rather he felt distinct, and that distinctness exposed him, made the real him apparent to everybody, when often he wanted to be submerged in the mass, to be the same as everybody else, and so hidden, and not marked out as responsible.

He already had some idea of what was meant by sin. His family all went to church and he could remember being taught his prayers by his mother back in the days of the bombs. She would say a phrase and he would repeat it. He liked that and when she tried to persuade him to say the Our Father by himself, he had not wanted to because he thought the repeating game was much more fun. He could also remember his early attempts to think about God, but he became so engrossed in the misnomer, Holy Ghost, that his picture was of an amorphous mass with a kind of rounded head and deep-set black eyes, all rather threatening. He knew who Jesus was and he liked it when his teacher read to them from the Gospels in school (*Peter Pan* was even better). He knew he had a soul and thought it was oval-shaped and fitted into his body somewhere between his throat and the tops of his legs. It was a silvery colour: it could become dented and dull but he never imagined it black. And yet this was all theoretical and had not much to do with the real him. Even when he made his first confession, the conditions for which he could repeat from the catechism (confession, contrition, and satisfaction), he did not really connect it with himself. Indeed, as he walked to school (part of which was used as a church) on that day, he told his sister, Alice, that though he knew exactly what to do and what to say in the confessional, he did not know what to confess; nobody had told him. She reminded him that he had told lies and had been disobedient, and that was what she always said, so he did the same. He added saying bad words and doing rude things but he did not tell her that. He did know, however, when he had done something wrong – but only in a vague way, despite his ability to define mortal sin and venial sin according to the catechism. All this was because it was really adults who defined sin: parents, teachers and priests said telling lies was a sin; disobedience and saying swear words were sins; missing Mass was a terrible sin. He knew you had to try to avoid these. Yet there were times when his behaviour was reprehensible and he was only vaguely aware of why until he was told.

A family that lived nearby was very poor, perhaps because there were so many children. One of them was a skinny little boy named Arnold who was fairly close to Jimmy in age but looked much younger. Sometimes they played together, but Arnold would run home at even the slightest hint of danger: he seemed to be afraid of everything. Despite his own fears and apprehensions, Jimmy showed no sympathy for this and he usually felt annoyed when Arnold cried for very little reason, or ran off because there was a minor threat. Sometimes Jimmy would deliberately try to frighten him by saying suddenly, "Here's Carter's dog!" or "Look out, Mr Robert's cows are coming!" (A daily event that he knew Arnold worried about). One Saturday, Jimmy was in the fold in front of the cottage when he saw Arnold coming down through the village, so he hid behind the gatepost until the little boy drew alongside, then he jumped out shouting, "Weeaar!" The effect was electric: Arnold leaped into the air with a scream that surprised even Jimmy, and ran off home in tears.

However, what Jimmy did not know was that his mother was watching through the front bedroom window. She threw it open and called Jimmy into the house. Only then did Jimmy sense that he had done something wrong.

"Why did you frighten little Arnold like that?"

There was no answer because Jimmy did not really know why, and now he felt afraid. Would she smack him again as when he was late home?

"C'mon, tell me. I want to know."

"I don't know… it was only a joke."

"Not a very nice joke, was it? Look how frightened he was. Do you like to be frightened like that?"

"No," he said, with tears beginning to well up in his eyes.

"No, and you soon come running to me if something frightens you, don't you?"

"Yes," he said, now beginning to cry.

"And what should I say next time you come… 'Go away, bully'?"

"Mam, I'm not a bully," he said, crying copiously now.

"Well, that's not how it looked to me."

The thought that anyone should think he was a bully he found very alarming. He considered himself a good boy and he knew that nobody liked Fatty Robson, who really was a bully. He did not want anyone to think he was like him! But he had been called a bully before and that was an occasion too painful to think about.

"Now stop crying and go out to play and if Arnold comes out you're to tell him you're sorry. Then I shall think better of you. And don't do that again – think of how you'd feel."

When he met Arnold again, he could not say he was sorry. That would have made him feel silly, so he gave him a rusty ball-bearing that he had found. After that he avoided him.

What was odd was that he could be quite moved by stories: he cried when he saw 'Lassie, Come Home' at the cinema in Ironbridge. Also, one day when he was on the stretch of the river where he had had his illicit swim, he heard a group of lads coming towards him shouting excitedly to each other and he hid in the bushes. Suddenly he realized that they were throwing stones at a duck, which must have had something wrong with it because it did not fly away. It must also have been confused because it did not make for safety on the other side of the river but persisted in trying to get away from the boys by swimming downstream. He

felt very sorry for the poor bird but was afraid that if he intervened they might throw stones at him. All that he could do was
to hope that the bird would escape a little further on where it
became difficult to get down to the river because the banks were
so steep and covered in brush and briars. Unfortunately, one
stone hit the duck square on the head and it fluttered to a stop, to
the triumphant shouts of the lads. Jimmy crept away.

It was not only animals he felt sorry for. It must have been
during Lent that he became acquainted with the story of the final
days of the life of Jesus, and it made him feel unhappy. The Passion
seemed to go on and on for such a long time and each thing that
happened to Jesus was worse than the last. As if scourging was
not bad enough, they stuck a crown of thorns on his head. Then
they not only kept hitting him, but they also made him carry a
heavy cross, and if he fell over they beat him again. He wanted to
shout, "Stop. Leave him alone!" He wondered why nobody tried
to defend Jesus, and he thought he had some inkling of how Jesus
must have felt.

Before the family had come together in the little cottage, he
had attended a different school from his brother and sisters. One
day a small boy was pestering him by pulling at him and jumping and swinging on him. Telling this child to stop had no effect
and finally he got angry and hit him. The little boy then howled
loudly. A group of girls had seen this happen: they called him a
bully and began to dance around him, chanting, not letting him
escape. The other boy took advantage of this and started to kick
him. When he retaliated the girls began to beat him.

It was a warm afternoon and the teachers must have allowed
an extended lunchtime and so the hell seemed endless. He tried
crying piteously, to no avail; he raged and threw his fists in all
directions, with the same effect; he lay on the playground and
curled up but they continued to beat him. They seemed to like it
best when he tried to run away. Then they could chase after him,
shouting and screaming, cut him off, surround him and beat him
again. And no one came to help; no one seemed to care. When,
at long last, he got to his class, dirty, red, still wet with tears and
still shivering from the prolonged anguish, the teacher told him

not to be silly and to go and wash his face. So he felt very sorry for Jesus, whose knees he noticed from the Stations of the Cross, in the church at Madeley where they sometimes went to Mass, were cut and bruised just like his always were from climbing walls and falling out of trees.

This was also the time when he learned about Hell, and then sin began to matter, because it meant pain and terror that went on and on. He learned that God sent you to Hell if you committed a mortal sin and then died – because you were to blame, you were responsible. God always knew. You could not tell him lies: he could see right through you. You always got what you deserved. Furthermore, in his mind, this was all linked in some way with his growing fear of death. He had only vague notions of how this in its turn tied in with disease, but the very vagueness allowed for greater unease, even deep anguish. His mother's fairly frequent telling to anyone who would listen of the events leading up to his father's death helped to create a feeling of impending misfortune or even doom. This was heightened by her sense of the dramatic, and those statements that were meant to convey the unexpect- edness of his death ("I never for one minute thought he would die") increased the apprehension that no one was ever safe. It was only later that he learned that his father had died from a probably avoidable peritonitis, but what he did know was that his death had been sudden and painful. He also learned that he'd had another elder brother who had died from diphtheria at the age of seven. Again, he knew the history of the illness and the effects it had had on everyone, and though he himself had been inoculated against the disease and his brother never had, any pain in the throat and he was convinced he was going to die. In fact, any pain, no matter how small, could build up into a panic: his whole family knew countless stories of friends or acquaint- ances who came home, sat down, said, "Oh! Mam, I've got such a funny pain in my wherever," and died within days, or hours, or even minutes! Yet all this took place within a loving, caring family in which relationships were secure, despite the turmoil of War. Nothing felt safer than sitting around on a cold night listen- ing to the wireless or talking, drinking cocoa and making toast with a fork in front of a glowing fire. Even outbursts from Aunt Mary as she mended her soldering gloves for the twentieth time – "If this bloody government want me to solder ammunition boxes, why can't they give me decent gloves instead of this bloody stupid ribbon to patch the soddin' patches!" – could not spoil the sense of security he felt. Moreover, one of the effects of the shortages caused by the War was that families had to work together in order to provide for their needs. He was happy cutting strips of old cloth with his sister for his mother to make a rag rug to go in front of the fire. Everybody had a say in the design, not only in the decisions about which colours to use where and in what shapes but also in whether his mother had made the shapes accurately. Bottling fruit, of which none of the adults had any previous experience (though they had made jam), became a cooperative affair, as did making shades for the gas-light from jam jars. Did you put the cold water in the bottom of the jar and the hot water in the bowl you stood it in, or vice versa? No one was ever sure, but they always managed to make the shade – to everyone's surprise.

He still needed his mother very much. He was young enough to hold her hand when they walked to Mass. If he woke in the night from a bad dream and went to her, he was still small enough for her to say, "Never mind then, come in with me. It'll soon be all right." Outside though, she could not be with him and there were times when he was engulfed with the fear that he had felt in the pantry – as when the big boys from the other end of the village locked him in the toilet behind the Methodist Church. They ran away and left him and no matter how much he shouted, "Let me out," no one seemed to hear. In desperation, he kicked the door violently and screamed and yelled but to no avail. By the time the church warden came along quite by chance, Jimmy was reduced to quiet sobbing. He received no sympathy, nor even a chance to explain how he got there. He was clipped around the ear and told to clear off and not come back if he knew what was good for him. He avoided going by the Methodist Church after that. He also disliked walking to school by himself because he had to walk past some houses where very tough kids lived.

They never did attack him, in fact they barely noticed him, but he always expected them to. Even so, despite the anxieties, living in the country was mostly a time of happiness.

When the younger of his mother's two sisters had been with them for about a year she married a local man who was not in the forces because he was hard of hearing. He worked on a farm nearby. Jimmy got to know him very well and liked nothing better than to go with Fred up to Hay Farm. This was usually when he was using machinery, such as the heavy roller, on which Jimmy could ride: he would sit happily on the sturdy frame, with his legs dangling as Fred, walking behind, controlled the three horses by means of the long reins. Up and down, up and down they would go, but he was never bored and at lunchtime he would sit with the men in the stable eating the butties his mother had prepared for him and drinking cold tea from a lemonade bottle, just like Uncle Fred. The other farmhands seemed to talk mostly about what they had heard on the wireless and read in the *Daily Herald*, the latter being their chief source of information about horses. Despite the fact that only a very limited number of race meetings were licensed during the War, the men studied form sedulously. Their bets, however, were paltry.

One lunchtime, when Alan was at the farm too, the farmhands got very excited about a rank outsider (thirty to one) that had caught their attention because its name seemed significant: it was called Smokey Joe. About a week before, one of the men, Joe Partridge, had left the farm because he reckoned he could earn more money on the railway, but that morning he had come back, because, he said, he had spent all his time as a GWR worker burning off the grass on every embankment and every cutting from Bridgenorth to Shrewsbury. He could stand the smoke no more. Hence the excitement over Smokey Joe. Everyone was going to bet on it, so Alan and Jimmy did too. By scraping together what they could and begging a few coppers from Fred, they were able to put on sixpence each way. Alan wrote the bet and signed it 'Tom,' because it had to be placed illegally with the bookie's runner who operated out of the nearest pub. So, at seven, Jimmy became a gambler. Needless to say, he and Alan lost their money:

Smokey Joe disappeared without trace.

Jimmy did not mind; he was so glad not to be at school but to be on the farm with Fred, and especially he loved being with the horses. More often than not, Fred had two big horses, Dragon and Boxer, with a mare, Jolly, between the two. They all three were very gentle, so he rarely had to be firm with them. The only time they were difficult was towards the end of each day when they sensed that work was nearly over. Then they would start to rush as though they believed that the faster they went the sooner they would finish. Fred had difficulty turning them at either end of the field but he would heave on the reins and curse and they would comply. Once work ended they became docile again and Fred would lift Jimmy on to the back of one or other of them to ride the short distance to the stable. The first time this happened Jimmy was too near Dragon's neck and when the horse bent his head to sample some of the luscious grass on the side of the farm track, Jimmy could feel himself sliding towards the animal's ears. It was quite frightening because he was an awful long way off the ground and he did not know how Dragon would react to having a child on top of his head all of a sudden. But, in his wisdom, the horse, sensing the child's apprehension, lifted his head and Jimmy wriggled further back. Jimmy sometimes wondered why his uncle never put him on Boxer's back; he seemed as gentle as the others. But one evening he discovered that this horse had a sense of humour.

It was getting towards the autumn and the apples were begin-ning to fall from some of the trees in the extensive orchard. The various children who, like Jimmy, came to visit the farm from time to time had been told that they could pick up the windfalls, but they were not to touch what was on the trees. Jimmy decided he did not want to nibble round the wormholes any more, so he had taken apples off several of his favourite trees. With his shirt stuffed, he sneaked through the yard and went to that part of the road on the furthest edge of the farm where he was hidden by fairly high walls on either side. What he did not know was that Boxer was on the other side of the wall. Jimmy was completely unaware of him until he put his head close to Jimmy's ear and neighed very loudly. The lad sprang into the air like a jack-in-the box, scattering apples all over the road. Fortunately he returned to earth on his feet and whirled around to see the horse looking at him quizzically. (Jimmy later swore the animal was smiling.) His immediate sensation was terror. Then he felt angry: Boxer had made a fool of him.

"You bloody stupid hoss!" he yelled, but the horse merely snorted, turned and cantered across the field, the metal of his shoes glinting silver as his huge hooves thundered over the ground. He turned again, neighed and jerked his head up and down. Jimmy gathered up his ill-gotten gains and slunk off home.

He was to see Boxer's sense of fun again during the following winter, but this time it proved infectious. There had been a fortnight of continuous frost and the ground was so hard the horses could not work it. There was not even any carting for them to do and they had remained in the stable. One sunny afternoon, when the temperature rose fast, the bailiff decided that all ten horses should be let out into the back paddock to get some fresh air. Jimmy wondered why some of the men were muttering at this idea. He also noticed that once the horses were in this small field next to the yard the men stood on the road outside and leaned on the wall, watching. He soon realized why. These giant shire horses began to play like kittens. They raced around, butted each other, bit each other and even rolled on their backs with their legs in the air, kicking wildly. Boxer lived up to his name by rearing up with his forelegs punching as rapidly as if he were hammering a punchball. Dragon accepted the challenge and the pair of them sparred like featherweights. Jimmy had never been to a circus but he was sure this was just as good. He sat on the wall, delighted. After a while the horses calmed down and began to nibble at the grass where the frost had disappeared. Gingerly, the men went into the field and gently began to drive the horses back into the farmyard so that they could return them to the stable. Someone had thoughtfully closed all the gates leading into this large area, except the one used by the horses. It was just as well, because when everyone thought that all was quiet, Boxer neighed loudly and sped off around the Dutch barn. The others took up his cry immediately and ran after him. The men scattered because soon the yard was like a scene from *Ben Hur,* with these huge animals zigzagging round the buildings and dodging each other at breakneck speeds. For a while, none of the men did anything, in the hope that the horses would tire themselves out, but in the end they had to try to do something because it was getting dark and the temperature had begun to fall rapidly. Their tactics seemed to be to try to break the run of each particular horse by jumping out in front of it and then dodging back into their bolt-holes as though they were dealing with bulls in a French bull fight. At first this seemed to make the horses worse: this was good sport. Then, gradually, the pace slackened and some horses, like the gentle Jolly, made their own way to the stable. The crazy hour was over, but Boxer was the last to go in. Jimmy felt elated, but when he thought about it afterwards, he shuddered at how dangerous it had all been. Living in the city could be dangerous too, as he was about to discover.

Chapter III

T HE FIRST TO GO was Grandma, because Granddad had at last found a house. However, she had not been home very long when she took ill. So, Jimmy's mum had to go to look after her. Though Jimmy felt worried about his grandma, this feeling was overwhelmed by the anxiety he experienced because his mother was away and Aunt Mary was in charge. However, this did not last long because suddenly Grandma died. All the adults went home for the funeral and Jane had to manage the house.

Life seemed almost as strange as it had in the days immediately after the bombing. Everyone talked in whispers; no one seemed ever to laugh or even smile. And the gloom increased when the women returned from the funeral, because not only had they been visibly shaken by the death of their mother, but also their sadness was made all the more palpable because they were dressed completely in black – even the younger sister who had not been long married. They now talked in low tones about the details of the illness, the death and the funeral: if they thought the children would not hear, they were quite wrong because the earnestness of their conversations made everything they said distinct. This added to the apprehension that Jimmy had about sickness and death. He thought he ought to feel sad at the death of his grandma, but he found that he seemed to feel nothing and was almost ashamed that, if anything, he felt glad – because his mother was home again. When he did think about Grandma he knew that she was in Purgatory. He did not think this was very fair because his grandma had been so good: he could never imagine her committing really bad sins.

He had a secret place where he could hide from everyone. It was inside a double hawthorn hedge, which must have been neglected because it was overgrown. However, inside there was a hollow, which, though it was worryingly dark, was completely hidden and also dry. On one side of it there was the railway line and on the other the field sloped away, so if you checked carefully before you went in, nobody knew you were there. Jimmy sneaked in and said the little prayer he had been taught. "Eternal rest grant unto Her, O Lord, and let perpetual light shine upon her. May she rest in peace. Amen." This gave him some comfort because he was certain her stay in Purgatory would be shorter.

His brother, Alan, then returned to Liverpool to live with Granddad so that he could go to the school their father had attended. However, the return to the city began in earnest when his sister, Alice, also went to stay with an aunt and uncle, again, so that she could attend a particular school. Once more the family seemed to be breaking up and the unhappiness that this caused his mother, though she hardly showed it, had an unsettling effect on everyone. So it was that the thought of returning to the old home became stronger, especially as by now it was clear that the War was at last reaching its final stages and there had been no raids on Liverpool for years.

Returning home, however, was a great disappointment: everything was so drab and grimy, not only the houses but the people too. He wondered if it had been like this before the War, but he could not remember very clearly. He thought that it might be because of the bomb sites: even those that had been cleared were eyesores. But it had to be more than that. There were other factors – such as the pervading smell of burning. Sometimes this was of wood and so was not unpleasant, but mostly it seemed to be much more pungent and he imagined that it was caused by smouldering flock beds thrown out because children had wet them over and over again.

Life in the old house was not easy either. A great aunt and uncle, their daughter and her husband had been living there since they too had been bombed out. There was not enough room for all of them but accommodation was hard to come by and it was clear that they would have to endure the inconvenience for some time. His mother got a job but unfortunately it involved shift work. He seemed to see her hardly ever and yet he still felt dependent on her, especially because the new circumstances were very threatening, especially in the world outside. School was the worst. In the little village school he had attended, classes had been small and he had known all the children and the teachers – and they him. Even those he had regarded with suspicion or deference were as innocents compared with those he now found himself among, in a very large all-age boy's elementary school which, built in the Nineteenth Century, looked from the outside and felt from the inside more like a prison than a school. The place teemed with lads of all shapes and sizes, many of whom looked decidedly scruffy, and some of whom smelt as though they washed only rarely. The preferred form of footwear was black canvas pumps with thin rubber soles, but in the summer, he would later discover, a few came to school in bare feet. They regarded him with suspicion and at the same time contempt. They were very inquisitive and very direct in their approach.

"Who are you?"

"Where do you come from?"

"Why do you talk funny?" (Because of his Shropshire burr.)

"Why have you got that tie on?"

Others behind the inquisition group, asked questions of them and of each other.

"Who's he?"

"What's he doin' 'ere?"

"Why does he talk so funny?"

"Is he from Wales?"

"Aah, go 'ead, hit 'im."

He was entirely surrounded and very scared. One of them suddenly pulled his tie; another pulled his cap, the only one in the school, down over his eyes. Several of them shoved him or hit him, but not heavily. Then, suddenly, they lost interest, left him against the wall and went off laughing and chattering and jostling each other.

But he had one stroke of luck on that first day. He was not put in Standard Three because there was no room, and in Standard Two the only place vacant was next to the lad who, he was later to realize, was cock of the class and of several other classes too: he could fight everybody! He didn't look particularly tough but he had very bright brown eyes that seemed to take everything in. Though Humble was clever, being successful in class was not one of his priorities, but he wanted to avoid trouble, so it wasn't long before he realized that his new benchmate was quick, and could provide correct spellings, could check sums fast, and knew answers to obscure questions like where Toronto was. Jimmy had a kind of protector but that didn't stop him being frightened, because this boy went home to lunch and so when the school disgorged at twelve o'clock, Jimmy had to stay with another boy, who the class teacher, Miss Taggart, had asked to show him where the dinner-centre was. They ran: nobody ever seemed to walk.

"C'mon, hurry up, and we'll miss the crush."

"What crush?"

"You'll see, soft lad."

That Jimmy was regarded as an encumbrance was made even clearer when they got to the centre, which, to his chagrin, was in another school even bigger than his own. There were wrought-iron gates ten foot high and very obviously locked, but boys were streaming over them and dropping down on to the steps on the other side. By the time he was over and running up towards the school, his guide had disappeared. He didn't know what to do or where to go and felt it must be obvious to everyone that he was a stranger, particularly in his cap. Just as the panic set in, some other boys from his class rushed by saying, "C'mon, lad, stay with us, you'll be all right".

So he followed them. At the school it was confusing because there were several queues, but he saw the others had joined the shortest and fastest-moving, so he did too. What he did not know was that it also contained the smallest kids, the infants: he had not spotted that you had to walk with your knees bent. He stuck out even more because of his cap. When he got to the door a very large dinner-lady, a type of official they didn't have in small country schools, and in a massive blue uniform, grabbed him by the ear and threw him out back into the yard.

"Where do you think you're going? This is the babies' line. Get out you big cheat!"

The lads in the other queues laughed and jeered.

"Aah, soft lad!"

"Now, hat."

"Hatty – hatty – hatty."

"Who's in the babies, then?"

He staggered, red and close to tears, down past them until another boy from his class said, "Come in here, lad, by me, and you'll be all right".

He'd heard that before, but this time he was in the right line. However, when, after a long wait in a heaving mass, they got inside, it was bedlam. You had to dash to a place which, because you sat at benches, was to be got at only by pushing and shoving. Then the first thing you did was to pick up your knife, fork, and spoon and spit on each of them to establish your right of possession. Finally, if you didn't know the two lads at the top of the table, you got little dinner and less pudding.

But he survived the first day at the centre and got back to the relative safety of Standard Two in time for afternoon school. Like all the boys in his class he fell in love with Miss Taggart. She was not only beautiful, with her black hair and blue eyes, but also calm and quietly spoken. Her eyes twinkled and she seemed to like them all, smelly though some of them were. When they tried to joke with her she could always cap whatever they said. No one ever tried to play her up, and all the boys wanted to please her by doing their best. The work was not hard, at least not to Jimmy, because he should have been in Standard Three, but the other boys thought he was very clever. He made some friends, especially among those who lived near him; he became less apprehensive about them, but he no longer wore his cap or his tie. His accent began to change.

Then, just when school seemed to be less threatening, he got a severe shock. Summer was approaching, the days were brighter and so two boys decided not to come to school. They played truant for a fortnight before they were brought into school by their mothers. As the class was settling down to do sums one fine morning, the Headmaster brought the two offenders in. He was carrying a stick. He told the class what they had done and went on and on about how heinous a crime truancy was, especially, he stressed, because it could lead to other misdemeanours. He then told the class that he wanted to make an example of these two so that everybody would learn the lesson. He called the tougher of the pair over to him and made him hold out his hand. The violence with which he struck the boy barely seemed credible, and that was only the first of six. The lad's face was contorted as the cane hit him each time, but apart from that he hardly flinched. The other boy, however, was almost subsiding as he watched. When his turn came, he was already crying loudly.

"Oh, please, Sir, don't hit me."

"Hold out your hand."

"Oh, please, Sir."

"Hold it out!" came the roar.

He held out his hand and the Head struck him just as violently as he had the first boy. The scream which followed evoked no pity. There was more pleading and crying and promises that he would never do it again, but the Head insisted that the whole ritual had to be completed. The class, even Jimmy's tough benchmate, looked on in horror, and Miss Taggart's face went deathly white, framed as it was by her jet black hair. The hideous process seemed as though it would never end. Jimmy felt it was happening to him: the vicious slap of each stroke terrified him and made him wince. Long after it was over, even when the crying had stopped, he could not get it out of his mind. Though he swore to himself that he would never, ever play truant, it seemed as though life had become completely uncertain again: you did not know when terror might strike and there was nowhere to hide.

Life at home got worse. His mother's job entailed not only long unsociable hours but also hard physical work. She became ill. The doctor said she needed a complete rest: maybe, with peace and quiet, she might recover. He wanted to go to her, really so that she could comfort him, but no one would let him. His elder sister took on again the care and worry of the whole family, and she, being young, was overburdened, especially as her wages became the mainstay of their income.

Sometimes, because of the stress, she became understandably bossy, which put further stress on the other three, who, once good friends, now bickered with each other. Then their cousin, with whom they shared the house, had a miscarriage. The whole house plummeted into misery and gloom. One rainy evening, sitting on the unlit stairs, he could hear his sister complaining to his inattentive brother, while his cousin, in her grief, wept upstairs: he was afraid this was not the peace his mother needed. She would become so ill she would die. His place of refuge would cease to protect him. The thought became unbearable. Despite the rain, he crept out of the back door, his mac over his head, down what was left of the rear entry, and back round the half-cleared debris where his grandmother's house had once stood, and into the street. It had been a cul-de-sac, but the bomb had made it a shortcut through to a street that ran at right angles to it. The bottom of the street had no pavement but the kerbstones were still there, shaped in an elegant curve. Because of a blocked grid a large pool had formed, which, at its worst, was about a foot deep. Throwing bricks into it was a little boy from the next street. He watched this child for a while: he had no coat so his jersey and trousers were soaked. A couple of other children were also looking on from the doorway of the house opposite. The girl seemed concerned.

"Eh, Billy, why don't you go home out of the rain?"

"It's all right; I've got me rain hat on."

And sure enough, on his head was a girl's bathing-cap. Somehow this seemed typical of the children he now became acquainted with, for he discovered that, though they had a veneer of city slickness, they were naive. A boy in his class had a deformed hand and when he asked another boy about it, the reply was that, "He sat on it when he was a baby".

Anyone with a different accent was 'from Wales'. A boy behind him in school always claimed that whatever you were doing he could do better. If you were drawing he would say, "I used to be very good at sketching, like".

The 'like' at the end of sentences was a kind of addiction, which many children suffered from. There was a more virulent form of it: 'Y'know wharra mean, like?' Another grammatical virus was 'well' as in 'Well, I said to this kid....' In questions it could appear twice: 'Well, wharra ya gonna do, well?' Also things were never 'the same,' they had to be 'the very x-same,' though he never discovered where the x came from. These children copied each other's forms of speech and adopted words even when, he was sure, they knew they were wrong. For example, a propeller became a repeller!

Yet that evening, he began to talk as they did: he was becoming one of them. He wandered over to the boy and girl standing just inside the lobby: they chatted about how daft Billy must be, and he began to forget the unhappiness he'd felt when sitting on the stairs five minutes before. Indeed, it was about this time that, like most of the other kids, he began to spend virtually all of his waking hours out of doors. Home became a place you went when you were hungry or tired: you remained there only under duress. In later years he would reflect on this and think how right Rousseau was to call this period in a boy's life the age of the savage, because he became almost as wild as his new companions. He learned to climb up and run along the high backyard walls and to jump from one wall to another across the alleys. He even plucked up the courage to 'belly-band' the very wide gaps; this meant throwing yourself off one wall and wrapping your midriff round the one opposite. The dinner line ceased to be a problem: he could push and shove and sneak in as good as the rest. He spat on his spoon and shouted loudly if he thought his share was too small. And, though he knew he'd never be cock of the class, he learned to fight. At first, it was just a case of hitting when you were hit, but gradually it dawned on him that many lads were as cowardly as he and merely to adopt a threatening posture was enough to make most of them leave you alone. But he also learned to be wary because once, at the Pit, the local playground, he began to hustle another boy who was slow to get moving along the monkey-ladder. When he got to the end of the ladder himself, this boy was waiting for him and, without even murmuring, hit him several times very fast and very hard, so hard that he had to go off in a corner and cry, but he did not run home as he might have done earlier. When at last he decided to re-join the others, one of them said, "Why did you pick on Tommy Black?"

"Tommy Black? Is that him?"

"Yeh, didn't you know?"

"Course I didn't. He looks soft."

"Well, he isn't and now you know."

He began to play football in the street, and soon was as competent as most of the others, so that when teams were picked he could be sure he would be chosen fairly early. He even went to a 'derby' game at Goodison Park. A big lad from up the street asked him who he supported. He knew there was a team called Liverpool so that is what he said, but Georgie got hold of him by the throat and said, "Not in this street!"

At first he was shocked and quite worried until he realized Georgie was joking.

"You didn't know about Everton, did yeh?"

"No."

"Tell you what, well. Everton are playing Liverpool on Saturday. Ask your Mam if I can take yeh. You can come with me and our Alfie."

"Ah, can I?"

"Yep: it'll cost nine pence in the boys' pen."

Sure enough, on Saturday, Georgie and Alfie called for him and they set off for Goodison Park. Once on the main road, they joined lots of other boys and men striding purposefully along, and as they got nearer the ground the crowds became denser until down the side of Stanley Park they filled the whole road, even the verge the trams ran along. In fact that's where they were when a tram nosed its way through behind them. As the entrance passed by, Georgie jumped on the step and pulled Jimmy and Alfie after him. The conductor, instead of throwing them off, simply said, "Hang on, lads. You'll be all right!"

The mass of people at the ground was amazing, with great long queues winding seemingly in all directions, but controlled by policemen on big horses. Georgie hopped through the crowds, dragging them behind him. The line for the boys' pen was not too long, as many lads wanted to go in the ground proper, and there was no police horse to stand on your toes. The height of the windowless walls viewed from outside, the narrowness of the poky turnstile, and the dash up the dark stairs, meant that Jimmy was unprepared for the sight that hit him when he emerged into the bright light of the ground. He could never have imagined anything so big, or so full of people. The stands, with their powerful stanchions and cantilevered roofs, with their blue and white fronts, seemed gigantic. The crowd was alive and so animated, so full of expectancy, even joy. The drabness, usually so prevalent in those early post-war years, had fallen away: everything and everybody seemed brightly coloured, even though there were really very few red and white or blue and white scarves scattered through the crowd. But it was the pitch that stood out most of all, despite the blue haze of tobacco smoke. It was so big and such a vivid green in the early autumn sunlight. Its white lines were clear and bright and even the goalposts and nets appeared to glow. Then there was the noise: in spite of the march thumping out from the loudspeakers, you could hear a cacophony of human sound, from deep murmurs through chatter to laughter and shouts. When the players came out, this changed to a unified roar. And the players were larger than life and so smart in their blue or red shirts and white shorts, with stockings to match. (When his school had played St Francis de Sales, not everyone had a shirt and very few had shorts or even proper football boots.)

Afterwards he could remember very little about the game, except that Billy Liddell split his shorts and had to change them on the pitch to the whistles and cat-calls from the fans. However, he would never forget the effect of 55,000 voices shouting "Corner" in unison, or better still, "Goal!" He did know that the result was 2–2 and that from then on he would be an Evertonian.

Sometimes when he played football in the street he saw himself running down the wing for Everton. However, this was more likely on the occasions when he went with a gang of lads to play in Stanley Park. This was only if they had acquired briefly a caseball, or casey, as they called a real leather ball. Usually this was when a teacher allowed someone to look after the ball over-night after a games session (also in the park), probably because he didn't want to go back to school with it and didn't want to be seen on the tram with it either as he went home.

Once, when they were coming home from the park, the lads decided they would like some balm-cakes (baps elsewhere) from a baker's on the way. They already knew Jimmy was one of those who wouldn't steal, so he was detailed to actually buy one. But he had additional instructions. The balm-cakes were laid out on shelves along the side of the shop.

"Can I have a balm-cake, please?"

"Right-o, son, take one. That'll be a penny."

"Not one of them. Can I have a hot one, please?"

"Yes, but I'll have to go and fetch one from the bakery. Hang on a mo."

As soon as she left the shop, grubby hands darted forward to snatch balm-cakes. When she came back they were all standing innocently and exactly as they were when she'd left.

"Thank you, Mrs," he said as they all went out.

Some kids would steal anything. He saw one take a Christmas pudding in a decorative box as it stood on the counter right in front of the shopkeeper. Another stole a tin of evaporated milk on the way to the Saturday matinee. They had to punch holes in it with a rusty nail and a brick before they went in. Once inside they took it in turns to suck the milk out as they watched *Flash Gordon's Trip to Mars* (black and white, but shown with a green filter over the projector). However, they also took useless things and things they would never need, just because they were there for the taking, like an old paintbrush, stiff with paint, hanging on a wall, which one of them saw as they ran along the top. They could also tell lies without looking in the least bit guilty and they were very good at protesting their innocence. Jimmy, on the other hand, looked guilty even when he hadn't done anything.

He was afraid to steal, mostly because he would have been mortified had he got caught, but also because he knew it was wrong and the catechism said you could be forgiven only if you made restitution, so what was the point of stealing if you had to give it back? The catechism dominated the religious teaching he got in school, the result being that he developed a legalistic, almost hair-splitting, notion about wrong-doing. For instance, it said that to miss Mass on a Sunday or Holiday of Obligation was a mortal sin. However, what was important was that you were physically there: paying attention (to the Latin that you didn't understand anyway) did not seem to matter too much. Also, you had not actually missed Mass if you got there in time for the Offertory, and you could leave before the last Gospel.

There was a children's Mass. It was at nine o'clock on a Sunday and the Headmaster was always there. This meant that on a Monday morning, when the Mass register was taken, most of the boys told the truth about whether they had been or not, because Mr Smith, they thought, would know if they were telling lies. Actually, there were other Masses and Jimmy usually went at eight o'clock with his mother, who had gradually recovered from her illness. The Head rarely saw him. The taking of the Mass register was always embarrassing because those who hadn't been, though they were not caned, were shamed by the teacher and told they had committed a mortal sin.

The school also made sure that the boys went to confession: each week a couple of classes were taken across captive to church and put in rows next to two or three confessionals. You couldn't choose which priest you went to, so you hoped it would be Father O'Dowd and not Father Hanley. The former was easygoing and never seemed surprised at anything you might have done, but the latter quizzed you in a loud voice, and even repeated what you said, before he admonished you.

"Six times, did you say? And what do you think will become of you if you keep doing that, me lad?"

The squirming, grimacing boys outside would nudge each other and even those who were dreading their turn, and most of them were, would grin sheepishly. Yet, like Jimmy, they all probably tried to tell the truth in there, because they had all been taught that really it was God who was listening and He would know if you told lies. Moreover, they were at the stage when they were obsessed with rules: rituals had to be carried out to the letter. Cricket was the game that best illustrated this, for they spent most of their time arguing about whether or not someone was out, or whether each one had a fair share of the bowling, according to rules and conventions, their notions of which were only vague. LBW caused trouble but once it was established (wrongly) that leg meant only up to the knee, it had to be the same for everybody. You had seven turns at bowling because this was 'six and an over,' which was their interpretation of 'six an over'. But you had to abide by the rules. So they understood that in confession you had to do things properly, because to make a bad confession was to plunge yourself deeper into sin and the threat of hell. Actually telling the truth in confession became more difficult as they got older, because sex began to figure in their interests.

They had bizarre notions of the facts of life. On being told the basic mechanics of how 'some white stuff goes out of a man and into a woman' to make a baby, Jimmy was at first disbelieving because it seemed so hilarious. However, that seemed more likely than a theory put forward by one of his acquaintances that somehow the man had to penetrate a woman to break her eggs! Yet despite their naivety they told each other the crudest jokes to do with what they regarded as the rudest bits of the human anatomy, both male and female, and how they functioned.

Generally, the lads would not deign to play with the girls, but any one of them felt flattered if his name were called out as the girls played 'the girl of the golden city,' when they would hold hands and move around in a circle. One of them would whisper to her friends the name of a boy and stand in the middle, looking coy. Then they would sing their song. At one point the words went: "Andy Jackson (or whoever) says he loves her; all the boys are fighting for her; she goes courting one, two, three etc." The boys pretended not to care if their names were not mentioned, but they did. As autumn came and the evenings got dark earlier, they sometimes played 'Catch a girl, kiss a girl,' but their kisses were little more than pecks. One of Jimmy's friends once asked him if he had ever felt a girl. At that stage, as a nine-year-old, Jimmy was uncertain what this meant, but he imagined it happening in a clinical way, or perhaps as it might occur in a cattle market, or maybe in a slave market: it seemed an odd thing to do. The notion didn't have the impact it would have later. But they were all becoming more aware of girls – and of their own bodies.

Part of their shared mythology was that you could have terrible problems, for example, in school medical examinations. They related tales about boys who, touched by nurses or female doctors, found themselves acutely embarrassed and were hit and thrown out or made to go and wash themselves in cold water and told: "Control yourself, you dirty little beast". The morality of all this was confused in their minds. They had no guidelines, and so confession became more difficult for them (the Catholics, that is) as they got older, especially as the words they used in the street did not seem appropriate in the confessional.

There was another way in which confession could bring problems and it did for Jimmy. The catechism taught that it was a sin to take part in 'the services or prayers of a false religion,' but in his naivety, Jimmy thought this meant to go into the church even of another denomination and for whatever reason, especially as he had heard his mother and his aunts complain that they could not attend weddings of friends because they did not take place in the Catholic church. They were horror-stricken if they knew of a Catholic being married in a non-Catholic church.

One evening in the autumn, when the nights were drawing in, he heard some of the other children in the street say that they were going to see a slide show in the strangely-named Police Mission in a street nearby. Not having any real idea what this show was about, nor even of the form it would take, he found the notion more and more attractive as the time for the show grew near: he dearly wanted to go with the others. He began to wonder whether this would be a mortal sin, yet it didn't seem possible. He worried and worried and still wanted to go. When they set off, he went with them, but almost as though he were in a trance. Once inside, he felt a little reassured: there was no altar and so perhaps this was not a church at all.

A tall thin man came to the front. He looked like pictures

Jimmy had seen of Dr Crippin. He spoke through his nose. Though the other children found this funny and many of them sniggered, Jimmy felt afraid. They were told by this gentleman that he had just returned from Africa where he had been engaged in missionary work. Jimmy felt even more apprehensive. He thought all real missionaries were Catholic priests and he had an uncle who was a Mill Hill Father, but this man had been teaching natives how to be Protestants! He now began to feel very unhappy. He wanted to leave but daren't: the other people in the church or hall or whatever it was might realize he was a Catholic and turn on him. Then the lights went out and the first slide was shown. The picture was so poor, so grainy, that without being told you would not have known that it was of a river in Central Africa. Others of a similar quality followed, but painfully slowly because each one was accompanied by a long explanation from the lanky missionary. Just occasionally he himself appeared in one of the pictures and he at least was recognisable – not only because of his whiteness but also because he was so much taller than his black charges. At first, time dragged and Jimmy grew more and more afraid. That is until the other kids began to get restless: the long, boring descriptions of the indecipherable pictures were not what they had been led to expect. Where were the tigers, lions and elephants? Then a really tough lad, Archie Casey, began to laugh in a derisory way as each new picture was shown. The other children responded with spontaneous laughter of their own and then continued to make a noise by talking at the same time as the missionary. The adults in the audience, who no doubt were regular members of the congregation, began to tut-tut and even tell the children, in stage whispers, to be quiet. The chatterers, who felt a certain security in their numbers, took no notice. And soon the lecturer could hardly be heard, even though he was shouting. Finally, a stout man with a moustache and a watch and chain went to the front, interrupted the speaker, called for silence, and then asked all the children to leave. Jimmy was both relieved and ashamed. If his mother should find out that he had been thrown out along with the others she would be appalled, but at least he could now get out. However, the ordeal was not yet over. The children scrambled out of the benches and began to proceed in a disorderly way down the aisle to the door, which was at the front of the chapel, when the missionary held up his hand and stopped them. He told them how ungrateful they were and warned them of the wrath that was sure to come down on them for their behaviour. But, he said, their real misfortune was their ignorance and so, he said he was going to pray for them, there and then. For some reason, the children, even Archie, became silent and even perhaps contrite. But Jimmy was aghast: here it was – the great sin – he was taking part in the prayers of a false religion, and there was nothing he could do about it because he was trapped right in the middle of the group – where he had placed himself in the hope of not being recognised by some adult who might tell his mother, or worse still, his teacher or the priest.

When he got home and was asked where he had been, he used his usual tactic of simply saying "nowhere". But he knew he looked guilty and his mother probed further. Though it was out of character, he did what his sister, Alice, did: he refused to say anything and so was told to go to bed. He felt so wide awake that he knew he would not be able to sleep. He kept going over and over in his mind the events of the evening and the questions kept coming back: had he committed a terrible sin? Was he on his way to hell? He tried saying an act of contrition but he knew that this would not lead to forgiveness if his sorrow was only because he was afraid of the punishment. You had to be sorry because you had offended God and no matter how hard he tried to make himself believe that this was so, he found he felt nothing, except that he would die and then spend eternity in hideous physical pain. He tried reading his favourite book, *William the Pirate*, but this did not help, especially as the candle in its candlestick seemed to be too far away and provided insufficient light. He tried one of his brother's strategies: he took the candle out of its holder and stuck it instead on the bed post, which had a flat top. Now he could see better and before long, William began to work his charm and Jimmy became engrossed in the doings of his ragged hero. Without even realizing it was happening, he fell asleep – only to be rudely shaken awake by Alan, shouting.

"What do you think you're doing, you stupid little bugger? Are you trying to set the house on fire!?"

The candle had almost burned down to the wood of the post. Jimmy rolled as near to the edge of his side of the bed as he could and tried to keep his weeping silent. He was so unhappy, but he got little sympathy from his brother who thought the crying was the effect of being woken up.

"Oh, shut up, you silly little twit, and go to sleep."

Jimmy wished he could.

At first, when he awoke the next morning, he remembered nothing of the night before, but then in a rush it all came back to him and he felt afraid again. Over breakfast he was preoccupied: was he guilty or not? Nobody noticed because he was usually silent at that time and anyway they were all concerned with their own efforts to get ready for work or school. However, on his way to school himself, he met some other kids who were kicking the remains of a deflated ball as they went along and as he became involved in this, he forgot his troubles. Then, once he was occupied with his sums and his spellings, life began to feel fairly normal. That is, until just before dinner time, their teacher got a message that they could all go across to church to confession, and all too suddenly Jimmy was confronted with the problem of how he could confess his awful sin. He wanted time to work it out but they seemed to be rushing headlong to the brink and, worst of all, the way the class filed into the benches meant that he was the first to go in to the dreaded Father Hanley. In the dark of the confessional, he felt even more confused and found himself repeating the usual formula.

He'd told lies, been disobedient, said bad words and so on. Then he paused and there was silence. It grew longer until at last the priest asked if there were anything else. Jimmy could not bring himself to say that he had taken part in the services of a false religion. The priest asked again – quietly, but with the same result.

Then, suddenly, he roared, "I said, is there anything else!?"

Jimmy was by then too traumatised to speak and Father Hanley said, "Right. Make an act of contrition, then get out and for your penance say three Hail Marys."

Jimmy came out of the box to find all his class and his teacher staring at him. He went to the front where you said your penance and though he did go through the words of the prayer three times they meant nothing because he was now certain that he was in a state of grave sin because he had omitted to tell of a serious offence and so had made a bad confession. His life was over. It could never be the same again.

The next few days were miserable and Jimmy could see no way out of his dilemma because he knew that if he went to confession again he would have still greater difficulty telling the truth: now he would be even more afraid of the priest. Yet he was certain that if he died he would go straight to hell. Consequently he became afraid of everything – just crossing the road became a trial: he might be run over and killed. At night he was afraid to go to sleep because he might never wake up. But the worst aspect of his situation was that he felt cut off from everybody else: they were all normal and could go to heaven and he could not. Moreover, there was no one he could tell, not even his mother. Especially not his mother.

Occasionally, when playing with the other kids in the street or the school playground, he would forget. Then it would all flood back over him and he would wander off quietly by himself. It was during one of these wanderings that he found himself thinking about the dedication under one of the stained glass windows in church. It said, 'Pray for the Soul of J.C. Baxter' – or did it? Did it say 'James C. Baxter'? He felt he wanted to find out straightaway but did not know why. He wondered whether the church would be open and decided to go and look. It was and he went in and made his way to the Lady Chapel. He found that the dedication said J.C., not James C. He knelt down and thought about saying a prayer, but God would not be listening to him. He also wondered who J.C. Baxter was and how he knew J. stood for James. Suddenly, everything seemed so awful he began to cry. What he did not know was that the new young curate, Father McMurray, was also in the chapel and he, hearing Jimmy's sobs, came to investigate. At first Jimmy did not know he was there until Father McMurray said, in a very quiet voice, "What's the matter, sonny?"

Jimmy, startled and shocked, looked up, but could only cry all the more bitterly. The curate sat down next to him and after a while, as Jimmy tried to quieten his crying, he said, "Wouldn't you like to tell me? I'm sure you'd feel better if you did."

Jimmy managed to splutter out, "No. I can't."

"Well, if I promise not to be shocked at anything you tell me, do you think you could try – just a little?"

Jimmy thought about this and for a long time there was silence. Then, all of a sudden, it came pouring out between the sobs.

"I went (hic) to a service (hic) in a false (hic) religion (hic) and when I went to (hic) confession (hic) I didn't tell the priest (hic) and now…"

"Now what?"

"I'm going to hell!" wailed Jimmy.

Father McMurray knew he shouldn't laugh but he could not help it and what a loud belly laugh it was. Jimmy was so surprised at this that he stopped crying and stared at the priest in wonder – or was it horror? Then the priest controlled himself and said, "Dear, dear me. One thing I can tell you straightaway is you are not going to hell."

"I'm not? But it was a bad…"

"Have you got a hanky?"

"(Hic) No, but me mam gives me a piece of rag."

"Well, you dry your eyes and wipe your face and blow your nose and tell me the whole story. Then, I bet you a penny that I don't think you're going to hell and God doesn't either."

"I haven't got a penny."

"Never mind. Just tell me."

As Jimmy wiped his face with his none-too-clean rag, he began to recount the whole tale. The curate listened carefully but his permanent smile sometimes became a broad grin. When it was finished he said, "What's your name?"

"James Thompson, but everybody calls me Jimmy."

"Well now, Jimmy, you've been a bit silly, but you haven't done anything bad enough to go to hell."

"But I made a bad confession."

"Tell me… er… when you were in the confessional, were you afraid?"

Jimmy thought about this very carefully and he could remember everything so clearly that the sinking sensation he had felt at the time came back to him.

"Yes, I was very scared."

"Did you go in there boldly, telling yourself that you were going to deceive the priest?"

"Oh, no! I was just scared all the time and didn't know what to do!"

"Well, don't you think that it was not the real you in there: you weren't thinking straight, were you? I bet you felt very confused, didn't you?"

"Yes," said Jimmy, very quietly.

"You know, don't you, that when you are in there you have to be clear about what you are doing."

"Yes."

"And you weren't?"

"No."

"Now, that's why I think you didn't commit a mortal sin. In fact, you probably didn't commit a sin at all."

Jimmy sat and looked at his dirty knees. He did not know what to say, but he knew that a sort of calmness had come over him and he felt very grateful to Father McMurray. However, he now wanted to get out of church and run as fast as he could – anywhere, but probably all the way home. Then the priest tousled Jimmy's hair and said, "Tell you what, why don't we go into the box? We won't go over it all again but you can say an act of contrition and I'll give you absolution – even though I don't think you need it. And then you can stop worrying about it altogether."

"OK… er… I mean, yes, Father."

The curate smiled his broadest smile and said, "OK. Let's go."

At the end, Father McMurray said, "I'd like you to go up to the Lady altar and say just one Hail Mary, and as you say it, look at the statue and think about Jesus' mother, because he was once your age and she looked after him. She'll look after you too. Will you do that, Jimmy? And always remember that God the Father doesn't want to punish you, He wants to love you."

"Yes, Father."

When he knelt at the altar, he did try very hard to do what the priest asked. Then when he got up and turned round, the priest had gone. Jimmy ran all the way home and as the air rushed past him he felt so light he thought he might fly.

There were other worries for Catholic children in the city at that time, because Orangism flared up again after the War. To be Catholic or Orange was rather like being Evertonian or Liverpudlian, but in a more virulent and dangerous way. Even those who rarely attended Mass felt they owed allegiance and undying loyalty to their clan. In Jimmy's street, people were divided: a sizeable minority was Catholic, but most families were Orange. Usually, neighbours were friendly and even helpful if a family got into difficulties, but in the summer as the Twelfth of July (the anniversary of the Battle of the Boyne) approached, and especially if the weather were good, relations could become very strained. For example, there was the question of decoration. The Protestant families wanted to put up orange and purple bunting, but as the Catholics refused to have anything to do with it, there had to be gaps, which spoilt the effect. Strange anomalies arose. One year, prolonged rain washed all the colour out of the decorations and by the time the weather cleared and it was worth replacing them, there was little paper left in the shops. What remained was either white or pale yellow and so these were put up. No Catholic dared to point out that they were the colours of the papal flag. But probably neither Catholics nor Protestants knew that in 1690 the Pope celebrated Mass in thanksgiving for William of Orange's victory at the Boyne, because besides defeating James II, he also, in effect, defeated Louis XIV, whose ambitions were seen as dangerous to the Papacy.

Jimmy found the feuding very worrying. Once, on Netherfield Road, he had seen a crowd of very angry women banging on the door of a Catholic apartment, calling the woman inside dreadful names because, they claimed, she had been seen deliberately flashing her green knickers from the balcony where she lived as the Orange bands went by. On another occasion, as the lodges made their way along Shaw Street, a Catholic area, he had seen sods of earth thrown from behind the onlookers on to young children as they marched along. Sometimes he got glimpses of the futility and crassness of the feud. One Easter Monday he went with some other boys to see the lodges assemble in Shiel Park (named after a prominent Catholic!). Many of the men were very drunk and he felt apprehensive so he decided to go home. As he made his way to the gate, having left his friends behind, he came across a man done up in a sailor uniform, talking to a group of young girls in long white dresses. He had difficulty in standing upright and his speech was slurred, but Jimmy could make out what he was saying.

"Now I'm gonna tell youse why I'm an Orangeman. Yes, why I'm an Orangeman. Just listen and I'll tell ya." Long pause. "I'm an Orangeman because... " Another long pause. "I'll tell ya. I'll tell ya. I'm an Orangeman because..." A third long pause, and a look of intense perplexity came over his face. "I don't know why I'm an Orangeman!"

The little girls giggled and Jimmy ran home, afraid someone somehow would realize that he was a Catholic. He got there safely on this occasion. However, even home could be threatened. One Twelfth of July, everyone was out except a great aunt who, after the departure of the cousins, had come to live with them. A gang of boys, playing next to the house, on the debris that had never been cleared properly after the War, was unearthing bricks with crowbars (usually the remains of old iron railings). They chanted as they worked, "We're the Orange Lodge! We're the Orange Lodge!"

Aunty Mary was disturbed by the bumping and banging, not the singing, and came out to tell the boys to clear off. They misunderstood and thought she was complaining about the chant. Knowing she was a Catholic, they began to bait her, calling her "dirty ould pape" and telling her to go back in and play with her beads. Mary, though nearly eighty years old, was not in the least intimidated, at first. In her young days she had even barracked George Wise as he harangued a semi-religious political meeting outside the nearby children's playground (the Pit). She had provoked such a disturbance that she had had to be escorted home by the police: a gang of kids didn't bother her.

However, at this particular time feelings were running high and the boys became more threatening. Finally, one of them threw a brick. It missed her but she did draw back because she saw others were reaching down to the ground. She just got back inside as a hail of stones struck the door. Then they ran up the path and banged on the door with their bars. For a while, she cowered inside, afraid to look out of any of the windows in case they threw stones at them, but eventually she did take a peek from behind the aspidistra and the lace curtains. What amazed her was that adults she knew as nice people were standing watching, apparently unconcerned: they were either tacitly encouraging the louts, or were afraid to protest. Quite late in the evening, but long before the rest of the family returned, somebody must have contacted the police, because two constables arrived and dispersed the mob. Great Aunt Mary was very distressed for several days and would not go out, though usually she did some of the shopping. The whole family was under stress. The feeling that you weren't safe in your own house or welcome in your own street was strong. Even discreet questions about possible ringleaders were met by hostile silence from habitually gossipy neighbours. Were they afraid or were they ashamed? Jimmy began to feel the old fear creeping over him. The self-confidence that he had displayed as a street urchin began to fade away. After a time, something like normality returned to his relationship with the other children in the street, but he was never again as carefree as he had been, and apart from one or two who went to his school, he felt wary of them all.

There were also threats from other quarters. Back in the days when they lived in Shropshire, his brother had made a toboggan, with steel bed-laths nailed to its wooden runners. He no longer used it but he was still proprietorial about it: Jimmy was allowed to take it out on sufferance whenever it snowed, provided he was very careful with it. Because the laths were rusty, it would never run as well as other sledges at first, but with use, it became very fast, as the runners polished up. One good place to take it was Mere Lane, where there was a wide pavement on a not-too-steep slope, next to the cinema, and here he could outrun any other toboggan. That is, until the day an older boy pushed him off it and refused to give it back. Jimmy, in a panic, ran home to tell his brother, so that he would know it was not Jimmy's fault the toboggan had gone. To begin with, Alan's anger was directed at Jimmy, who pleaded, "Come quick and you'll catch the lad who took it".

When they got to Mere Lane the boy was just arriving back at the top of the run, pulling the toboggan behind him. He was nearly as big as Alan.

"That's him there."

"This lad here?"

"Yeh."

"Eh you, did you take his sledge?"

Before the boy could answer, Alan hit him hard in the stomach and as his head came down, he hit him twice in the face. The boy fell and rolled in the snow with blood spurting from his nose. Alan turned to Jimmy, telling him to bring the toboggan home and leave it there. As they trudged off, the boy, still sitting in the snow, shouted, "I'll get you, kid! You'd better watch out!"

Alan told Jimmy to take no notice, but he was not the one being threatened.

The following Friday, Jimmy was sent, as usual, to take Granddad his washing. This meant walking to a stop in Oakfield Road to catch a tram to Wavertree. To get there you had to go down St Domingo Vale. As Jimmy ran down there with his fat parcel, he saw a group of kids standing on a doorstep and recognised one of them as the lad his brother had beaten up.

"Hey, that's the kid I'm after," he shouted.

"Let's get him," cried the others.

Jimmy, already trotting, sped up so that soon he was running as fast as he could. Fortunately for him, the houses had fairly big gardens and the gate to this particular house was fastened. The group got all tangled up as they struggled to get out, so Jimmy had a good start. However, as they approached Oakfield Road, they were gaining on him, so although this was a busy main road, he took only the briefest of glances each way and ran across, because there was a tram at the stop he needed. It pulled away with him on it, just as the mob arrived. He was safe. Nevertheless, he could no longer use St Domingo Vale and this meant that every week he had to take a detour to get to the next stop towards Granddad's. However, he not only avoided that street but several others round about just in case. Yet in a way this had positive results, because he found the fare was less and so he could make a few coppers out of the journey. This encouraged him to walk even further before he got the tram. Then he began to take shortcuts. In fact, whereas before his geographical knowledge of the city had been dependent on the tram routes, he now realized that they rarely followed the most direct course to their destinations. A more exact image of the network of streets began to establish itself in his head, and he could think of a line, as the crow flies, to his Granddad's, and try different streets and combinations of streets to get there. He could walk all the way and save all the fare. His mother knew this: it was, along with the three three-penny bits he always got from his Granddad, his only pocket money.

Then, one dark evening, he took one shortcut too many. He tried a back entry to see if he could find a way to a particular street that ran very near his Granddad's. As he turned a corner he was confronted by four lads, one of whom had a pot-stick. They surrounded him, and, menacing him with the stick, asked him what was in the parcel. He gasped; he could not speak; his legs and back tingled; he felt his heart beating in his throat and his eyes opening wider and wider. This all had an effect on his assailants, who each took half a step backwards. He saw his chance and suddenly bounded between two of them and ran and ran. They followed but he got to Granddad's: up the path and kicked at the door, just as he had done in the air raid so long ago. Even before the door opened, they had run off and his aunt (the dreaded Shropshire Aunt Mary), who still lived at home, flung open the door and glared at him.

"What's the matter with you, banging on the door like that?"

"Some lads are after me."

"Where? I can't see no one."

She didn't seem to notice the state he was in. "Come in and don't be so daft!"

That evening he got the tram home. From then on he avoided streets he suspected had rough kids in them and used mostly main roads. He also avoided the company of certain lads in school, though this was easy because his class was divided into ability groups, represented by rows of desks, and he was always in row A, where other pupils from aspiring families were likely to be found. He was now in a class with children of his own age, and no longer had an advantage: there were other boys cleverer than he, but he could hold his own, especially in the weekly tests in arithmetic, spelling and dictation. However, one Friday, Mr Wade called out as he marked the sums.

"Jimmy Thompson, your work is getting very untidy. You watch it next week, lad."

"Yes, Sir."

The following Friday, as he did the tests, he took special care. Unfortunately, as he was putting ten in the pence column, he momentarily lost concentration.

"Wow!" said Mr Wade, as he marked the papers, "Jimmy Thompson has got sixteen in the pence column. What does that mean, lads?"

"A mortal sin, sir," chorused row D, at whom he was looking significantly.

"And what shall we do with him then?"

"Cane him, sir!"

"OK. Come out, Jimmy."

Jimmy went cold all over. He felt the colour drain from his face. He tried to protest his innocence, but his throat had seized up, he was so near to tears. The teacher remained seated at his desk, but reached behind it to get his cane. Jimmy held out his hand tentatively and Mr Wade lifted it higher very gently with the cane. The hand seemed both leaden and tingly, as though Jimmy could feel the pain already. In fascinated terror, he watched the cane lifted up. He saw it waver in the air, as though Mr Wade was taking careful aim, and then, swish, down it came with sickening effect on to his hand. He did not believe he could hurt so much, and he snatched his hand back and tucked it instinctively under his armpit. Despite the burning sensation, he tried very hard not to cry: he knew that the whole class was watching to see how he took it, because he had never been caned before. He could feel the tears in his eyes, but he kept his teeth clenched and his lips tight together, and when he got back to his place, he looked hard at his book, and neither to left nor right. Very slowly the pain eased, but his hand remained sweaty, and when at last he looked at it, he could see a fiery red weal right across it, which still smarted if he stretched the skin back. Writing was not easy. Later, in the afternoon, he got his papers back and looked at the offending sum. There, sure enough, was the sixteen in the wrong place. He checked the arithmetic: the pence column came to one and ten-pence, and he'd carried the one into the shillings correctly. Why then had he got sixteen in the pence column? At last it dawned on him: he'd started off writing the zero of the ten, but he had concen-trated so hard on the neatness that he'd lost track of what he was doing and it had become a very tidy six instead. He wondered if he would always do things like this. Would he get the cane again for carelessness? How could he be certain of what he wrote if he had to think of several things at once? That helpless feeling came over him again, as though he had no control over what happened to him, and he was afraid. From now on he must check every-thing, but he knew that even if he did, the cane was still a possi-bility. In fact, he was to get into trouble only once more during his time in the elementary school and it was only on reflection, years later, that he realized how serious it could have been.

It was when his class, Standard Four, did a trial run in the Review, a year early, along with Standard Five, who were taking it in earnest, to see which of them could be entered for the Scholarship. He was sitting next to Andy Claverty from the other class. There was a sum he could not do and Claverty whispered how to do it. It was easy. A little later, two boys were discovered collaborating: the teachers made a big fuss, and Mr Wade said that if anybody else had been cheating he would be able to tell. Jimmy went cold all over, because Mr Wade knew that his class had never done conversion of weight. Should he put his hand up and confess? If he did, Andy would also get into trouble. He felt his chest go tight: he couldn't write; he could hardly move at all. Then tears began to form and he had to struggle with the sob that was welling up from within him. He tried to cry quietly, but finally he had to give in to a noisy intake of breath. Mr Wade came and stood over him.

"What's the matter with you?" There was no reply.

"What's the matter, lad?"

Still Jimmy could not answer. He remained with his head over his paper. He could only watch the teardrops falling on to the ink, making it run.

"I can't help you if you don't tell me what's wrong."

Finally he looked at Andy, and said, "Claverty, do you know why he's crying?"

"Yes, Sir."

"Then what is it?"

"I think it might be because I told him how to do a sum, Sir."

"Oh, yes?"

"But I never done it for him, Sir. I only told him how to do it."

Without saying anything, Mr Wade collected up both sets of papers, and left the boys sitting disconsolately.

"I'm sorry," Jimmy spluttered. "I'm sorry."

"Never mind, kid. I'd finished anyway."

Jimmy ran all the way home at lunchtime, and avoided all the other kids. His mother now worked part-time in a dinner centre and had left his lunch ready for him so he did not have to speak to anybody. But he worried: he would not be allowed to do the scholarship as his brother and sister had done; he would not go to the grammar school; worse still, he had stopped Andy Claverty from doing the scholarship too.

Even when he had forgotten the pain of this terrible day, he went on worrying about what he had done to Andy, but he need not have concerned himself so much, because the teachers thought very highly of Claverty and he was entered anyway. Later, Jimmy heard that Andy did take the scholarship, but he failed, or rather, he was judged not to have the aptitudes that would allow him to benefit from an academic education – as the jargon of tripartism would have it.

But if Andy had been allowed to do the scholarship, then Jimmy would also be able to, and so he need never tell his mother that he had been caught cheating in school. Indeed, when he moved up to Standard Five, he found that his new teacher, Mr King, seemed to like him, and he got on very well. He was never first in the class but was always in the top six or so. When it came time to do the examination in February, off he went to the grammar school his father had attended. His brother had taken him to see the school one Saturday afternoon, but it was closed. Nevertheless, they did get inside, because as they passed a side door, it was opened by an acquaintance of Alan's, who must have committed some heinous crime, because he had been doing a detention. All three sneaked in and walked along the bottom corridor as far as the hall, which they peeked inside: Jimmy was suitably impressed and so they crept out of the front door, looking up at the large main staircase as they went.

On this particular day, Jimmy discovered that his brother was not the only rascal in the place: this other lad was something of a wag. He looked the part because, though he was tubby, his blazer was pulled tight across him and all the buttons were done up. Moreover, instead of being the sober maroon sort, bought in Horne Bros, it was the pinky variety, got from George Henry Lee's: it seemed to glow. On his head he wore a much too small cap and yet it was pulled down hard so that he had to lean back to see under the peak. The effect of this was further exaggerated by his cheap wire-framed glasses, which looked as though they had been squashed on to his face so that the lenses pointed in different directions. Underneath this there was a permanent grin. His trousers were too short and narrow at the bottom, so that you could see his wrinkled and rather grubby yellow socks and very large boots. He seemed quite unaware of how ridiculous he looked. At his suggestion they decided to walk down London Road, into town. Halfway down they came to an amusement arcade on what had been a bombsite. It was a very temporary building. The wag peeped inside and decided it was crowded enough to suit his purposes, so he pulled Jimmy and Alan in, saying he wanted to show them something. They started to fumble in their pockets for pennies, but he told them to wait until he had demonstrated how to beat the slot-machines every time. He went up to a particular kind of machine: it was the sort that had a ball-bearing that you flicked up towards a row of holes in a line. Only the two end holes were the ones you lost in and in the middle were six or seven win holes. However, there were small steel bars either side of each hole and the ball always seemed to hit these and bounce into the lose holes. He put his penny in and flicked the catch that sent the ball up the machine. Then he pressed the glass on the front, just over the win holes. This trapped the ball, which he then dropped where he wanted. So they set to work on the slot-machines, making sure that they never played any machine too long, taking perhaps only three wins from each one. Gradually their winnings began to build up, and their pockets to sag with the weight of the pennies. However, they had to keep an eye on the attendant, and it was this which gave the game away: they, and especially Jimmy, looked furtive; he became suspicious and tried to follow them. At first, this was to their advantage as all three were operating in different alley-ways between the machines and they kept moving, but before long Jimmy began to get scared. He went and stood by Alan, who told him to go and play elsewhere. When they looked up, there was the attendant, with his long bunch of keys, staring intently at them.

"What are youse two doin'?"

"Nothin', just playin' the machines."

"Well, it doesn't look like just playin' to me."

"Well, we are. See!"

At this Alan sacrificed one of his pennies, which he put in the machine and flicked up into a losing hole.

"Even so; go on, gerrout, the pair of yer."

"Ar-Ay! We haven't done nothin'."

"Clear off if you don't want a kick up the arse."

Jimmy was ready to bolt, but Alan held his arm and together they left the arcade, slowly and carefully, so as not to jangle the coppers in their pockets. Meanwhile, Sartori, for this was the inappropriate name of Alan's pal, was milking the machines for all he was worth. However, it was not long before he emerged through the swing-doors, rather more swiftly than they had, propelled as he was by the boot of the attendant. But he was still smiling, and unperturbed.

"How much did you make?"

"I don't know. Let's have a count up."

They started to count the pennies. Jimmy had three shillings, but the other two had much more, and to his amazement they pooled the lot and did an equal share out: he'd never felt so rich in his life. You could buy a lot for 4/9d., and off to town they went to see if they could spend it.

So the dreaded scholarship was not quite as terrifying as it might have been: he knew the school and he knew some of his brother's friends. However, he was still very apprehensive. Moreover, his propensity to check and double-check everything meant that he finished neither the arithmetic nor the English papers. He did complete the intelligence test, but unlike the other two papers, he did not know whether he had the answers right or not in many instances. Then came the long wait.

Sometimes he was certain he had failed: how could they give a scholarship to someone who did not complete important parts of the examination? At other times he felt more optimistic: he knew such a lot of his answers were right, and he knew his brother and his friends were not so different from him.

Then one morning, after prayers, Mr King, grinning broadly, asked certain boys to stand up – and the last of these was Jimmy Thompson.

"Now, Standard Five, I want you all to give these boys a rousing cheer because they have all won scholarships to grammar schools."

There was some half-hearted clapping.

"C'mon, lads you can do better than that: they've passed!"

The clapping got a little livelier, and there was a feeble attempt at a cheer, but it had an undertone of sarcasm to it. Jimmy looked around. He saw some very disappointed faces – Connolly for instance, who according to the boys' reckoning was the cleverest in the class. How could he have failed? And Jimmy's friend, Albert, who was just as good as Jimmy in everything they did at school.

"Well, I think you four should go home straightaway to tell your parents. Will there be anybody there if you go now?"

"Yes, Sir," all chorused.

Once outside, they all went their separate ways. Jimmy had only a vague notion of what time his mother went off to work in the dinner centre, so he ran as fast as he could, but in fact he met her at the top of the street, talking to several other women. She spotted him, and did not look pleased.

"What are you doing out of school?"

"Mr King sent me home to tell you I've won the scholarship."

His mother smiled, but before she could say anything the other women broke into "Oohs" and "Aahs," and "Isn't he a clever boy?"

Jimmy felt both embarrassed and proud at the same time, but he kept watching his mother's face: the news seemed to give her double the pleasure, because it was delivered whilst she was surrounded by so many friends and acquaintances. Later that day, his brother and sisters congratulated him, but they each maintained that they knew all along that he would pass. If only they knew how much he doubted his own ability.

The period between getting the scholarship and actually going to grammar school was a kind of limbo in which time stood still: nothing seemed real; nothing seemed to be achieved; and especially at school, nothing seemed to matter. Indeed, Jimmy felt quite ashamed of himself when he came only eighth in class, even though he thought that was about where he should have come.

Nevertheless, he knew he was on the brink of something, though he did not know what it was. That his life was about to change he was certain; that all sorts of things would now become possible, he felt sure, but he had only the vaguest notions of what they might be.

Each evening during that summer, when he went off to bed in

the back attic, which he shared with his brother, he would look out over the rooftops at the sunset over Liverpool Bay. He knew the bay was there even if hidden by the houses, but he could see the clouds and imagined that they were an extension of the land stretching out to sea in the form of promontories, bays, peninsulas, and then breaking up into islands both large and small, as he imagined the landscape when they sang, 'The Road to the Isles' in school, or as it must have appeared to David Balfour in *Kidnapped*. The clouds were black or various shades of grey and the sky creamy gold or yellow running into blue tinged with pink, but after a while the whole scene began to take on a reality of its own as though viewed from a high mountain. He could even imagine himself sailing out to the west through these islands to seek his fortune, he knew not where. At other times he saw himself having adventures in such an archipelago, like the two young men in *The Riddle of the Sands*.

Sometimes, during the day, he would go into the front attic, which did not have a window but a skylight: you had to set up the stepladder to see out of it. However, once you were up there it was like being in a separate little room, but you had to remember that its floor was only the platform of the ladder. From this vantage-point you could see over many more roofs to the water-tower in Brunel Street, way off in the distance. There was also a church with a steeple and another large building, which he pretended was a prestigious college, like the one in *Tom Brown's School Days.* He imagined that attendance at this college would somehow transform him, so that when he grew up he would be able to do an important job that would make him rich and famous. The sides of this little room were whitewashed and one day he had an irresistible urge to write his name up there. He then decided to provide himself with some companions: Jingleberry Dunnings was one and Hotchpotch Pompcoynings was another. They were later joined by Willibert Peachead and Hortense McDogsbreath. One Saturday afternoon, when nearly all the family were sitting in the kitchen doing nothing in particular, there was a terrible crash somewhere upstairs. They all ran up to see what it was. When they got to the front attic they found Alan in a heap on the floor and all tangled up in the stepladder. He had gone up there to look out of the skylight with binoculars, which really belonged to Granddad, but he had discovered Jimmy's companions and he had started laughing, forgotten there was no floor to the little room, and lost his footing. He was not really hurt, only shaken. Jimmy felt guilty, but he was secretly glad, because it meant that to some extent he had got his own back on his brother for all the terrifying tales Alan had told him about the grammar school. Especially frightening were the descriptions of the effects of the ferula, the thick strap used by the Jesuits to punish all misdemeanours, even the most trivial. It was with some trepidation as well as excitement that Jimmy approached his new life.

Chapter IV

"That's my piece of toast. Get your maulers off it."

"Why is it yours? It's on the table."

"'Cos I made it."

"So?" And Alan bit into it.

"Mam, tell him. He's eating my toast."

"Oh dear." (From the back kitchen.) "What's the matter with you all this morning? It's anybody's toast. There's plenty of bread. Make some more."

"Why should I? I made that for me. I got up early and he never makes the toast."

"What's the matter, little baby? Did naughty Alan eat the little diddum's toast, then?"

"You leave me alone!"

"Is baby bunting feeling liverish this morning, then?"

"Aaagh! LEAVE ME ALONE!!"

"Temper – temper – temper – little boy!"

"AAAAGH!!" And Jimmy ran out into the street.

"Oh, why do you have to provoke him?" said their mother, coming in from the back kitchen. "You know what he's like in the morning."

"Well, he's worse, this morning."

"Only because you can't stop teasing him."

But Jimmy did feel worse. In fact, he knew there was something wrong. He ought to feel elated. He had a new college blazer, cap and tie, which he had been allowed to wear to church on Sunday, even though his first day at the grammar school was still a week away. He kept feeling hot and then cold. Everything he did seemed to take a huge effort and he knew he was bad tempered. And his head felt itchy. He scratched. Then he noticed he had pimples in his hair. He scratched harder and this time drew blood, so he went back inside to his mother.

"Mam. Look," he said, beginning to cry.

"What's the matter?"

"I've got pimples on me head."

"Show me." She scrutinised him. "There's one or two on your face too. Have you got them anywhere else?"

"I don't know."

"Pull up your shirt… Ah yes, there are. We'd better go to the doctor's."

It was chicken pox, and because of it, he had to miss the first two weeks of the term, and that made his first day at the new school more traumatic than it need have been. Alan took him into assembly and showed him which line to stand in. He even had a word with the prefect, who put him at the end of the line and told him to follow the others when they marched out after prayers. This was not as easy as it seemed because, just like the boys in the elementary school, his new companions ran everywhere unless somebody told them not to. As they dashed up the stairs, 1A, 1B and 1C got all mixed up and he did not know the faces well enough to tell one class from the next. Fortunately, their rooms were next to each other and even a simpleton could tell that 1B was the middle one. So that was where he went. Then the embarrassment really began: everyone went to a desk and sat down, but he could only stand in the front and be stared at. There was a desk with nobody in it and had he been less tense he might have asked if it were free, but instead he stood on one foot and then the other and got redder and redder. When the teacher finally arrived, he strode in and said, "Who are you and why are you standing there like a ninny?"

"He's the new boy," at least half the class shouted, before Jimmy could speak.

"Can't he talk for himself?"

"No, Sir."

"Yes I can, Sir."

"What's your name?"

"James Thompson, Sir."

"And do you know which class you are supposed to be in?"

"Yes, Sir. 1B, Sir."

"Then, gentlemen, he's in the right place, is he not?" Cheers and shouts broke out, and the teacher looked very stern. "Pipe down, all of you." And then, turning to the boy behind the empty desk, which was on the end of the front row, he continued, "Does anybody sit there, lad?"

"No, Sir."

"Right, park yourself there, and have you got a French exercise book?"

"No, Sir."

"Have you got a scribbler?"

"Yes Sir. My brother got one for me."

The teacher looked at him sharply and said, "Is he the Thompson in 5S?"

"Yes, Sir," said Jimmy proudly.

"Right my lad, we'll have to keep a careful eye on you too."

Jimmy felt his heart sink. His first day in the school and already he was a marked man and all because of his brother. He'd half expected this from things his brother and his friends had said. Perhaps the teacher was joking, but Jimmy took him seriously, and felt afraid for the future, and especially the ever present threat of the ferula.

Most lessons on that first day had awkward openings for him as teachers quizzed him about who he was and whether he had books or not. They also all gave him extra work, supposedly to help him catch up, though he had no difficulty understanding any of the work, as everything was still at a relatively simple level and, apart from the algebra, it was all in the textbooks. He did go home with instructions to learn *je suis, tu es, il est...* etc., and *amo, amas, amat...* and so on, and to make sure he knew them for the next day. This got him into the habit of doing his homework thoroughly. As the term wore on and he became more acquainted with the routines, his fears and apprehensions receded. Latin was easy as long as you learned the declensions and conjugations and were careful to choose the right bits from them when you translated the ludicrous sentences you were given for homework. French was a little different because of the pronunciation but, as they learned it out of a book, he and his fellow pupils were able to cling doggedly to their Liverpudlian vowels and consonants. Three teachers of French, one of whom was a Sixth Former waiting to go up to Oxford, followed each other in quick succession and all colluded in this. Algebra and geometry were new and quite exciting because they were thoroughly taught in a way that included problem-solving.

Science, a subject Jimmy was looking forward to, was a disappointment, its only novel aspect being that it was taught in the chemistry lecture theatre. It could have been taught in any old classroom because it was confined to Botany (in the first term), and entailed nothing more than copying stamens and cotyledons and other bits of plant life from drawings in a textbook and taking down notes from the blackboard. P.T., on the other hand, was different from anything he'd done before because it took place in a real gymnasium, which had wall-bars and beams and ropes, as well as boxes and all the other paraphernalia; and you were punished if you did not have the correct kit. Art too came as a surprise, again because it was in a room specially designed for it. In fact it was a late autumn afternoon lesson in this sunny room, using real poster paints, of which each pupil had his own set, that brought home to him just how different this was from the cramped, dark, elementary school he had recently left. He began to think he might learn to like this school. However, there were dangers.

The worst was the ferula, which, within very few weeks, most of the boys in the class had experienced for one reason or another – perhaps not doing homework, or doing it badly, and that meant carelessly. It was rarely given to discipline pupils because mostly they were well-behaved and minor misdemeanours such as talking in class usually resulted in the imposition of lines. What was cruel about the ferula was the ritual that had built up around this particularly barbarous form of corporal punishment. It had become contradictory, or perhaps had been subverted, or maybe even perverted, because it was clearly meant originally to ensure that justice was done, that vindictiveness was avoided, and appeal allowed for. By the late 1940s, it provided for none of these. An individual teacher could not administer the ferula in his own classroom, as Jimmy's elementary teachers had the cane. If he wished to punish a boy he gave him what was called a bill. This was a small square of paper on which was written the date, the name of the miscreant, the number of strokes – three or four (in the First Form) or six or even nine. However, twelve or even twice nine, and in the mythology, twice twelve, were not unknown. The teacher then signed it. Most often bills popped up out of exercise books when homework was given back, but if a teacher decided during class that a bill was needed, he might invite a boy to write one for himself. How Jimmy dreaded the words, "Write yourself a bill for six". The boy then took the bill to the Head, if he were in the upper school, or to one of the two Deputy Heads, if he were in the lower. This was supposed to be the point of appeal, but Jimmy never heard of anybody persuading a Deputy Head to even consider waiving a bill. They always signed them and often added a sermon too, and were not unknown to utter threats as well. "This is the third time this week you've been punished for not doing homework, would you like me to add to this bill?" The boy then took the bill to the P.T. office at the back of the gym and there joined a queue of nervous wrecks waiting to be punished. Inside was a scholastic, i.e. a young man at that stage in his training as a Jesuit that required him not only to teach but also to undertake the most unpleasant duties attached to the teacher's role. To Jimmy they always appeared very large, very fit and very strong. When the boy entered this claustrophobic cell with its smell of stale sweat, rubber from old plimsolls, and leather, the scholastic transferred the details from the bill to a large black 'punishment book'. He then took the ferula out of the drawer, held the pupil by the wrist and administered the strokes first to one hand and then the other. He put the bills into a box, which he would later deposit in the staffroom so that teachers could check whether or not boys had been punished. If a pupil delayed too long, the master would double the number of strokes. Now this system may have had the dubious merit of making lads face up to difficulties quickly, but it could lead to alarming situations: one of Jimmy's acquaintances managed to assemble a whole collection of bills. On the way home from school he discussed how he might get through the ordeal:

"I've just had six. I could go down and get the four from Checker tomorrow at break, but then not have any at lunchtime, just to give me hands a rest. Then at afternoon break I could get the six from Pegleg. The trouble with that is Brum might double his six, 'cos I haven't had them. Who do you think will check up first, Pegleg or Brum?" And so on.

In the end it all became so complicated that the Deputy Head had to commute the set into a composite bill for twelve, and delay the punishment for several days so that Walter's hands could recover first. The trouble was that it was too easy for teachers: they did not have the unpleasantness of delivering the punishment themselves. Setting aside the danger of sadism among teachers, it would have been a salutary experience for most of them to have done their own dirty work. Scholastics tended not to order the ferula very often for their pupils. Having once kept a bill over a whole weekend, Jimmy found it so unnerving that from then on he always got ferulas as soon as possible.

So, at first Jimmy worked diligently, partly to obviate the danger of the ferula, but also because he felt compelled to catch up with the others. He paid attention in class and did his homework so conscientiously that he surpassed them. But he was almost obsessed with the need to avoid careless mistakes: he checked and double-checked every little detail, so that sometimes the work took twice as long as it should have done. This meant that certain things he learned very thoroughly, but others he never really learned at all, because he always checked them in the textbook. Fortunately, in the first year, this did not matter too much because the subjects were relatively simple, and the logic of things like theorems and grammar rules were such that you could work out the answer, and so he came top of the class in the Easter examinations, and by a considerable margin too. He managed to stay top when it came to the summer exams but, ominously, by a much narrower margin.

By avoiding the ferula he found himself promoted to 2A

in the second year. Life then started to become more complicated. First of all he was faced with the problem of catching up
again, because 1A had obviously progressed much faster than
1B, perhaps because the pupils were brighter, classes having
been set up according to marks achieved in the scholarship.
However, Jimmy found that many of his new companions were
no sharper than the ones he had left behind, and so it must have
been because the teachers believed that these pupils were more
capable. Whatever the cause, he faced difficulties and ones he
felt less inclined to deal with: he wanted to rest on his laurels,
so convinced was he, briefly, of his own ability. At first all went
smoothly and he coped with the work very well, but then he
became cavalier in his attitude to homework. One reason for
this was that he had two sets of friends: one at school and one at
home, because the school friends all lived miles away. He usually
stayed late after class to play football in the yard, and this meant
that time when he might have done his homework was lost. Once
he got home, friends would be calling for him who were at either
the old all-age elementary schools or at the new (old really, but
renamed) secondary moderns, and they had no homework. In
the early stages, one of these could be relied on to help with the
maths, because he caught on quickly and could calculate accurately if Jimmy told him what to do, but gradually he got out of
his depth, and could not help. Jimmy began to leave some of his
homework till the next morning. He could lean on the piano in the
hall before assembly and do it there. One morning, however, the
prefect moved him off the piano. His French homework was left
undone. He tried to do it during Latin, but the teacher obviously
suspected something. He tried again during maths, but got only
two of the five sentences done. He thought he might still get away
with it because the French teacher never collected the books. He
would ask an individual boy for his version of the first sentence
and then he would write the correct version on the board. He
would move on to another boy for number two. You could always
write the correct version in your book. Jimmy hoped he wouldn't
be asked and right up to sentence four his luck held. He was then
devastated to hear, "Thompson, give us number five".

There was a long pause as Jimmy stood up very slowly.

"Apres… apres un… apres un certain temps…"

"Thompson, what are you doing? Are you trying to compose number five now?

"No, Sir."

"Then have you developed a stutter overnight?"

"No, Sir."

"Bring out your book."

Jimmy did and his teacher peered at it.

"Ah, Thompson. It's very strange, isn't it? We have two sentences badly written and riddled with mistakes, two that are completely correct, and one that doesn't exist at all. Would you like to tell us why, Thompson?"

"No, Sir."

"Do you mean you won't tell us or that you don't know why?"

"I don't know, Sir."

"Oh, but you do know… Let me tell you just the same. Not only are you lazy and don't complete your homework, you are also a cheat and write in versions composed by other boys. Furthermore, you are a liar, because you know all this very well. Take this away and write yourself a bill for six."

At last the Damoclean sword had fallen and the whole class knew it: apart from Gibbons, who was a genius, Jimmy was the only one who had not had the ferula. Suddenly life had become unreal. As he walked back to his place he looked at his feet: they seemed miles away. When he took up his pen it didn't seem to belong to him. Even his hands seemed to be part of someone else. He had shrivelled up into a ball somewhere in the back of his skull; such was his state of shock. His hands and his pen and his exercise book were outside in another world, a world of ordinariness, from which he was now cut off. He wrote the bill somehow, though his writing was shaky and spidery. He still had one vain hope: that the teacher would forget to sign it at the end of the lesson. He did not. At break Jimmy took it to the Deputy Head who countersigned it without even looking up from his desk. Jimmy now faced a dilemma – should he get them now? What if he cried? Could he go back to class weeping? How the others would jeer. No. He'd go at lunchtime. But that meant two lessons of desperation. Fortunately it was double P.T. next and so he could at least be active and he wouldn't have to concentrate. Even so, the next eighty minutes were miserable. At the end he changed very slowly out of his P.T. kit – so did the others: they wanted to stay and see. Also as he glanced towards the half-glass doors he caught a glimpse of faces from 2B, his old class. They had also found out and wanted to see how smarty-pants took the ferula. Then a queue of ashen-faced waifs began to form outside the P.T. office to await the arrival of the scholastic, the aptly named Mr Birch. Some lads shuffled; some shivered and yawned; one picked and rubbed at his nose, as though it were the source of his woes; others stood hunched up. Jimmy joined them. He wanted to be brave but it was so difficult with all the others in the queue twitching and snuffling, and with most of 2A and 2B looking on. Mr Birch arrived and strode in, asking the first to come in and shut the door. Before long this child almost fell out of the office, bent double, with his hands tucked under his arms. The next went in. The rest considered the signs and conferred with each other. "Is he laying on?" The general opinion was that indeed he was – several left the queue, which meant that Jimmy reached the front all too soon. When he went in he found the stench almost over-powering and he worried that he might be sick. The formalities gone through, Mr Birch took his wrist and Jimmy looked away. The ferula descended. There was an intense burning sensation, and then his hand went numb. The second and third strokes followed in quick succession. Mr Birch turned him round and grabbed his other wrist. Again the burning and the numbness. But then the pain was so intense that he nearly cried out. In a twinkling he was outside and Mr Birch was shouting "Next!" There was a ring of expectant faces around him, all staring hard to see how he was taking it, but what surprised him was that he was not crying, even if there were tears in his eyes. He kept his hands open but thrust in his trouser pockets. Somebody put his bag on his shoulder and he walked stiffly out of the gym, down the corridor, out through the back courtyard and into the alley to Shaw Street. By then he was alone. He began to cry and he prayed and prayed that the pain would go away, but like a burn it kept on and on. He was almost home before it subsided and even then he still smarted, especially if he clenched his fists. Once in, he washed his hands in cold water and this gave him some relief. He looked at them and arched them so that the skin was tight. Where the strokes had overlapped he could see dark red stripes. Mr Birch was obviously an expert.

Jimmy did his homework very thoroughly for the next three weeks, but then got the ferula again, this time for misbehaviour. It happened on a Saturday morning and in the very last lesson of a week in which he felt he had done well. 'Egg-in-the-nest', so-called for one very obvious reason, was head of Maths, and took a class as lowly as Jimmy's only because it was the A stream. He was a tall, middle-aged man, rather stiff and formal, reminiscent in shape and carriage of General De Gaulle, though more portly. He always wore a dark pin-striped suit and black shoes with steel tips, so that you could hear him coming. On this particular Saturday he was uncharacteristically late, and so was the teacher who should have been taking 2B next door. Both classes were making a noise and there was some horseplay too. Boys, scrapping half-heartedly in 2B, crashed against the partition between the two classes and Jimmy climbed upon his desk to see what was going on, as the top part of the partition was glass. Boys on the other side began to make faces at him, so he did the same at them. At this point Eggo came along the corridor – silently because, inexplicably, he was wearing suede crepe-soled shoes. Without looking at anybody in particular, he stepped across the room from the door to the dais, saying, in his nasal way, "Come out all those boys fooling about".

But by the time he had turned to face the class, everybody, with the exception of Jimmy, was sitting down. In flagrante delicto, he had no option but to climb off the desk and go up to the front. Jimmy was just about the shortest boy in the class: he seemed to have to bend his head right back in order to look up at this giant, as he stood on the dais. The teacher, in his turn, had to look down his nose to see Jimmy.

"Well, you're a very honest little fellow but you're very unfortunate too because you are the only one I can chastise to set an example to your rowdy companions. You'd better write yourself a bill – but for three only."

This did not have quite the same shattering impact on Jimmy as the first bill, but it was still very unsettling. He found it difficult to concentrate for the rest of the lesson but so did all the others. Partly, this was because it was last lesson on a Saturday, partly because they had escaped Jimmy's fate, but mostly because of Eggo himself: the suede shoes were not the only items of his dress to appear unusual. He was wearing a light check jacket, with what, for him, was a florid tie and brown trousers. He taught them only briefly and then set them some examples to work through – "for homework which you may begin now". They were truly amazed. But the intrigue developed even further. Now seated at his desk, he took up the textbook and held it close to his face. He peered at it: the boys peered at him. Then he took a pair of nail scissors out of his pocket and began to trim his pencil thin moustache. After a while he became aware of the fact that they were all looking at him. With great aplomb, he carefully put the book, and its concealed mirror, down, looked round at them with ever-widening eyes and said, "Have you not got enough to do?"

Their heads went down over their books and shortly after, the bell went. Eggo hurriedly signed Jimmy's bill and left. As they packed their bags with weekend homework and decamped, the class was full of their Maths teacher's strange dress and behaviour. All sorts of theories were expounded: he had won on the pools; he had gone mad; or he was taking up a career as a crooner. But the favourite, though most unlikely, was that he had a girl-friend, who lived over the water somewhere posh like Hoylake. Why the latter details should figure in this was never explained. They were taken as self-evident. Because of all this Jimmy nearly forgot the ferula, but every so often the memory and its attendant sense of dread flooded back like a cold douche. He saw the Deputy and then went down to the gym but he got there too late: Mr Birch had been and gone. His feeling of relief was tinged with regret, because he had missed the chance to get it all over with and he knew his weekend would be wretched. At break on the

Monday he was first in the queue.

During the rest of the second year he more or less held his own. He could understand the work and he usually did his homework sufficiently well to avoid punishment, but he had few friends at school, and those he did have he rarely saw outside. Matters might have been different had he got into the Chicks football team. He had nearly managed it in the first year but was too small. In the second year he felt certain he would be included, but the place he coveted was taken by a first year boy of outstanding ability. So on Wednesday afternoons he hung around his own neighbourhood instead. Though he was no longer completely acceptable in the old street gang, these were the boys he played football with down at the Pit. Sometimes he went with them to the swimming baths, and quite often to the pictures. But he had a strange sense of not belonging fully to either world.

At the beginning of the third year the situation improved and to Jimmy this seemed to be linked to the fact that he began to serve Mass. All the others in his class who lived near enough began to serve too, because this was the wish, not to say command, of Father Tomkins, their Form Master. To begin with they served in the college chapel in pairs, a learner with an experienced altar boy, and they served only Father Tomkins, who said Mass in a steady and dignified way, so that you could keep up with the Latin, and had time to think about what you were doing. However, the Jesuit house responsible for the school also ran a parish: there were a large number of priests to be served at seven o'clock each morning, and the sacristy, organized by a scholastic, was like the H.Q. of an army under siege. Altar boys, the squaddies, were drafted wherever they were needed, to plug the gaps, and it was no good protesting, "We're Father Tomkin's servers". You were given a small cloth, a cruet of wine and one of water on a flat dish, pushed into line and told where to lead your priest – either to the high altar, or the Lady Chapel, or the Bona Mors Chapel, or wherever. When the church clock chimed seven, a line of priests emerged from the vestry and the servers, mostly boys from the parish, slotted into it. No altar boy knew which priest he would serve, and no priest knew where he was going until led there. This could be nerve-wracking: one morning Jimmy got the Headmaster to lead to a side altar he'd never heard of before. He went to where he imagined it was, only to discover it was already occupied. Fortunately, there was another next to it. The Head said Mass faster than seemed proper: before Jimmy had finished any of the responses in the psalm, he had begun the next part. They were back in the sacristy in a quarter of an hour, but the priest explained that if he said Mass slowly he lost concentration.

On another occasion, Jimmy arrived at church with very little time to spare and found that all the cassocks his size had gone. Of those left even the smallest was much too big, but there was no alternative so he trooped off, like Mickey Mouse in the Sorcerer's robe, to an obscure altar, leading a strange priest, and carrying the cruets in one hand while holding up his drooping skirts with the other. They arrived without serious mishap at a tiny chapel next to an aisle in the transept from which it was separated by only a high railing. On the other side of this, seated on a bench that was fixed to it, was a scruffy old lady with a very large bag. She must have been a regular, because she knew where the light was and Jimmy obviously didn't.

"It's over there on the side of the pillar on the left," she said in a loud, hoarse voice. Jimmy found it, switched it on and put his cruets down on the little table nearby. However, he had forgotten his long skirts and had not realized that on his way to the light he had had to make a step up. Blithely striding back to take up his place at the right-hand-side of the patiently waiting priest, he put his foot in the hem of the cassock just as he arrived at the step: over he went, with his skirts whirling round his head, and crashed into the railing.

"My God, son, what are you doing jumpin' around like that? Are you trying to knock the church down?" said the old lady.

"Oops-a-daisy," said the priest, lifting up Jimmy and straightening out his cotta. "Are you all right, laddie?"

"I think so, Father," said Jimmy, trying to get his bearings.

Mass began, and all went well, until Jimmy had to transfer the Book from the Epistle side to the Gospel side of the altar. This time he remembered the step and his long cassock, yet still got his foot stuck in the hem, but without falling over. He waggled and waggled his foot but it would not come out: he could go neither backwards nor forwards. The priest waited and waited. Jimmy felt his arms would drop off.

"What is the matter now?" said the priest at last, turning round to see the predicament. He called to the lady, "See to him, can't you?"

She came and pulled up Jimmy's cassock, and matters proceeded. However, after her sortie on to the altar, the old lady felt that she was part of the service and could relax into familiarity with Jimmy. She rummaged noisily in her capacious bag and emerged with crackers, cheese and a knife.

"Ay, lad, I bet you've had no breakfast, have you?" she said, without making any effort to lower her voice. "Do you want some of this?" she continued.

But Jimmy ignored her. That is until she said even more loudly, "OK, then dip your nose in it."

"Shh, the priest is trying to say Mass!"

She was quiet for a while and thankfully right through the Consecration, but then she broke in again with, "You know, you remind me of my son... he was like you... you know, always jumping about and falling all over the place and that... got into trouble in the end... he's in Walton Gaol now, y'know?... Ay, he wouldn't listen either."

Jimmy got up and went over to her. He knelt down so that he could whisper to her. "Listen, Missus, you'll have to be quiet, or you'll have the priest getting upset. He has to concentrate when he's saying Mass."

She gave him a faraway look, but it did the trick and she didn't speak again until they were coming off the altar when she gave them a cheerful, "Tarra, well".

When they got back to the sacristy, the priest asked Jimmy if he had ever served on that altar before.

"She's always there; you just have to ignore her. But don't worry, you did very well. Make sure you get a cassock that fits you tomorrow. God bless, now."

Jimmy liked serving Mass early in the morning. He had

not realized before just how alive the city was at half past six, with people of every description, but mostly workmen, scurrying to catch trams and buses; dashing into shops to buy newspapers and cigarettes; or simply walking to work. He liked it especially in the winter when it was still dark: for some reason the street lights seemed brighter, and strangely, so did the people. They spoke and sometimes even called to each other across the road. If he went into a shop to buy gumdrops, the newsagent was cheerful and seemed to know all his customers well. But probably what he liked most was that he felt, for the first time, that he was part of the adult world. When he strolled home afterwards, there would be a different set of people about; more women and children; people he felt sure had office jobs; and even early shoppers. He felt superior to all of these and he hoped that they realized that he was from the elite who had to get up very early to do important work. Once he knew the ropes and was familiar with the situation of every altar and the idiosyncrasies of every priest, he liked being in church.

He never questioned what he was expected to believe. His sense that as a Catholic he was beleaguered was still strong and this was not only because the family was surrounded by Orangemen, but also because of the way the Church interpreted its terrestrial situation after the Second World War. The notion that it was in a life and death struggle with Communism was carefully nurtured by the Jesuits and, of course, to some extent this was true. The imprisonment of Cardinal Mindszenty in Hungary was played upon as an example of what would happen if the might of the Soviet Union were allowed to hold sway in Western Europe. Details of how the Cardinal had been treated were published in the Catholic newspapers, which his mother brought home from church, and they found an echo in a story which his R.I. teacher read to the class during one Lent term.

It was about an Elizabethan boy who found a secret way into the grounds of the Tower of London. Down a short shaft he sees a man's hands (the title of the story) protruding from a grill, which formed a small window to a prison cell. Fascinated by them, the boy returns several times and finally talks to the man, who is

Edmund Campion, a Jesuit, and about to die for his faith. Then there comes a time when the hands are torn and bruised and the wrists are swollen and cut: Campion has been on the rack. He cannot talk. A few days later the boy sees him hanged, drawn and quartered. Jimmy was struck by the equanimity attributed to Edmund Campion in the story and the determination of the boy, despite what he has seen, to become a Jesuit. He wondered how he would behave if he were faced with torture and a painful and prolonged death. He fervently hoped persecution would never return, and if the hymn 'Faith of our Fathers' was sung he felt like a hypocrite as he sang the words: "How sweet would be their children's fate if they like them could die for thee". He was terrified of such a fate. But the real dilemma was that if you were not prepared to die for your faith, you faced the horrors of Hell, which were worse because they were unimaginable and forever.

He noticed that on the days he served Mass, he also seemed to avoid trouble in school afterwards. Whether this was mere coincidence, or perhaps because he organized himself better, he did not know. He never thought about it in such terms: he simply assumed he was protected in some way. Consequently, when he was not on Father Tomkins' rota, he went to Mass with his mother who went to their own parish church most mornings. There were still difficult times at school: he never seemed to catch up in subjects like physics and chemistry, even though he wanted to very much, because these were the subjects his brother had been so very good at. Indeed, the Head of Science was obviously disappointed in him, because he fell below his brother's standards: he also seemed to know if Alan had helped him with his homework. Nevertheless, for a time, in all the other subjects, he met with a measure of success.

He also played football for a school team, though there were only a few games. The 'Chicks' was composed of boys who were under twelve years of age on the first day of the Christmas term and the 'Juniors', fifteen. There was nothing in between. Then a priest, Father Smythe, himself a Liverpudlian, came to teach chemistry at the school and he was often to be seen leaning out of one of the windows in the house, watching the boys play during break. He decided to get up a team that he called the 'Intermediates' and he arranged half a dozen fixtures with other schools. He had watched the rather diminutive Jimmy play in the yard and decided that he wanted him to act as a tearaway centre-forward, to play the kind of football Jimmy played at home in the street.

"Look, Jimmy, I'll tell you what I want. If you get the ball in your own half, or just inside your opponents' half, I want you to bang it out to either of the wings. If you get it in the penalty area or within spitting distance of it, I want you to put your head down and go for goal, then if there's half or even a quarter of a chance I want you to whack it at the goal."

"But what if no one's on the wing?"

"Don't you worry about that. I'm going to get two wingers who will know that you are going to pass it to the wings without looking. They'll be off and running at the drop of a hat – and they'll be fast. And what's more they'll be told to centre it to Jimmy Thompson as soon as they are level with the penalty area so you've got to be ready."

"But what if it's a big centre-half?"

"Look, lad, I've seen you jump and head. And anyway, if you put yourself about it will worry them, even when you don't get the ball."

All the players had simple instructions like these so that everyone had a limited number of things to do. All the defenders knew how to cover each other. There were also ploys at set pieces. For corners, the two biggest lads went up from the defence and stood close to the opposition's goal-line. The forwards all hung back beyond the penalty spot. The winger was told to try and loft the ball over that spot. As the ball came over, all the forwards ran towards the goal and jumped at the ball. The effect on opponents was devastating: just being organized was enough to unnerve them; leaping together made them think the ploy was even more complex than it was.

The team won every game it played and by a considerable margin too. Jimmy scored regularly, though there were times when he missed as many as he hit, but Father Smythe told him not to worry: Jimmy was playing the way he had been told. The two wingers were from the year below him and regarded him as something of a star. They expected him to pass out to them if he got the ball and they saw their next job as supplying him with passes from which to score. The team spirit was very high. Father Smythe never complained: he gave them positive encouragement instead. Jimmy wished all his teachers could be like him. Unfortunately, they were not and when the football season ended so did the euphoria.

He began to backslide again and because this went on for several months, school became more difficult, and he began to use every possible excuse not to go. This made matters worse: lessons missed created problems in later ones so that there were times when he could not do the work, not because he was lazy, but because he didn't understand what he was supposed to do. The threat of the ferula loomed large. His family began to realize that something was wrong and his mother became less inclined to write excuse notes for him. Home was not the safe bolt-hole he thought it was because he could be turfed out of it and sent to school. So he began to feel very insecure and not at all sure how to resolve the dilemma. In the past, the only way to avoid trouble in school had been to do your homework thoroughly and carefully, and to pay attention in class so that you knew what to do. But these ploys no longer worked because he had lost so much ground. He thought about playing truant, but the awful memory of what had happened to the two lads in the elementary school was still a powerful deterrent.

Moreover, when he moved up to the Fourth Form, he fell foul of his new Form Master, Father Burden, who took the class for both Latin and R.I. He was the worst martinet Jimmy had ever met. Each lesson began with an oral test of a chunk of grammar set the previous day. As much of this was revision of work done lower down the school, he expected all answers to be perfect at the first time of asking: the slightest mistake could result in a bill. Jimmy was terrified, so he learned the grammar. Then the correct version of the homework just returned was put up on a green board, written in an ultra-neat italic hand in yellow chalk.

You had to look at the board and nowhere else; a sideways glance could result in the ferula. But Jimmy was so frightened that he didn't even blink either. This meant that when he had been looking at the board for a while the letters would begin to dance and his view would begin to blacken, at first around the edges, but then towards the middle.

Jimmy tried to keep a low profile, but he had an accident on a bike which resulted in him having to wear a collar and cuff on his right arm: he wasn't able to write very well. He had an official note saying he was excused written homework. Burden saw this as malingering. He told Jimmy to do his homework in rough, not to hand it in, but to have it ready for inspection. At the end of the next lesson, pronouncing the 'th' in Thompson as in 'the', he called Jimmy out. With a sneer he picked up the piece of paper (torn out of a rough book) between his finger and thumb and said, "What do you call this?"

"It's my homework, Father."

"It looks very tatty to me."

"You said to do it in rough, Father."

"And that's the same as tatty, is it?"

"I wrote it with my left hand, Father."

"And I suppose you tore the piece of paper out with your left hand too?"

"Yes, Father."

There was a pause. Burden glared at him over his glasses.

"Thompson, you're a plausible rascal."

He then proceeded to question Jimmy on the tenses of all of the verbs in the subordinate clauses in the homework. Then, looking Jimmy square in the face again, and opening his eyes even wider, he said, "I'll expect neater work tomorrow".

Jimmy did his homework with his right hand, even though it was swollen and the doctor in the hospital had told him not to use it. He also got his mother to comment on how neat she thought it was. The next morning in the hall he took it out of his bag to check it with others in his class. Just as he was holding it up for Gibbons to squint at it, a clown in one of the Fifth Forms behind them squirted a water pistol at it. Jimmy's immediate reaction was to wipe the back of his hand across it: he smudged almost every word on the page. This time his work was collected with all the others so he had to wait two days to discover the outcome. The lesson in which they got the work back was a double and Burden brought the books in and stood them on his desk. He did not give them back until the very end and he returned them individually, commenting on each piece. Jimmy's was the last of all. Burden picked it up, again between finger and thumb: he exuded disgust. Jimmy almost choked with apprehension. Burden laid it carefully, almost precisely, on Jimmy's desk and said, "Had a little accident then?"

He then walked straight out. Jimmy looked at the work: there were no mistakes in it.

There could be no doubt that Burden was out to get him. In fact he had said as much. His chance came when he was examining the grammar on a day when Jimmy really was sick, but his mother had made him go to school anyway. A quarter of an hour into the lesson he was so certain that he would throw up that he dared to ask if he could go out. He was told that he could but only when he had answered some questions. Again, Burden left him to the end, this time of the grammar quiz.

"Right then, Thompson, Let's see what you can do. On your feet."

Jimmy knew he would get asked the adverbs because, though there was a kind of pattern to them, it hindered rather than helped the learning.

"Ubi"......"Where"

"Thence"......"Inde"

"Whither"......"Quo"

"Hinc"......"Hence"

"Unde"......"Whence"

"There"......"Ubi... er... Ibi"

"Aha! You're not sure. I'll give you five more. Any mistakes and it's nine ferulas."

"Hic"......"Here"

"Quo"......"Whither"

"Ibi"......"There"

George Timmons

"Thither"......"Er... er... Ist"

"Too late – nine ferulas. Now you can go out."

Jimmy got to the top of the stairs before he was sick; what seemed to be gallons of water poured out of his mouth and down the steps. Just then, Ollie, the school keeper's assistant, came up the stairs.

"My God. What's goin' on?"

"I'm sorry, Ollie, I couldn't stop it."

"Couldn't you wait until you got to the basement?"

"No."

"Well, why didn't you come out earlier?"

"I asked but Father Burden wouldn't let me."

"Oh, him! ... Never mind, lad, you go down before you're sick again and I'll see to this. You look terrible."

When Jimmy went to get the ferulas, he discovered that it was Mr Birch, and the consensus was that he was laying on. He was surprised that he did not care: he had that feeling of separateness, when his body seemed not to belong to him, when the real him seemed to be far away. Mr Birch gave him the first four on his left hand and when Jimmy tried to struggle out of the cuff so that he could present his right hand, Mr Birch said, "Leave it".

"But Father Burden..."

"He won't find out and if you say nothing, neither will anybody else."

Feeling grateful for once, Jimmy left the office. There was nobody else waiting to be punished.

Though from then on he always did enough to avoid trouble, he lost interest in school and this was not only because of the injustice and spite that he had experienced. Indeed, this was not so very important. What did matter very seriously was that he felt education was not having the effects he expected. He had imagined that grammar school would somehow change him, make him intelligent, perhaps even wise. Yet he felt more stupid and more confused than he had before. The knowledge he had gained seemed not to amount to much and most of it was eminently forgettable. That it was bitty was perhaps his own fault, but that it was incoherent and seemingly unrelated to the real world could

Safe Haven

not be blamed on him alone. Unless, that is, he really was not very bright.

However, what was much worse was that he felt that he did not know how to think constructively. Given any new problem, he did not even know where to start, or how to go about finding out how to begin. Quite how he should have been transformed by the school he did not know, but surely, by now, after four years, something should have happened.

Had there been a tutorial system or if the Form Masters had been more than mere recorders of marks, then someone might have realized that he was in difficulties. Without help, he had no idea how to catch up with the work he had missed. Much of what he should have learned could probably have been forgotten with impunity, but he did not know that and so was daunted by what seemed a mountain of work. He also imagined that the complexity of the missed learning was greater than it really was, and this added to his feeling of helplessness. So he did nothing, but as a consequence felt even more guilty: it was his fault alone that this situation had arisen. He began to wonder if the underlying problem was indolence. In fact, he did nothing because he did not know what to do – but he thought matters were the other way about, and this was the case even on those occasions when he could see clearly what had to be done, knew how to do it, and got on with it. Yet he still felt guilty and saw idleness as his besetting sin.

Nor was this the case with schoolwork only. As the youngest in the family, and especially when he was little, his brother and sisters did things for him, even when he wanted to do them for himself. Moreover, not only was his brother four years older, he was also very skilled at making and repairing household items. To make matters worse, on the one occasion when Jimmy tried his hand at electrical repairs, he blew all the fuses in the house. This alone was enough to discourage him, but he had to contend with the jeers of the others too. Despite, or perhaps because of, his low self-esteem, and also because Father Burden had warned him that he would look carefully at all his papers, Jimmy did some work for the summer examinations – and he made especially sure that he revised for Latin and R.I. In a perverse way this in turn was to have an adverse effect on his sense of his own worth.

Chapter V

O NE FACTOR IN JIMMY's dislike of school was what he saw as the freedom of the friends at home, many of whom had left school and were working. They had money, could buy some of their own clothes, could afford cigarettes, and in the evenings their time was their own: they were not obliged to do homework. Also, they could do something about their new-found interest in girls. In fact, Billy Wilkins, who lived opposite, even went dancing at the Grafton on Saturday afternoons. When Jimmy asked his mother if he could wear his best suit and go with Billy, she laughed and shook her head, making him feel silly. He could only fantasize about what might happen if he went.

Jimmy was very shy of girls and could be thrown into paroxysms of embarrassment if confronted by them. As he walked to school, by himself, he met several as they made their way to a local secondary modern and they all seemed to know that he would blush furiously when he saw them. They played on this and would link arms so that they stretched right across the pavement, and he had to step into the gutter to pass them. They rarely said anything, but they all grinned as they approached him and giggled after he had stumbled by with his hand in front of his face to try to hide his blushes. Crossing the road achieved nothing: they were on both sides. On one occasion he tried a different ploy and stopped to look into a shop window. He feigned deep interest, but really had no idea what he was looking at, until one of them said, "Ay, there's that college-pudd'n with the satchel looking at the dirty books".

"Are you gett'n a good eyeful, lad," said another, and this was followed by, "He's not as posh as he thinks, is he, ay?"

Only then did Jimmy realize that he was standing in front

of the second-hand bookshop, which did have books with lurid and suggestive covers, though these were not even mildly pornographic by later standards. All that he could do was to continue to stand and stare, feeling fiery red. He also felt guilty: he had been found out because he did stop regularly at this window in the hope that the covers of the books would be more revealing than usual.

Friends of his sisters' and girls from his street that he had known for a long time he could talk to easily enough, but those he was really interested in he felt very apprehensive about.

One particular girl, whose name he knew was Bella, he used to see most evenings as she went home from a friend's nearby. He wondered if he were in love with her because he often found himself thinking about her when he least expected it. He would daydream of situations in which they would be thrown together so that she could become his steady girlfriend, and all those lads who were bigger than him, or who had more money, who smoked and shaved and were tougher, would be envious because she really was very beautiful. He wondered what he could do to make her notice him in particular, because usually there were several other lads around when she went by. He had no clothes he could wear to look smart, except his Sunday suit, and that was getting too short. Moreover, his family would ask embarrassing questions if he wore it on a weekday. Perhaps he could sneak out in it one evening, he thought … and he thought again … and again: it was risky, but he would give it a try.

When he looked in the wardrobe, however, the article that caught his eye was a greeny-blue jacket of his brother's. Alan was now working and could afford such luxuries: it was also fashionably styled, having the long lapels referred to at that time as 'the drape'. His brother was also of an age when it is essential for young men to drink too much, and this jacket had suffered considerable abuse during Alan's Saturday night forays. Jimmy tried it on. Beer and sick had been sponged off regularly, but Jimmy thought the stains hardly showed at all. It was too big but not by that much and if he drew himself up to his full height and a bit more, it did not look too grotesque, and it was certainly more eye-catching than his skin-tight, so-called best suit. His hair needed attention, so he took some of Alan's Brylcreem too, but he was rather generous in the amount he put on. Never mind, there would be less chance that his hair would blow about in the wind (if there were any). He crept downstairs and out of the back kitchen door. This meant he could go up the back entry and so avoid being seen in the street. Fortunately, when he got to the shop doorway where the lads usually assembled there was nobody there: he had the field to himself. He stood as tall as he could with his legs firmly apart and his hands behind his back, so that his chest stuck out. Then he waited… and waited… and waited. After a while he began to feel uncomfortable in this posture. He had to relax and walk about a little. Then he took up his stance once more. Just as he thought he would have to move again, he saw her coming along the road and his immediate reaction was to stiffen and hold his breath. However, she was walking very slowly and he began to realize that if he did not breathe soon he would burst; he could also feel his cheeks burning. He tried to avoid taking in a sharp and obvious gulp of air, but then became aware that he was making a whistling noise with his teeth: he closed his mouth. By this time she was nearly alongside him, and he noticed that she was smiling. In fact her smile was getting broader and broader. Encouraged, he tried to speak, but no appropriate words entered his consciousness. He had become a goggle-eyed stuffed fish. As she glided by she could contain her mirth no longer, but the laugh she tried to stifle came out as a contemptuous snort. Her head came down and her hand came up to her face, but nothing could suppress her hilarity and she all but staggered as she broke into peals of laughter. Jimmy could do nothing but stand rigid and stare ahead until she was well past him, then he fell back against the shop door. When he had recovered sufficiently to move he ran home down the back entry as fast as he could. At least he got in without being spotted by any of the family, but when he saw himself in the wardrobe mirror he knew why she had laughed at him: what half an hour ago he had convinced himself looked smart was now very clearly ridiculous, because the jacket swamped him and the Brylcreem had run so that the whole of his head was shiny with grease. He put the coat back, wiped off as much of the hair cream as he could and went and did his homework, even though he found it difficult to concentrate, so full was his mind of every embarrassing detail of this debacle.

He was now certain of two things. The first was that he must avoid running into Bella ever again, and the second was that it would be safer hunting girls from within a pack of boys bolder than himself. As he couldn't go to the Grafton with Billy Wilkins, he thought the best place would be the Pit because lots of boys and girls gathered there in the evening when all the little kids had gone home to bed. Even though the cocky watchman had locked up and left, it was still easy to get in. He knew many of the lads and even some of the girls too because they came from the streets round about. If it were daylight nothing much happened; the boys would play in a sluggish fashion on the monkey ladder, the parallel bars or perhaps the maypole; the girls would be even less active, though they might push each other half-heartedly on the swings. However, after dark there would be some mixing of the two groups, though usually it took the form of innocent laughing and joking.

Occasionally, there would be some pairing off, but Jimmy never understood quite how it happened and would have found it difficult to pluck up the courage to try it, and anyway, he told himself, he just liked being in the mixed company, and getting to know the girls.

Then one evening when he went down quite late to the Pit there were only a couple of boys there and one girl. They were sitting on the swings, talking. He joined them but there was no swing for him, so he leaned against the stanchion. One of the lads he knew as Ronnie and the other had the nickname 'Oscar'. Jimmy did not know his real name but he did know that, like him, he was a grammar school boy. On the other hand, unlike him, Oscar was very self-possessed, articulate, and much more audacious than the majority of the boys who frequented the Pit. Jimmy knew the girl lived in a street near him and that her name was Jenny: he had noticed her. After a while, Oscar pushed on to the swing with Jenny, who, despite the discomfort, did not object.

Jimmy sat on the swing Oscar had vacated. Oscar had his arm around the girl, but she continued to include the other two in the conversation. She looked at Jimmy and said, "Doesn't your mam work in the dinny in Alsace Street School?"

"Yeh."

"Ah, she's nice. I like her."

Then Oscar interrupted, "Let's play Truth or Dare".

"OK," agreed Jenny for all of them.

At first the dares were innocent and the truths banal, but as it got darker they became riskier, and Oscar said, "I dare Jenny to let us walk her home".

The others smiled at this apparently innocuous suggestion when he added, "The back way".

There was a pause. All three boys looked at her. She seemed not to be able to make up her mind. Then with a lob-sided smile she said, "OK, but you'll have to behave yourself, Oscar Jarrom".

This meant that they finished up in the dark back entry behind Jenny's street, but before they got to her house, Oscar said in a whisper they could all hear, "I dare Jenny to let us give her a feel".

"Ar-ay, no. You're awful, Oscar Jarrom. No, I won't."

"All right then, give us a French kiss."

"No! Stop it or I'll go straight in!"

They walked on slowly and carefully until they were quite near her backyard door. She stopped and said, "You can all give me a long kiss, and then I'll have to go in, or me mam will shout".

"I'll go first," said Ronnie.

"And I'll go last," said Oscar craftily.

Jenny and Ronnie moved on from the other two and began kissing. Oscar was silent for a while and then he told Jimmy that he had been with Jenny before and that she had let him touch her breast. Jimmy never knew whether to believe him on not. Shortly, Oscar began to call softly to Ronnie to hurry up but he had to do so several times before Ronnie gave up and came back down the entry. As he got to them he told them quietly but eagerly that her blouse was open. Jimmy felt conflicting emotions as he walked towards her. He was excited at the prospect of kissing Jenny and at the possibility that he might discover for the first time what a girl's breast felt like. On the other hand, he was apprehensive at the thought that he ought not to do it because it might be a mortal sin. One way or another, he was shaking when he got to her. Then he realized that he did not know how he should go about getting into a clinch with her, and the fact that it was so dark did not help; he couldn't see where she was. Jenny solved the problem for him. She put her arms around him and gently pulled him towards her. He responded in the same way but held her very tight as he kissed her in the hope that she did not realize he was shivering. Then she pulled slightly away from him and they simply stood close to each other. He began to wonder if this was an invitation to be bolder, when he thought he sensed that she was pushing against him very gently. Should he or shouldn't he? Would she or wouldn't she let him? He began to search for her blouse: it was undone as Ronnie had said. As he put his fingers in he could sense her warmth before he had actually touched her. Then, just as he came in contact with the edge of her bra, she whispered very quietly in his ear, "I'll tell your mam".

He pulled his hand back as though it had been scalded, and Jenny giggled. He was now in a state of confusion. Should he go? If he did, would he look foolish? Should he go anyway, because he ought not to be there trying to do things that were wrong? Then Jenny made him feel even more as though he were out of his depth, when she said, "That'll teach you not to be a naughty boy".

At that point Oscar began to call to them to hurry up, but just as he pulled away, Jenny put both her hands around his head, softly drew him down, brushed his lips with hers and said, "Never mind, ay".

He began to walk back to the others, thoughts tumbling in his head. Why had she stopped him touching her? Had she let Ronnie? But why had she kissed him so tenderly? Was he no longer in a state of grace, his soul on its way to perdition? His feelings were also contradictory: elation because he was sure her gentleness was significant; disappointment because he still did not know what it was to touch a breast; and even fear that he might have to suffer the consequences of his intention to commit a serious sin. Without a word he walked past the other two, and made his way home. Nobody asked him where he had been and he went upstairs and lay on his bed, staring at the light from the street on the ceiling, not having lit the candle and there being no electricity in the attic. He thought of what Oscar might be doing and his mood turned to gloom. Then, as he contemplated all that had happened, he began to worry. It didn't feel as though he had done anything terribly wrong, but one of the clever-clever types in his class had said that any sin against the sixth or ninth commandment was mortal. He thought about the definition of a mortal sin. It had to be a serious matter and you had to have a clear intention to do it. Was what he tried to do a serious matter? One of the Jesuits in an R.I. lesson had said that the body was the temple of the Holy Ghost and to use it, or someone else's, for your own selfish pleasure was to abuse it, even to violate it. Was his desire to minimise what he had done merely a way of dodging the issue, of treating his conscience as Henry VIII had done (according to their history lessons)? Then again, he had only kissed Jenny. Perhaps he never intended to do anything else. He knew he was kidding himself and, anyway, he hadn't tried to 'avoid the dangerous occasions of sin'. He'd better go to confession. Then he thought about the embarrassment of that. What would he say to the priest? "I intended to touch a girl in a naughty place but then didn't" sounded daft. In fact it was daft, but he couldn't say "breast" to a priest. Then he remembered that Father Croft (the Temple of the Holy Ghost man) had also talked about 'unchaste touches': Jimmy had thought he had meant touching yourself but he now realized that the phrase covered literally a multitude of sins and he had actually come into contact with her bra, so he could use the formula without telling a lie in confession. He felt a certain relief at this, but then reflected a little more. What if he met Jenny again and the opportunity arose to find out what he had still not discovered? At confession, could he make a firm purpose of amendment?

At last he fell asleep, and very deeply, but then in the middle of the night a high wind came in across Liverpool Bay and the rattle of the windows woke him up. The house had not been unaffected by the bomb that had destroyed his grandma's house next door: it shook in the wind. Indeed, you could feel a tremor in the attic if someone slammed the back door. Above Jimmy's head was a beam that he never felt certain about. What if it were to come down in the wind and crush him to death? He was convinced it would, as a punishment for his wickedness, and he would go to hell. To assume that he would survive till morning, meet Jenny, commit more sins with her and then go to confession, was presumption, which along with despair, was forbidden by the First Commandment. He was trapped again and there was nowhere to run, no one to turn to. His fear and misery were wrapped around him: he felt stifled. He looked up at the beam. If it did come down it might hit his brother and not him – and stop him snoring. After a while he went back to sleep, but fitfully, and he dreamt he was running down back entries away from he knew not what. Each one ran into another and there was no way out. He seemed to come to a wall that had crevices in it, which meant it could be climbed; it appeared to offer a way out. However, the ascent was never-ending and when he tried to look down he found himself peering into an abyss, which paralysed him with fear.

Fortunately, when Alan got up for work he woke Jimmy who, to his great relief, realized he had been dreaming. He thought he might get up but instead he dozed for a while. That led him to think about Bella and Jenny. He tried to put these 'impure thoughts' out of his head but they always came back again, and so there was another sin to confess. However, when he got up he made up his mind to go to confession and then to be good ever after. The opportunity came on Saturday morning at school because at break several of the priests from the parish came out to 'hear'. This was the best time to go because they didn't know you. Moreover, they could never get through all those who wanted to confess and that meant you could be late for fourth lesson with impunity. Also, he went to Father West who was never shocked and never commented on anything you might say, so the 'unchaste touches' formula worked well.

He managed to stay out of trouble for several days and even to keep all traces of 'impure' thoughts out of his head, so that he could go to communion on Sunday. This good phase lasted almost a week. Then he thought he would go to the Pit again: it would not be an occasion of sin, because he would talk only to lads, and perhaps a few girls – casually. When he got there he met Ronnie, who told him how much Oscar was boasting about what he had achieved with Jenny once the two softies had gone home. Before long he saw Jenny and she was coming towards them, smiling. He thought at first her smile was for Ronnie, until it was quite clear that she was looking at him, and she kept on looking even though it was Ronnie who spoke first.

"Have you heard what Oscar is saying about you?"

"Yes, but don't believe a word that Oscar Jarrom says. He's a liar," she said, still looking at Jimmy.

"But what happened after we'd gone?"

"Nothin'. He tried it on but I told him I'd shout for me dad and so he went home." She was no longer smiling but continued to stare at Jimmy with what was now almost a pained expression, as though she were trying to will him to believe her. Ronnie laughed and then jeered, "I bet. We all know what Oscar's like."

For the first time she turned to Ronnie and said angrily, "Well, I didn't let him and he's a liar!"

She immediately turned her attention back to Jimmy and seemed anxious that he should not disapprove of her. At last he spoke, but felt so nervous because of his growing awareness of her concern that he should like her that his voice seemed to him to belong to somebody else.

"If Jenny says she didn't let him, then she didn't let him."

He tried to give Ronnie a piercing, if not quite menacing, look and to his surprise Ronnie backed away and said, "OK, OK, I was only joking".

They were standing by the maypole and all were feeling sheepish, when suddenly Ronnie broke the spell by leaping forward, grabbing a handle and swinging off into space with a Tarzan yell. As he came back round, the other two had to step aside to avoid his flailing feet. They nudged together, but as they broke away, each looked into the other's face and smiled. Jimmy felt an exhilaration he had never experienced before, but he did not know what to do next. Jenny said, "Ooh, look, two swings are empty. Quick, before somebody gets them."

They ran across and sat down. If they did swing it was hardly noticeable. Both were content just to be there, but after a while Jenny said, "Where've you been all week?"

"I've had a lot of homework," he half fibbed.

"Oh I see," she mused. Then more earnestly, "Why did you run away that night?"

"I didn't."

"But you disappeared."

"Well, I thought that was what we all agreed."

"Yes, but you left me with that Oscar!"

"I didn't know what else to do."

"Well, I don't like him really... You won't leave me with him again, will you?"

"No. Honest, I won't," he said in astonishment.

They were quiet for a while and watched the others coming and going. Jimmy was glad Oscar was not there and hoped he would not suddenly turn up because of what he might say. He knew he still couldn't quite believe Jenny, but he did not want to think about it, and certainly not argue with Oscar about it, so he said, "What's it like at your school?"

"Not bad really now we're in the leavers' class, and I'm doing R.S.A. typing and the Preceptors' exam so I haven't got time to mess about."

"Does that mean you have homework?"

"Ooh, no. Nobody would do it! I suppose you've got a lot of homework?"

"Yeh, but sometimes, like tonight, not so much, and at the weekend I do it on a Sunday."

"What you goin' to do when you leave school?"

"I don't know and anyway that's goin' to be ages yet. What are you gonna do?"

"I'm going to try to get a job in an office. But not here."

"Why not?"

"'Cos we're leaving. Me dad's got a job in Coventry and we're goin' when he finds a house."

Jimmy felt a terrible wave of disappointment and he must

have looked crestfallen, because Jenny took hold of his hand and said very gently, "Never mind, ay".

There was a pause before he said, "You always say that".

And they both laughed. He thought how much he liked her face when her eyes shone and her white even teeth showed. Despite the disquiet he felt because she might be moving away and the fear, still niggling at the back of his mind that this evening might be an occasion of sin, he experienced a surge of happiness and he felt that somehow the world had been transformed. Though it was becoming quite dark there seemed to be a glow everywhere that he couldn't remember ever seeing in the city before: it was more like the late evenings he remembered in Shropshire when everyone was out working in the fields helping to bring in the harvest.

She stood up and said, "I'll have to be getting home, or me mam will shout".

They climbed out through the railings. Once they were in the street he grew bold enough to take her hand. Then after a while he said, "Shall we go the back way?"

Jenny did not reply, but that was the way they went. Neither of them spoke until they came close together by her back door and then she said, "You're not goin' to be like Oscar, are you?"

"Not me," he whispered.

They kissed for a long time but only very gently. Finally he said, "Will I see you tomorrow?"

"Yes, please... but not in the Pit."

"OK. Where?"

"Let's go to Stanley Park."

"Right, I'll see you at the top of Granton Road, at half past seven."

As he made his way home, he kept checking over the events of the evening to make sure that it was all really true: she liked him. In fact she seemed to like him a lot. She wanted to be with him and only him; neither Oscar nor Ronnie, but him. He had a girlfriend! He could hardly believe it. And he would see her again tomorrow. And the night after that. He'd only kissed her and so that was all right too.

To his surprise, everyone was in the kitchen when he got in. There was no special reason for this: it just seemed to have happened. His mother, sitting in her usual armchair in front of the fire, was listening to the others, but she looked up and said, "Hello stranger. Where've you been?"

"Nowhere special."

"What have you been doing then?"

"Nothin' much."

"Then why are you grinning all over your face?" said his brother.

"It's not a crime, is it?"

"Oh, don't you two start," said Jane and his mother added, "No, don't upset him. I'd rather have him grinning like a Cheshire cat, for whatever reason, than grumpy like he usually is."

"I'm not grumpy," he said smiling more broadly than ever.

"No, not much!" somebody said and everyone laughed.

In that instant, he realized how important his family was to him and how secure he felt when they were all together like this: he was safe. Here was his mam and his brother and sisters and they were all great. Suddenly he was flooded with a feeling of generosity, but because he had nothing to give anybody, all that he could do was to say, "Does anybody want a piece of toast?"

"And are you going to make it, then?"

"Yep!"

"Wowser! Wonders never cease. We'll all have some."

As he went off into the back kitchen, he heard Alice say, "What's got into him?"

"He must be in love... He hasn't got a girlfriend, has he?"

Then Jimmy broke into a Danny Kaye song:

"You can take the moon,
Gather up the stars,
And the robins that sing merrily.
Put 'em in a box
Tie 'em up with ribbon.
Throw 'em in the deep blue sea,
'Cos love and I we don't agree."

He could hear them laughing so he went on singing as he plonked the bread on to the grill pan and shoved it under the grill with a crash.

"Hey, mind what you're doing out there," cried his mother.

"OK, kiddiewinks," he shouted. "Don't worry, Wonderman has it all under control."

The next afternoon, Jimmy hurried home as soon as school finished at twenty past four and did all his homework before tea, so that there would be nothing to spoil the evening: he wanted to have no cares, no worries, no lurking threats to bother him. After the family had eaten he even helped with the washing up, so that the sink would be clear for him to scrub his face and clean his teeth, which he did long and hard to make absolutely sure his breath was fresh. He even cleaned his shoes. He ignored the pointed comments of the others and refused to answer any questions: he was "just going out, that's all".

It must have been about twenty-five past seven when he got to the top of Granton Road. There was nobody there but he was not surprised, nor concerned: everybody knew that women were always late. Half past seven came and went. He was still relaxed about it, but a little later he walked along to the Skyliner Milk Bar so that he could look through the window at the clock. At twenty to eight he began to feel uneasy. At a quarter to he had become quite anxious, and by five to he had become positively gloomy: he hadn't got a girl after all. By eight o'clock he was feeling angry. Who did she think she was to stand him up and make him look such a fool? But then he felt sure something must have happened, and the words of a George Formby song came into his head: 'She wouldn't leave me flat; she's not a girl like that'. Perhaps he'd got the time wrong. Or maybe her father had found out about them and thought he was like Oscar: Jenny might be locked in her room sobbing. Don't be so daft! He might not know her very well but he was certain she was not a girl like that either. And anyway, how could her father possibly know about him or Oscar? Disappointment flooded over him as he recalled how excited he had been at the prospect of seeing her, holding her hand and walking with her.

He wondered what he should do. To go home would make him feel more miserable, and the family were sure to suspect something. Go across to the Pit. That prospect was even worse, and what if he met Oscar? Perhaps he should go to Stanley Park by himself. Just as he was about to go down Granton Road to make his way there, he became aware of a girl about ten looking at him. He stared back at her and she said, "Are you Jimmy?" and without waiting for an answer, gabbled, "Our Jenny can't come out tonight. Me mam's sick and the baby's sick and me dad's away and she's got to look after us."

"Can't she come out at all, not even later?"

"No, she's already had a row with me mam, because she said she was goin' out, and now me mam says she's got to stay in all week."

"Did she say anything else?"

"Yeh, she'll see you outside the Everton on Saturday in time for first house pictures."

He went to the park feeling less aggrieved but still miserable. The lawns and the flowerbeds by the pavilion looked bright and colourful in the evening sunlight but he was sure they would have been even more beautiful had Jenny been with him. He walked along to the bowling greens, sat on a bench, and watched the old men playing calmly, without any fuss. He wondered what it was like to be old, but then thought perhaps you had to earn whatever it was they had: how many of them had been stood up by girls when they were young? Then he watched a group of young lads playing football, their coats and jerseys laid down for goalposts. They looked hot and sweaty and totally engrossed in the game: he envied them, because, he thought, they did not know yet how to be miserable like him. But one day they would. You had to live through it sometime, so there was no point in going back to be like them. He went home.

The next day on his way home from school he looked to see what was on the grandly named Everton Picturedrome on Saturday. It was Clifton Webb in *Cheaper by the Dozen*, and the first house began at ten past five. He remembered that the prices were nine pence and one and six, so he knew he would have to supplement his meagre pocket money if he were to be able to afford two expensive seats and two six-penny choc ices. He surprised his brother and sisters by offering to do jobs for them but that did not result in any appreciable increase in funds. Saturday afternoon found him climbing the stairs to Great Aunt Mary's room, because he was still one-and-tuppence short of his target.

"Hello Aunty Mary."

"Hello, Jimmy... Why aren't you out playing football or something?"

"Well, I'm going out tonight to see this special film... If I can afford it."

"Haven't you had your pocket money?"

"Yes, but I've had to use some of that to buy a new scribbler for school... and... er, a new pen."

"Oh, I see."

There was a silence and then...

"Aunty Mary?"

"Yes, Jimmy."

"You couldn't lend me two bob, could you?"

"Glory be to God. No, I couldn't. Where am I going to get money like that for you to spend on the pictures?"

"Ar, go on Aunty Mary. I'll give it you back, honest."

"I'm an old age pensioner, y' know, with hardly enough to buy me few bits and pieces."

"But I promise to pay you back next week."

There was another pause in the conversation, and then, "Well, are you sure, now? You will be able to pay me back?"

"Yes, really, truly, I will."

"I've heard that before... and from all the men in this family."

"But I've always paid you back, haven't I?"

"Well, I suppose so."

And with that she lifted up the first two of her many full-length skirts to reveal a cloth bag fastened to her waist by a cord. From this she extracted a very old leather purse secured with an elastic band. She took out a two shilling piece, which she gave him, saying, "Now, remember, I want it back".

"Thanks, Aunty Mary. I'll give it back next week, but don't

tell me mam." He almost fell down the stairs in his excitement because everything was beginning to work out just as he had hoped. He now had to convince his mother that he was going to the pictures with some of the lads... from school, because she knew hardly any of them. All was well and she agreed to let him have his tea early. He also had to go through the rigma-role of getting ready: using the sink when nobody else was about; sneaking Alan's Brylcreem; polishing his shoes surreptitiously in the back yard. Then came the business of waiting outside the cinema. And once again she did not turn up! He went through all the emotions of the evening earlier in the week: excitement, apprehension, anxiety, gloom, and then intense annoyance, espe-cially as the film had already started. This time, however, no little sister turned up. Instead, he decided to try to find out what had happened. Boldly, because he felt so angry, he went to her street. At first he simply stood at the top looking down to see whatever he could. There were some children playing but nothing much seemed to be going on.

Walking, almost marching, purposefully, to make it look as though he were passing through, on his way to urgent business elsewhere, he made his way to her house. As he approached it he began to think that something was odd: it looked different from the others. Finally he realized it was empty. At first he thought he must be in the wrong street; next he wondered if he had got the wrong house: perhaps she had never lived here. He'd only ever been to the back of the house before. But this was the number she had told him. By this time he had stopped walking and was standing, looking confused: he became aware of his open mouth and the kids staring at him. He had to confront them.

"Does Jenny Mack live down here?"

"Not anymore."

"Eh?"

"They went away yesterday," said one.

"'Er dad's got a job in Coventry," said another.

"Oh."

He was so astonished he did not know what to think, but what forced itself into his head was that she ought to have let him know. Surely, she could have got a message to him. She could not have felt for him what he felt for her, otherwise she would have let him know. Perhaps, after all, she preferred Oscar. And then he remembered her smile and the way she looked at him. It was so perplexing. ...Oh! Hell!

It began to rain and gloom descended around him and within him. Nothing seemed real; a psychological ferula had lacerated him and he had shrivelled up inside his own skull: he was looking out at the world down the wrong end of a telescope. Then there was a shaft of light – of course, she would write to him and explain everything and tell him that she loved him! He was so certain! And so it was that with this comforting thought in mind he somehow got through the weekend. On Monday morning, he actually went and met the postman in the street, but there was no letter. On Tuesday he waited till the postman came, in case he looked silly: there was no letter; nor yet on Wednesday; nor Thursday. By Friday hope had faded and after that so did love. He never found out what had happened to her.

Fortunately, he could forget all these concerns once the long summer holiday came, because he could leave them all behind and be part of quite a different life. His Uncle Fred was now bailiff at the Hay Farm and was entitled to live in the big house: there was plenty of room and so children from all parts of the extended family assembled there in the summer. However, they were all expected to contribute to the work of the farm, especially if a crisis arose.

On one occasion, Fred found himself without sheepdogs. When he got up one morning at half past five, as he usually did, he discovered that the dogs had wandered off to chase rabbits. This was because no one had remembered to chain up Paddy, a large male dog, the night before: everyone knew that if he and Lady were loose together, she would take him off. The only other dog available was little more than a puppy and but half-trained: by himself he would create more problems than he solved.

So it was that Jimmy and the three other children who were staying at the farm were chased out of bed at what seemed to them a ridiculously early hour, and with nothing more than a hunk of bread and dripping and a mug of milk were herded down the banks – a series of pastures that formed one side of the 300-acre farm, where the land dropped down towards the river. The hedges and ditches between these meadows had never been made up for years and so, as far as the sheep were concerned, there was just one big field, half a mile wide and nearly two miles long. Without dogs, working such a large area was not easy, but as the weather was hot there was a grave danger that the sheep would become fly-blown, so they had to be inspected and counted every day. A small area near the farm had been separated off with hurdles so that the sheep could be driven into it through a narrow opening. Everybody had to go to the far end of the banks and then, in an extended line across the width of the pasture, walk slowly towards the farm, driving the sheep before them. Provided everyone went slowly, all was well, but any precipitate movement always seemed to make the sheep double back through the gaps and you had to start again. In the last field, everyone had to merge towards the hurdles. Again, hasty movement could cause the bolder sheep to break for it, and once the human line was breached the other sheep scattered too. At this stage there were fewer children doing the herding because Fred and Alice, the most responsible of all the children, were at the gate counting furiously. Their numbers had to agree and if they didn't, another count was made as the sheep were driven back out – and then back in again.

It all took most of the morning, but it did work: several sheep had to be treated with McDougal's Maggot Oil. Jimmy was very impressed with Fred, not only for his patience with the children but also his skill. He could pick out a sick sheep on what seemed to Jimmy to be very little evidence, grab it with his crook, and turn it over on its back in order to control its struggling and then deal with it quickly. In a flash he could trim the ends of a sheep's claws and then pour in the oil. To Jimmy's surprise, out crawled the maggots, to be squashed between finger and thumb. Later in the day, one of the children would be dispatched to Ironbridge to get yet more supplies of McDougal's, but that was after they had returned to the farm for bacon butties – and the bacon was home-cured and in thick slices. Jimmy then made the mistake of jibbing at being sent to Ironbridge. He said, "But I'm on my holidays". The others never let him forget it. Again, he wondered if he were incurably lazy.

One job that was unpopular with all the children, and so for which there was a rota that nobody could argue with, was clearing the slurry out of the cowshed. There were only ten cows and these were meant to provide milk for the farm and its workers but even they created a lot of mess and Fred insisted that the shed should be kept as clean as possible, especially as it was he and just one of the women workers who did the milking there. To clear away the slurry there was a wooden sweep about a yard-and-a-half wide and a foot high, on the end of a hefty broom handle. This was easy to manage where the floor was flat, but, on the cobbly bits, if you got stuck, you could get a nasty blow in the ribs. Everything was swept out of wide double doors, which were on the level of the floor on the inside but because the shed was built into rising around, they were four foot above the ground on the outside – where there was a big mound of manure. This too had to be shifted periodically out into a field where it waited for the muck-spreading season. Similar, but less smelly, work had to be done in the stables too because, even in the early fifties, much of the work was still done by horses.

There were easier jobs, such as collecting the eggs, when the only risk occurred if a broody hen was still sitting on one of the nests and as you put your hand under her to collect the egg she pecked you. Feeding the pigs was a bit messy as you had to make the slop for them and when you tried to put it in the trough they were so keen to get to it that they could nearly knock you over as they pushed and shoved, squealing and grunting in their anxiety to miss nothing. Mixing food and giving it to the young heifers was better and for this you had the experience of putting mangols into a huge chopping machine on which you had to turn a very large handle: there was something very satisfying about watching the chopped mangol fall through to your bucket. Unlike the pigs, these animals were shy and stood back nervously when you filled their trough.

There were also useful things to learn. The couple of petrol tractors used on the farm were maintained by the men themselves and everyone joined in, giving advice on what needed to be done, and so you learned how to check oil and water levels, clean plugs and leads, top-up batteries and so on. Once harvesting began, everyone worked, and often very long hours – even into the night, especially when there was an early moon. To Jimmy this still seemed romantic: getting everything in made you feel that something special had been done and that you were all blessed by that achievement. There was also the excitement when the last triangle (for such it always seemed) of wheat or barley was being cut in the centre of the field. Then the rabbits would have to emerge and race to what they hoped was safety. It rarely was because there were so many dogs and shotguns waiting for them.

It was not all work: Jimmy could still wander through the woods and along the banks of the river, through the secluded paths he remembered so fondly from his early childhood during the War when the bombs and the anti-aircraft guns were far away. In the evening, life in the enormous farm kitchen seemed to Jimmy bliss, with games of darts and dominoes, Newmarket (with matches for stakes) and the wonderful stories that the adults still told in the days before television. There were also expeditions to the cinema with fish and chips in newspaper on the way home. Also, one sunny day, they all went to the Royal Agricultural Show, which still moved from county to county and that year was in Shrewsbury.

Towards the end of the holidays, Jimmy felt sadder and sadder at the idea of having to go back to the city and to school, the thought of which he was beginning to find more than irksome even though he would be entering the Sixth Form.

CHAPTER VI

NOT HAVING HAD ANYTHING to distract him meant that he had done some work for the summer examinations and he made especially sure that he revised for Latin and R.I., because Father Burden had warned him that he would look closely at these papers. He did not do brilliantly, but all his marks were between 48 and 58. However, this was to lead to certain difficulties later.

In the days of the School Certificate, boys in 4A were entered for it even though they were still only fifteen, so that they could go into the Sixth Form a year early. This encouraged them to stay on. When the General Certificate of Education was introduced, an age limit of sixteen was imposed (mostly to discourage Secondary Modern pupils from entering for it). So, in order to keep his Sixth Form numbers up because they earned a bigger grant for the school, the Headmaster tried to persuade everyone from 4A to go into the Sixth Form anyway, and to take three 'O' levels at the end of the first year and three 'A' levels at the end of the second. In this way, matriculation and university entrance were still possible and it was a system adopted by all the 'best' schools. However, there had been some resistance to it from parents and, as might be expected, from boys the year before when it had been introduced. Everyone in 4A knew that the Head had got very annoyed with those who had asked if they could go in the Fifth Form and take the usual eight or nine 'O' levels and then leave. It was therefore with some trepidation that Jimmy and his class lined up in alphabetical order outside the Head's office a couple of days after the full Fourth Form examination results were known, to discuss their futures with him. Jimmy couldn't help feeling he was waiting for the ferula.

Nor did he know his own mind: he wanted to leave school and technically he could, but somehow this seemed a waste – to leave without any qualifications whatsoever, and after all the misery too. And what kind of job could he get with no 'O' levels? In fact, the thought of any job made him feel very apprehensive: at least he knew what was what in school. Furthermore, his mother wanted him to stay on. She often talked about how his father had been obliged to leave the same school too early and to go out and earn money and how he had expressed the wish that his children should stay on at school as long as they liked. Well, Jimmy didn't like but he daren't tell his mother that. He decided that he would have to take the bull by the horns, face the music, beard the lion in his den, and ask to be put in the Fifth Form. His resolve was firm.

However, coming at the back of the queue was not conducive to his remaining firm. Some boys came out of the office very quickly and looked quite calm: as they chatted to the rest it became clear that they were the ones who wanted to go into the Sixth Form and to take 'A' levels that the Head thought were appropriate. Others were in there a long time; you could hear the Head shouting: they came out looking flustered. Usually, they had not got what they wanted, i.e. entry into the Fifth Form. Jimmy grew tense; he felt his back knotting up; he felt a trickle of sweat run from his armpit cold down his side. Soon he was telling Wilson, the only one left in the queue behind him, over and over again why he just had to go into the Fifth Form; why he needed eight 'o' levels now. Wilson wasn't listening and it was Jimmy's turn to go in.

The Head was sitting at his desk, poring over his lists of Fourth Form marks and prospective Sixth Form candidates. He did not look up.

"Name?"

"Thompson, Father." There was silence as he glanced across the sheet that contained the class marks. Then he scratched his bald head with the stem of his pipe.

"Humph," he said. Jimmy said nothing.

"Now, then... ahhh," he said. Jimmy shifted his weight.

There was another long pause as he scrutinised the marks even more intensely. He still hadn't looked at Jimmy, but then he raised his head, stared hard at him and said, "Look here, Thompson, you don't appear to be good at anything".

"No, Father," replied Jimmy, as a feeling of helplessness washed over him.

"Then on the other hand, you don't appear to be bad at anything either."

Jimmy did not answer, because he did not know what to say.

"So, what are we going to do with you?"

"I don't know, Father, but I could go into the... "

The Head cut him short by raising his hand as though he were a traffic policeman, before Jimmy could get out the words 'Fifth Form'.

"Ah, now I see; you can do Maths, Physics and Chemistry at 'A' level, and English Language, Latin and French at 'O' level. Good afternoon."

Jimmy opened his mouth to speak, but was glared at: he closed his mouth, turned around and began the long march across to the door. As he reached it he became aware of the sound of fingers being clicked. He glanced around, not really believing where the noise was coming from, but the Head, though peering down at the lists again, was crooking his finger at him. Jimmy walked back and could see that the Head was crossing his name off the Science list. He then wrote it on the Modern list, which clearly was shorter than either the Science or the Classics lists: there's nothing better than a good balance between the three kinds of 'A' level; and nothing quite like feeling you're a makeweight.

"Right then, Thompson, it'll be French, History and English Literature at 'A' level, with Maths, Latin and English Language at 'O' level."

He then looked up, jammed his pipe between his teeth, and actually smiled a smile of satisfaction at having made this momentous (and it was for Jimmy!) decision.

So Jimmy went to Sixth Form which was certainly an improvement on the lower school, for most of the time that is, and the change of status was made visible by the navy blue blazer which replaced the maroon: people in the street might just possibly think you were an adult. Not that Jimmy felt very grown-up, because he was still a little shorter than most boys his age and he looked younger than he was. Moreover, he was overawed by many members of the Modern section, some of whom already had 'A' levels, and were competing for scholarships to Oxford, Cambridge or other universities. He was amazed at how erudite they were and how articulate they could be: in the first lesson in French they read one of Madame de Sevigné's letters to her daughter, Madame de Grignan. Jimmy felt like hiding under the desk when the teacher asked for comments on its literary merits: he wasn't even sure he had understood it! Fortunately the senior members of the class were keen to air their opinions.

"Well, Sir, despite the formality of the style, the letter is obviously spontaneous and full of affection and solicitude for an inexperienced daughter as she enters into the heady atmosphere of the court of Louis XIV."

Jimmy understood this, but he doubted very much if he would ever be capable of uttering such a statement off the top of his head. And how did they know it was spontaneous?

Fortunately the years were not always mixed and for the 'O' level subjects, he was with what was left of his old class, with one or two others from last year's Fifth Form who needed to retake a couple of subjects. Furthermore, in some parts of the 'A' level work they met as the lower sixth. One of these was History and here for the first time he was taught by the most celebrated teacher in the school, Dr Grisedale, who related History as one long, very funny, story, and who strutted and strolled around the classroom like a cross between Mr Pickwick and Winston Churchill. He had a deliberately pompous comic style, punctuated by alarming idiosyncrasies: if he wanted to expand or deepen an explanation, he might suddenly yell, "To wit".

And he expected the class to respond, "To woo".

As one of the courses was Early European History, it dealt with the Barbarian invasions, so if he wanted you to write 'i.e.', he would say sharply, "The ancient cry of the Hunnic Avars," and the class would cry out, "Aye-eeee!"

In the same way, 'e.g.' was the ancient cry of the Goths (both Ostro- and Visi-). Because western potentates of one kind or another tried to exploit the savage tendencies of these eastern tribes. He would sometimes say, "So what did he do?" and the class cried out, "He summoned the Magyars!"

At which Denis Mottram had to stand up and issue a piercing whistle. So, History was interesting, except, that is, when it came to writing essays. He was never sure what he should write about and certainly had no idea how much he should write. Teachers simply assumed you could do whatever was required. Moreover, Grisedale seemed to give essay titles on subjects he hadn't taught, so you had to use the textbooks, which were often obscure to the point of impenetrability. He also found that you had to be more careful with the work and to hurry was to court disaster. One piece of work that he dashed off for Father Reilly, who took them for English, came back covered in red ink, not only because it said nothing of any significance about *Hamlet*, but also because it was shot through with careless mistakes. Jimmy was mortified to discover he had written 'incite' for 'insight'! Which made him feel more stupid than he really was.

Gradually he became more and more convinced that he would leave school at the end of the lower sixth. He knew he could get the 'O' level Maths and the English Language and he even began to think he could pass the Latin. For this they had a teacher new to the school who was very impressed by the extent and the accuracy of the knowledge that Father Burden had battered into them. He had a very relaxed teaching style and gave everybody individual attention. He also showed them how to use what they knew. Jimmy realized the importance of this when Mr Baker showed them how to turn English into Latinate English first, so that they used constructions that they already knew how to handle. As a simple example, 'He captured the city and burned it,' became 'He burned the having been captured city,' so you could use (in this case) the accusative absolute: *'Urbem captam incendit'.* Indeed, one evening, sitting in Aunt Mary's room where it was quiet except for the clicking of her four steel knitting needles, as she made socks (to go with her old-fashioned long lace-up boots), he worked quite happily for an hour and became aware only at the end that he was enjoying himself: that Latin could be like this surprised him. Nevertheless, he was not inclined to change his mind about school and he knew he would leave as soon as he could, and so in the 'A' level subjects he did the minimum possible amount of work, just enough to avoid trouble. If he could get away without doing it, he did. He was often absent.

At the end of the year, having taken the 'O' levels, he screwed up his courage and asked if he could see the Head. In an embarrassing, but mercifully brief, interview, the Head said, "Thompson, y' know, when young chaps like you come to me at this stage in their educational careers asking if they can leave school, I usually try to persuade them not to, but in your case I find that rather difficult".

And with that he opened a drawer in his desk and took out a short, antiquated, even anachronistic, leaving certificate, filled in the gaps very perfunctorily, handed it to Jimmy and said, "Goodbye".

Jimmy could hardly believe he had actually left school. As he walked home, he felt just as he usually did: everywhere looked the same and it did not seem that this was the last time he would walk this route, between these two particular geographical points. However, when he reached the house and told his mother, he realized what he had done. She was very angry.

"You've done what!?"

"I've left school…"

"And who said you could leave school?"

"Well, I'm old enough and…"

"And stupid enough! … Why didn't you tell me what you were going to do? … Just who do you think you are? …" she raved.

"Well, I'm not …"

"I can't believe it… you said nothing about it… you can't leave just like that."

"But I have done, and here's my leaving certificate."

"Leaving certificate! Leaving certificate! And what's that supposed to be?" She looked at it, not really reading it. Then she looked more closely. "This isn't anything… it's worthless… it won't get you a job..."

"Well, I..."

"And that's what you'll do, my lad. You'll get a job and you'll stick to it."

Just then, one of his sisters came in, asking what all the fuss was about.

"Do you know what this fellow has done? Eh, do you know?"

His sister turned to him but before he could say anything, his mother began to shout again. "He's left school... Just like that... Not a word to anybody. Well, he'll rue it, but he can get on with it... I wash my hands of it..."

And so it went on... and on... and on, until he almost wished he had stayed at school. Nothing he could say, nothing his sisters could say, would calm his mother. And there was nowhere to hide, nowhere to run to avoid it, no way to make it stop. He had to sit and listen. Even when there was a pause, he knew it would not be long before she started up again. And she did many times over the next two days.

However, the outburst did make him fully aware of the seriousness of his situation: he had to find a job... and he didn't know where to begin. He had no idea what he might do. In fact, he'd little notion of what you did in any job he could think of. What does an electrician do? He fixes lights and puts in sockets and does things in factories, but he had never seen a real electrician actually doing his job. Nor had he seen an engineer or a fitter or a joiner. He had only vague impressions of what they might do all day. Then he remembered that his friend, Albert, from his elementary school days, had a job in an office: he could ask him what that was like.

When he called at Albert's house, he was told he was down the yard, but when he got there, he could not find him, until a voice said, "Up here, soft lad".

"What'yer doing up there?"

"What does it look like I'm doin'?"

There were clouds of smoke around Albert, and he was sitting on the roof of the outside (and only) toilet, a sturdy building surmounted by a large slab of sandstone. Jimmy clambered up.

"Gis' a ciggy."

"No, smoke yer own."

"I haven't got any."

"Go and buy some then."

"I haven't got any money either."

Jimmy was not put out by this morose opening to the conversation: it was normal. He stretched out on the roof with his hands behind his head. Albert followed suit and blew smoke rings into the sky.

There was silence until Albert said, "Oh, here," handing Jimmy the packet of Woodbines.

"Orr, thanks Albie, I'll give you one back after."

"No you won't, you never do, and you've never got any money either."

"Well, that's what I came to see you about, in fact."

"You've got a hope. I've no money to lend you."

"No, that's not what I meant. What I mean is I've left school and I'm looking for a job."

"So, what can I do about that?"

"Well, tell us what it's like in your place."

"It's OK."

"Yes, but what do you have to do?"

They were silent again for a while and concentrated on their cigarettes, Albert especially as he tried to puff his down to the very end, without burning his fingers. He threw the minute stub into the back entry, careless of where it went, looked thoughtful for a minute and then said, "Well, today, I've balanced the petty cash; I've been to the bank; I've been to the Customs House; and I've been to Cock Tugs."

"What's cocktugs?"

"It's an office in Dale Street."

"What did you go there for?"

"Don't be so bloody daft … I went to order a tug!"

"To order a tug… you mean a boat?"

"Of course I mean a boat; a ship can't get into a dock without a tug and I have to make sure that every ship we deal with gets into dock all right."

"Why is it called a cock tug?"

Albert looked at him in amazement. "Have you never seen one when you've been to the Pier Head? It's got a figure like a weathercock on the top of the foremast."

"What else do you have to do?"

"We do everything for a ship when it comes into port. See, some shipping lines don't have an office in Liverpool, so we make sure that they can dock, unload, load up again, and leave, just as though we were their own office. We pay the bills and even the wages. We get all that money back and we charge them a fat fee as well."

"And can you do all those things?"

"Well, no. I'm only learning, but I can do some of them."

"Do you like it?"

"Some of the time… like tomorrow night, there's this ship due to dock and I've got to be there to meet it, so I can take the mail on board as soon as she ties up: that keeps us popular with the Captain and the crew… and you get ciggies. Last time I got two packets of Chesterfield, and a drink of whiskey."

"Wow, that sounds great. I've never been on a boat like that… I've only been on that aircraft carrier; do you remember when we were kids? We all went, when it was open to the public."

"Oh, yeh, but that's not the same."

There was silence for a while as they lay staring into the sky. Then Albert said, "Tell you what; do you wanna come with me when I go tomorrow night?"

"Arr, yeh. That would be great, but will anybody mind?"

"Naah. They'll think you're from Sivewright's, like me."

So the next evening about eight o'clock, they set off to walk down to the docks, a journey of no more than twenty-five minutes from where they lived in Everton. At the dock gate, they met a policeman, who asked them where they were going.

"To take this mail to the *Baron Belhaven*, when she docks," said Albert, showing the big bundle.

"And where is she docking then, lad?"

"Canada Basin."

The policeman consulted a list on the back of the door of his little cubbyhole, which was set in the wide tower of the dock gate.

"OK, lads, she should be tying up about now."

Jimmy was surprised at how big everything was when they got in. The road that ran along the inside of the dock wall was very wide and it had train lines set in the cobbles. There were tall, exceedingly long, sheds running at right angles to it flanking each quay, and everywhere there were cranes like giant praying mantises, peering down at them as they hurried along. Though they could see that there were ships in most docks, they did not see many people about, and when Jimmy mentioned this he was told that the dockers would usually work overtime only till about seven o'clock, unless there was a rush job.

When they arrived at Canada Basin, it was not what Jimmy expected, because, unlike the docks they had passed by, it was much bigger, more like a small lake and square in shape. And there was the *Baron Belhaven*, already secured and just having the gangway pushed towards it. Jimmy thought that, close up, she looked like a grand liner, but Albert assured him she was only a medium-sized merchant vessel, with two red and gold funnels to denote she was part of the Baron Line. Albert said this was a Greek shipping company and that all their boats were called Baron something or other. At the gangway they were confronted by a tall, stern-looking man, who, because of his uniform, Jimmy took to be a naval officer. He looked at them very closely and said, "And where are you two going?"

"We're going on board to take the mail," said Albert, pointing to the bundle.

"And where are you from?"

"Sivewright, Bacon and Company... Sir," he added, in the hope of mollifying this fierce-looking gentleman.

"That's all right. You can give it to me. I'll take it on board for you."

Jimmy began to feel disappointed: it looked as though they would not get on the ship after all. But that was to underestimate Albert's new-found confidence.

"I'm afraid I can't do that, Sir. My boss says I have to hand the mail personally to the Captain, as part of the service to our clients."

The Customs Officer, for such he was, glared at them. However, at that point there was a shout from the ship to say that all was ready for them to come aboard, and they set off up the gangway, the officer leading. As they scuttled along behind him, Jimmy muttered, "Are you sure this is OK?"

"Yerss, they're always like that... officious bastards!"

All three were ushered into the Captain's quarters, which to Jimmy's amazement were as large and as plush as anything he'd ever seen on the pictures, the whole of one bulkhead being covered by a brilliantly coloured tapestry of a tiger set against a burnished gold background. The Captain and the Customs Officer talked briefly in a jargon that Jimmy barely understood, but which he took to mean that all the booze and cigarettes on board would, with certain minor exceptions, be sealed away for the remainder of the ship's stay in the port. The officer then went off, leaving Albert and Jimmy ensconced in comfortable armchairs. The Captain turned to them.

"Now, you're the gentlemen I really want to see... you have what all my crew have been waiting for: letters from home."

Albert handed over the parcel, and the Captain called out something in Greek down a corridor. There was the sound of hurrying feet, and Jimmy was aware of what seemed like the gathering of the whole crew outside. The captain undid the parcel. Inside there were in fact two bundles: one for him and one for the rest of them. Somebody Jimmy thought must be the bosun took the second parcel and started to call out names, to which there were lively replies. The letters all passed to the crew, the Captain turned to them and said, "Now, what would you boys like... whiskey, gin, rum... brandy, perhaps?"

Albert, knowing the ropes, replied immediately for both of them, "Whiskey will be fine, Sir".

The Captain went to a drinks cabinet and took out an impressive decanter and two chunky glasses. He poured them very generous measures. Jimmy felt both excited and apprehensive: he'd never drunk whiskey before. However, Albert leaned over towards him and whispered, "Sip it; don't guts it".

When Jimmy tried it he appreciated the wisdom of the advice.

It had a powerful effect on the tongue; it made your throat hot and you could even feel it warming the stomach. He decided he liked it. After several more sips he felt that it was suffusing his whole body and he began to relax and enjoy his introduction to the good life, especially as the Captain also offered them his silver cigarette case, saying, again just like they did on the pictures, "Turkish on the left; American on the right".

Remembering how, just after the War, adults used to complain when the only cigarettes to be had in the shops were 'Pasha', Jimmy took a Lucky Strike. Someone dressed in a white buttoned-up jacket then came in bearing a small silver tray very professionally on one hand. There were three rather small cups of very black, almost viscous, coffee. Jimmy noticed that Albert put in three spoonfuls of sugar, so he did the same. He was glad he did, but he liked the strong taste and it went well with the whiskey. He eased himself back in the armchair. The whiskey was having its effect, and his head felt pleasantly muzzy. He could let Albert get on with talking to the Captain, while he luxuriated in what to him were palatial surroundings, though he had a nagging feeling that it would be all too brief. And it was: just then the Customs Officer came in with a peremptory knock on the open door. The Captain offered him a drink, which he refused with a great show of hauteur, saying, "And you shouldn't be giving strong drink to these lads either".

The Captain stood up, and he was a tall man. He looked the bureaucrat in the eye and said, "My crew would be very upset if I did not show hospitality to these young men. Moreover" (and he put great emphasis on this word, as though he were pleased to show the extent of his English) "might I remind you that this is my ship, that nothing illegal is happening and that they are my guests, which you are not!"

The Captain looked so fierce that Jimmy fully expected the Customs Officer to wilt, but he too stood tall, glared at the Captain, and said, "That's as may be, but they are under age, and you should not be encouraging them to drink".

And with that he suddenly swivelled round on his heels, bent forward, and peered over his glasses at Jimmy. "How old are you, lad?"

"Err... si... se... eighteen!"

"Yes, I bet..."

Jimmy felt more like ten years old. Why was it that just when you were becoming a little bit adult at last, some supposedly mature person had to come along and spoil it? Whereas, five minutes ago, he'd thought that he and Albert were being treated like real people, now he seemed once more to be not in control of his life, but blown about willy-nilly. He felt weak, and useless and dependent on others. He wanted to run away again. He looked at Albert, almost pleadingly, and was surprised to see that, far from being overawed, his friend looked angry. What's more he stood up and said, "Well, I'm eighteen" (which he was not), "and will shortly be called up for National Service" (which was not true either). "If I'm old enough to fight for my country, then I'm old enough to drink whiskey."

Albert did look as though he might possibly be eighteen, because he was quite a lot taller than Jimmy, had thick dark hair, and was wearing a military-style raincoat. This hid how slight he in fact was. His intervention also seemed to come as a surprise to the Captain as well as the Customs Officer. The latter actually stood back and this encouraged the Captain, who said, "If you've finished doing all you need to do, then perhaps you can now leave my ship and let me entertain my guests as I see fit". For the first time the officer seemed a mite crestfallen.

"Very well, Captain, but you should be careful, and so should you," he said, looking at Albert and then more intently at Jimmy.

When he'd gone, the Captain poured them another whiskey, and gave each of them a couple of packets of Lucky Strike. However, he did not say very much and Albert had the gumption to realize it was time to go. As they made their way to the gangway, various members of the crew grinned broadly at them and spoke to them in Greek. Jimmy began to relax again, and felt elated by the whole experience. Or perhaps it was the whiskey. Of one thing he was certain: he did not want to go home and neither apparently did Albert, because he said, "The tide will still be running and some of the smaller ships will only just be leaving now. Do you want to watch them for a bit?"

"Oh, yeh. That'd be great."

They walked along to the end of the basin, to where it linked up with the next dock. They crossed an iron footbridge, which was obviously moveable, then around several sheds and into a maze of smaller docks, which to Jimmy were confusing but through which Albert walked with the confidence of someone at ease in this man's world, a world of hard physical labour, a world of arcane skills and a world of international trade. They came at last to a narrow deep channel and Jimmy was surprised at just how narrow it was. Somehow they seemed to have travelled back a century because everything that now surrounded them stood in contrast to the concrete modernity and straight lines of Canada Basin. He even found himself standing under an ornate Victorian lamp post, which carried three elegant globes. The Harbour Master too, in his gold-braided peaked cap and uniform, looked like a throwback to another age: he was even using an ancient loud-hailer to shout at the Captain of a tug, which was hauling the last of the large vessels out into the river. His language was as colourful as his dress. The Captain of the ship itself did not appear to trust the Harbour Master, because, though the ship never once touched the sides of the channel, he had posted what can only be described as the ship's boy towards the bow, armed with a large hessian ball on the end of a rope. He kept up a barrage of shouting that rivalled that of the Harbour Master in loudness and expletives. The unfortunate lad ran from the port side to the starboard, each time throwing his giant pompom over the gunwale, only to have to pull it back again immediately and run to the other side. This was the last ship to need a tug: all the others were quite small and therefore manoeuvrable enough to get out under their own steam, though the Harbour Master kept up a stream of abusive instructions to them. Jimmy wondered where they might be going, but Albert said they were mere coasters and some would be sailing only to North Wales; others plied a trade around the coasts of England and Scotland; a few might be trading with Ireland or perhaps Europe.

As they made their way home, Jimmy asked Albert had he ever thought of going to sea, but Albert said, "What, and be like that poor twit we saw being chased from pillar to post by that pig of a captain. No fear!"

"Yeh, but all jobs wouldn't be like that."

"They would for us, you know. We'd be bullied whichever ship we were on. Mr Wade warned us before we left school. And do you remember when Freddie Moran went on that coaster to Limerick? He had a terrible time, and not only from the crew but also because the sea was very rough and each time the ship pitched the screw came out of the water, and made everything vibrate so much he thought the boat would fall apart."

So, a notion that had been forming itself in Jimmy's head began to fade almost immediately. What a pity! No visiting speakeasies (even if he knew what they were) in New York; nor exotic islands in the South Seas, with lovesick hula-hula girls; nor even battling heroically round Cape Horn in mountainous seas, which, after the Freddie Moran story, began to sound like a nightmare to be avoided. No, he'd have to think of another job, and Albert's seemed quite attractive, especially if it meant being out and about on the docks, being on ships, and running around the city to places like the Customs House, the Cunard and Liver Buildings. He began to look in earnest.

The best place seemed to be the Situations Vacant in the *Liverpool Echo* and, sure enough, there was a position advertised for a school leaver in a ship's brokers, just like Albert's place, though Albert reckoned he'd never heard of Clissold and Parkin, and he wasn't quite sure where Lantern Yard was, except that it might be one of those funny little places behind Dale Street. Jimmy bought a large white Basildon Bond writing pad, put a new relief nib in his dip-in pen and wrote a letter of application, with great care, claiming possession of three 'O' levels – Latin, English and Mathematics – and swearing undying devotion to whoever might give him a job. To his surprise he was called to interview.

On the day, the whole house woke to a feeling of excitement. Jimmy had pressed the trousers of his best suit with creases that looked as though they could cut. (Actually, this was not difficult because the material was wearing very thin.) As promised, his mother had done the stiff collar of his best white shirt with real starch, not flour, which she usually used with complete disregard for the comfort of her sons. Even Alan was prepared to help by lending him a tie. When he set off to catch the 17C bus, he felt nervous. By the time he got off he felt queasy. He thought, 'If I go on like this I'll be violently ill by the time I get into Clissold and Whatsit'. However, his mind was at this stage fully occupied with finding Lantern Yard, which nobody he asked had ever heard of. The question then became, not would he get there in time, but would he ever get there? Panic! Panic! He was getting very hot and sweaty and his stiff collar he was sure was becoming floppy. Then he met a policeman who did know where it was but said, "Why on earth do you want to go there?"

"I'm going for a job."

"A job? What kind of a job? A back alley sweeper?"

"No. An office job."

"An office job? There aren't any offices up there, lad. It's only a little crack." But Jimmy followed his instructions and sure enough he found the place and understood the comments of the copper: it was narrow and dark and full of litter. Even so he found a door too and it was open. This had to be it because there could be nowhere else. The stairs were gloomy and smelt as though they were visited regularly by drunks. What's more, they seemed to go on and on, round and round, up and up, forever. When at last he came to a landing at what he was sure must be the very top of the building, he found a quite impressive door, which even had a brass plate. Though it was very tarnished you could make out Clissold and Parkin. Feeling sick again, he knocked, but the very thickness of the door seemed to absorb all the energy of the knock, which sounded like an apologetic tap. There was no answer, so he knocked again, but this time much more vigorously. The effect was startling, because the door was flung wide open to reveal a very young-looking office boy, who glared at Jimmy from under a ragged fringe of greasy hair.

"Are you the bailiff or sommink, hammering like that?"

"Sorry. No, er... I've come for a job. Er... I've got an interview."

Then a female voice came from inside the office. "All right, Danny, there's no need to show off. Let the poor chap in."

He stood back, still glowering, and Jimmy went in. The office was Dickensian and dominated by two very heavy desks, one of which stood under a quite high window and the other at right angles to it along another wall, so that it too took at least some light from the rather dirty window. The desks were high and quite steeply pitched. At the one under the window sat a girl on a high stool. She was half turned towards Jimmy, and she said, "Are you here to see Mr Parkin?"

Before Jimmy could answer, she went on, "He's not back from lunch yet. I'm sorry there's nowhere for you to sit. You'll have to stand. And, Danny, you'd better have that cash book done before he gets back and no mistakes, please. You know what he's like."

Both the clerks then turned towards their respective walls, leaned over their desks and scratched away. After a while the girl got off her stool and went over to a small table, which had on it a typewriter. She rattled away on this for several minutes and then took out whatever it was she had written, opened the door to an inner office, and put the piece of paper on a large desk that Jimmy could see in the middle of the floor. She closed the door and climbed back on to her stool, to pore again over what appeared to be a huge ledger. Time went on. Jimmy's anxiety increased: he did not feel at all comfortable in this place. Nobody said a word. The pair of them simply worked away, though Danny sniffed wetly and noisily every so often. Then he heard footsteps, though not very sure ones, on the stairs. The clerks shifted on their high seats. There was shuffling on the landing and then suddenly the door was thrown open violently to reveal a large, over-dressed and very hot man, whose most outstanding feature was the amount of red hair on various parts of his face. What was left on his head was curly and stuck out on all sides. His moustache was large and hid his top lip completely. His side-burns were long and frizzy. He looked fiercely into the office and then strode in. Plainly he had been drinking. At first he did not appear to have seen Jimmy, because he peered intently at the girl and then the boy. He looked truculent. Then he saw Jimmy and was taken by surprise.

"Who're you?"

"He's here for interview, Mr Parkin," said the girl without looking up.

Mr Parkin looked puzzled. Then slowly his memory began to function and his eyes opened wide. His face cracked into a broken-toothed grin and he said, "Ah, yes lad. Come in. Come in."

The inner office looked as though it might have been impressive, once upon a time, but now it had an air of neglect and dilapidation. Old dog-eared sheaves of paper were everywhere in unstable columns: there seemed to be no working surfaces. On two sets of shelves there were ledgers, heavy leather-bound books, and box-files, piled up higgledy-piggledy. Mr Parkin took off his overcoat, threw it on to a rickety stand, sat down heavily in a swivel chair behind the mahogany desk and looked at Jimmy.

"So you want to come and work for us?"

"Yes, Sir."

"What are your qualifications?"

"Three 'O' levels, Sir. Like I said in my letter."

"What letter?"

"One I sent in reply to your advertisement, Sir."

"Ah... oh... yer..." Mr Parkin rummaged through some of the papers on his desk but to no avail. He looked up and seemed surprised that Jimmy was still there.

"What did you say?"

"Three 'O' levels."

"And what are they when they're out?"

Jimmy had no idea what to say, so he just stared in amazement at Mr Parkin, who for a while stared back. Then he frowned, gradually harder and harder, until his face went even redder and his eyes bulged. Then suddenly, he roared, "I asked you a question! You stupid boy!"

"General Certificate of Education."

The answer shot out of Jimmy's mouth, to his own astonishment, but it seemed to have satisfied Parkin, who then appeared to calm down. He said, "You haven't got a School Certificate then?"

Jimmy felt even more perplexed and frightened. This was worse than school, and this maniac might at any moment reach into his desk and pull out a ferula. That debilitating fear gripped him again. Once more he felt the real him shrink up into the back of his skull, leaving his body behind weak and limp.

"Well?" came the bellow.

"Er... no... I haven't got one."

"You're no good to me then, are you?"

Jimmy thought he ought to say something by way of explanation. "There's no School Certificate now. It's GCE instead."

"Is it? ... Oh... and what did you say you'd got?"

"Maths, Latin and English Language, Sir."

There was another silence, and Mr Parkin stared at the desk, with beetled brows. He kept on staring, and staring and staring. Jimmy could only sit and look at him with a smile so fixed it began to hurt his cheeks. The silence was becoming unbearable, when Mr Parkin snored. He actually snored! Then Jimmy realized this fearsome man was asleep, and he had no idea what he could do about it. He just sat there looking at this hirsute monster, when it dawned on him that he did not have to stay there. This was not school. Parkin was not his boss, not yet; and never would be, if Jimmy knew anything about it. Very quietly he got up and moved towards the door, while looking over his shoulder to keep a check that he could get out without disturbing Parkin. He crept into the outer office to find Danny and the girl looking at him with intense interest. He smiled weakly and said, "Mr Parkin seems to have fallen asleep".

"Asleep?"

"Yes. What do you think I should do?"

They looked as perplexed as he felt. They stared at each other and then back at Jimmy. The girl said, "I suppose you could wait till he wakes up".

In that instant Jimmy knew that he was going to leave immediately, because the thought of entering that office again and facing the fiery Mr Parkin was very disturbing.

"Er... no... I think it would be better if I left straight away. Don't you?"

"OK. Suit yourself. What shall I tell him when he wakes up?"

"Er... tell him I don't want the job."

"You wouldn't have got it anyway."

"Eh! Why not?"

"Well, the way things are going there soon won't be enough work for us two, never mind you."

"Oh," he said, and set off down the stairs, feeling very relieved.

When he got home, he told them all he had not got the job, because they wanted someone more experienced: he couldn't bring himself to describe what really happened and he didn't want his mother to start up again about him leaving school. She'd probably say that what had occurred was his own fault and what he deserved. He had to start looking again in the situations vacant, but all the advertisements seemed to be for unskilled work. However, just as he was beginning to despair, Uncle George paid a visit, and he was an underwriter with a marine insurance firm. He had useful connections and said he would speak to some friends about Jimmy.

Thus it was that a week later he found himself on a bus on his way to the Pier Head so that he could be interviewed by Johnson and Jackson, Marine Insurers, in the Liver Buildings. Again he felt very nervous, but this time had no difficulty finding the place, which was quite unlike the slum in Lantern Yard. He had always been impressed by the buildings at the Pier Head, and especially the Liver itself, but when he got inside was even more impressed: everything was big and clean and shiny. A man in a navy blue uniform, lots of medals and a white peaked cap, called him young fellah-me-lad, and asked if he could help: it did not look as though you could refuse his assistance. He was cheerful enough and gave Jimmy clear instructions as to which lift, which floor and which direction to go in when he got there. Jimmy followed them to the letter and found himself in a vestibule with a sliding window and a push-button bell, which he was invited to ring. He rang and immediately the window slid back and a young girl politely asked him what he wanted. He was told to wait. After a little while a rather elderly man in a grey suit, with grey hair and grey twinkly eyes came out, asked him his name, and invited Jimmy to follow him. As they went along the corridor, Mr Holmes, for such was his name, chatted pleasantly about this and that, so that by the time they entered a small office, bare except for a table and chair, Jimmy felt at ease. Mr Holmes placed a blue booklet on the table and asked him to sit down, and explained that here were a few tests for him to try. He lent Jimmy a biro and told him to bring the tests back to the outer office when he was ready, adding that there was plenty of time and no need to rush. He then left and Jimmy opened the booklet to discover that it contained an arithmetic test, which was much simpler than the recently taken 'O' level, an intelligence test, which was like an advanced 11+, and a general knowledge quiz. None of these presented him with much difficulty: there were some tricky diagrams in the intelligence test, e.g. a picture of a clock that the reader was told was a mirror image and then asked what the time was an hour and ten minutes ago. Many of the general knowledge questions were easy, but some he was not sure of; for instance, he didn't know whether to put Tass or Pravda for the Soviet News Agency. When he handed the papers in, Mr Holmes gave them to somebody else and then invited Jimmy to have a cup of coffee downstairs at what appeared to be a café. He even offered him a cigarette, which he took but, too late, wondered if that were wise. They then had an easy conversation about all sorts of things, except what working in marine insurance might involve. They talked about football, school, books, the cinema, current affairs and even the weather, until Mr Holmes excused himself and asked Jimmy to wait there for a little while. He was not long away and returned with the blue booklet.

"Now, you've done very well in the tests, and we've had an informative conversation, but I'm afraid we can't offer you a job."

Jimmy was nonplussed: everything seemed to have gone so well, especially as after the first few minutes of the process, he had not felt in the least afraid. Then Mr Holmes added, "This is no reflection on you. We simply haven't got a place for you. In fact we are going to be over-staffed, because two young men are coming back into the firm after doing their national service."

They sat in silence. Mr Holmes looked duly sympathetic. He continued, "We would have liked to have done your uncle a favour, and we think you would fit in here, but there's nothing we can do about it."

Jimmy felt helpless again, as though nothing he tried could ever meet with success.

"What will you do now?" Mr Holmes went on.

"I don't really know... I suppose I'll have to start looking in the *Echo* again."

"Listen, son, do you want my advice?"

Jimmy looked up into this old man's kindly eyes, but could say nothing.

"If I were you, I'd go back to school, and finish those 'A' levels. You're far from stupid, and I'm sure you could do well if you tried. Remember, firms like ours take some people at that level... we sometimes even take graduates. What's to stop you going to university? Have you thought about that?"

Jimmy smiled, and said, "Oh, no, I've never thought of anything like that".

"But I bet other boys in your class have thought about it, haven't they?"

"Well, yes, but they're..."

"No buts about it; if they can, so can you."

It was obvious to everyone when Jimmy got home that he was dejected and had not got the job. As he told them what had happened, they all became sympathetic: nobody blamed him or criticized him. When he told them that Mr Holmes had suggested he should go back to school, they all looked at each other and no one seemed to want to catch Jimmy's eye: they were all embarrassed and he did not know why, at first. Did they think that was what he ought to do? Or did they think that if they appeared to agree with Mr Holmes, he would get angry? He realized that they knew he had to decide for himself. He also became aware of how unreasonable he could be any time a member of his own family tried to help him. Now that he felt he needed their advice they were afraid to give it in case he saw it as interference. Telling him, they knew, made him explode. So, internally, he squirmed, but he had to make the next move. He said, "Perhaps I'll have to. What do you think?"

They all began to speak at once, but his mother motioned them all to be quiet and said, "Well, do you want to?"

"Not really, but maybe I'll have to?"

"You know what I think. I wish you'd never left in the first place."

The others all murmured their agreement, but then Alan added, "You realize that by the time you leave next year, you'll be getting on for eighteen and so the army will be looming up. No one will give you a permanent job."

"Unless you went to university like Mr Holmes suggested," said Alice.

"You have to do your national service first anyway," said Jane.

"Not necessarily, it depends what they offer at the interview."

"That's only for Oxford or Cambridge."

"Well, he's not going there, is he?"

Jimmy began to feel as though he were somewhere else, so he interjected, "Just a minute, who are we talking about? ... You're all going too fast for me. I'm not even back at school yet... and old egg-head might not have me."

They were silent again, and then his mother said, "Look. Why doesn't Jane write to the school, I'll sign it, explaining the situation, and saying we all want you to go back. Then if they take you, we can think about all the other problems later."

A week later Jimmy had an embarrassing interview, in which he was told in no uncertain terms that if he came back he would have to work very hard, attend regularly, and generally behave himself. (He wondered if they really knew who he was, if they thought Jimmy ever did anything other than behave himself.) Then the Head mentioned higher education and it became obvious that he considered Jimmy to be training college fodder: he talked about Hopwood Hall and Strawberry Hill, but Jimmy felt not at all sure about this, so he kept quiet except for the odd "Yes, Father". He wanted to go home and think about it.

Chapter VII

T HE SIXTH FORM YEAR always began with a retreat, usually led by a Jesuit notable specially invited for the occasion. That particular year it was a priest with an unpronounceable Polish name who hailed from Farm Street, the Jesuit Communications Centre in London. At first, the retreat was just as Jimmy had remembered from the first year: there were homilies on faith and morals, followed by periods of meditation when the whole Sixth Form would stroll around the playground, supposedly in silence. Most boys saw it all as some sort of joke. They grinned at each other, but would usually look away in case they burst out laughing – the J's might be watching from the house. Generally, they were silent: only occasionally did they whisper side-mouthed to each other.

The approach was oblique: talks on purity had lots of references to Our Lady, but never mentioned sex directly. This priest, however, introduced a question box. Few people used it and the questions that were asked were innocuous. Then, one afternoon, as they returned from a period of contemplation in the yard, it became immediately apparent that he was angry. What did they mean, he raved, by asking such a question? They all looked at each other, puzzled. What question? Nobody seemed to know. He glared down at them from his dais, his face red with fury. There was a long, embarrassed pause: it became obvious to them that he realized they had no idea what he was talking about. He would have to tell them what the question was, but it was clear that he was having some difficulty with this. Then he took a piece of paper out of his pocket and with his complexion now fiery, read out in a voice choked with emotion, "How far can you go with a girl before you have committed a mortal sin?"

This seemed to render him speechless. They sat there, stony-faced. It was a question dear to their hearts, but one to which they were already sensing they were not going to get an answer that they would appreciate. He strode up and down the dais, looking everywhere but at them. Suddenly, dramatically, he swung round and stared intently at his audience.

"I'll tell you how far… no distance at all! What do you want with girls? You should not be even thinking about them. The place for that is in marriage and is not appropriate to any of you at your age. Forget about it. Pray to our Blessed Mother to keep you pure. I will talk about this no further. You are dismissed." He marched out of the room.

They did not find this helpful. Most of his friends in the Sixth Form were as perplexed and as disappointed as Jimmy. They all took the opportunity to 'neck' with girls if they were presented with it. Some occasionally boasted that they had taken matters much further, but Jimmy thought they were probably exaggerating. If they were to take seriously what they had just heard, then they should not be even kissing girls. They began to discuss the question and there were those who actually took the same reactionary line as the priest. Jimmy realized only much later that really they were acting as devil's advocates: they wanted to see arguments drawn out that would permit them more leeway in making decisions about sexual conduct. The trouble with this for Jimmy was that they quoted sources such as the catechism, which had the force of holy writ, no matter how dogmatic, didactic and narrow they might be. He had not lost the legalistic approach he had acquired in pre-adolescent days.

Later, the true intention of the retreat leader became apparent. His obsession was communism, which, as he was a Pole, was not surprising. However, at first Jimmy and most of the Sixth Form found exceptional nothing that he had to say. They had always assumed that a grammar school education in a Jesuit college would result in them taking up occupations where they would have some influence. In positions of at least moderate power, they would behave as good Catholics, for the good of society, but also to enhance the reputation of the Church. Slowly it began to dawn on them that more was expected of them: they were to be the shock troops in the fight against the forces of the left. Jimmy began to feel uncomfortable about his projected role, and not only because it would make him responsible in some way. It was also because, if he had any political philosophy, it was left of centre: in his family it was assumed that people like them voted Labour. He understood that communist regimes in Russia and China were anti-democratic and irreligious, but this man seemed to see communists and subversives everywhere. This was very disconcerting: how did you know when you had met one? Finally, Jimmy decided that there was something very remiss when, in one of the last talks, they were told that they should "put all communists and fellow-travellers up against the wall and shoot them for the slime that they are". Wasn't this what fascists did? Jimmy was glad to get back to boring old lessons.

Though there were now only three subjects to think about, Jimmy found the work at school hard because he had missed so much. This was especially true of French, which he should never have taken in the first place. He also reverted to the habits of work that had been successful back in the Second Form, when in French and Latin he had checked every word. The trouble with this was he never really learned the stuff very well: he was always having to look up words and grammatical constructions, and he began to worry about exams, which he was now sure he wanted to pass.

He had an incentive: he wanted to go to university. At first this was almost out of a sense of perversity, because one evening when he was in the pub (under age, but that was half the fun of drinking) with Albie and several others who lived round about, he had a conversation with Freddie, who, besides working in a shipping office, also went to night school, where one of his subjects was History. Unhappily for Jimmy, it was Modern European History, about which he knew very little because his 'A' level course was in Medieval European. Freddie liked to talk about his course and was always surprised (and pleased) that Jimmy knew so little about it. However, on this particular evening they were talking about their possible futures and Jimmy mentioned that he might

George Timmons

go to university, though the chances were slim. Freddie poured scorn on the idea, saying that you had to be really clever to make it, and implied that Jimmy was not up to it. Though Jimmy too thought this, he was annoyed at being told to his face that he was stupid. There and then he resolved 'to show this bugger...' He began to take the work quite seriously, and to think of sending for application forms.

But where should he think of going? His direct grant grammar school being interested almost solely in its Oxbridge candidates, the rest were left more or less to their own devices, and Jimmy's were puny. Of course Liverpool had to be first choice, because most of those he knew who intended to go into higher education had applied there. However, Jimmy thought that he would like to find out how he would function away from home, and so the notion of going away seemed attractive, even if more than a little frightening. But where? The only person in his street ever to go to university was Bernie Reave, who came from the top end, i.e. the posher part, and he'd been to Durham and had worn a duffle coat and a purple scarf, which Jimmy thought looked very smart. That was a possibility. Another was Hull, and for this there were two related reasons. The first was that there was a connection with the school. This had come about because the founder of the university had established a scholarship in Classics, and somewhere in the distant past the Head had discovered this and used it as a consolation prize for those in the Classics Sixth he considered to be less well endowed; in other words, those who were not going to get into either Oxford or Cambridge. It also looked good in the school Magazine, because it could be entered as 'The Ferens Prize'. The second was that one day Grisedale had referred to one of these scallywags, for such they often were, and had warned the class that, "To go to Hull University meant running the risk of turning to gambling and drinking, or gambling and women, or drinking and women or even all three!"

He told them this with such glee that Jimmy thought it must be true and though he himself was very wary of gambling, the other two dangers seemed eminently attractive, so he decided to apply to Hull too. He sent application forms to all three, and soon had replies from each of them.

The first interview was at Liverpool. He was able to attend in a new sports jacket, bought specially for the occasion. After sitting in an outer office for ten sweaty minutes he was ushered into a narrow room, where sat two gentlemen behind a desk. They had their backs to the window through which poured brilliant afternoon sunshine. The features of one of these tutors he could just about make out. Of the other he could see nothing, because he was smoking a large pipe from which issued clouds of not unpleasant-smelling fumes. The first man addressed him in a friendly fashion and put to him questions to which the majority of answers were readily available: in fact, he had already written most of them on the application form. Asked which of his general interests had suggested to him that he ought to study History, Jimmy, in what he thought was a flash of brilliance, answered, "Politics".

"Ah, so you are interested in politics?"

"Moderately. Yes." Jimmy was now not so sure his answer had been so sensible. What was coming next?

"Perhaps you would like to tell me the subject of the White Paper issued by the Government yesterday?"

He had actually listened to the news that morning and knew that the Paper was on the National Health Service and so this is what he said, but was then asked, "And who is responsible for it?"

"The Minister of Health."

"Who is?"

Jimmy was stumped: he knew he knew the answer but the more he tried to recall it, the blanker his mind became. Then an apparently disembodied voice boomed from out of the cloud of smoke, and Jimmy learned how Moses felt before the burning bush.

"Mr Thompson. Are you interested in words?"

"Er… Yes."

"Then would you like to tell me what you mean by the word 'around'?"

"Well, there could be several meanings."

"Give me one."

"Er... one could be 'to go along the perimeter,' another could be 'to be out and about,' as in 'around town'."

"Now, suppose you were in Africa, trying to observe the habits of monkeys. You arrive at a tree, where you can see a monkey on the side nearest you, so you try to skirt round the back of him: you want to get nearer the monkey by approaching him while hidden by the branches. However, as you move round the tree, the monkey does too and you never get behind him. You both end up in the same place. Now, have you been around the monkey?"

This was not the sort of question expected and because the questioner was still hidden in wreaths of smoke made more impenetrable by the bright sunlight behind him, Jimmy was momentarily struck dumb. When he became conscious of the fact that his mouth was open, he decided he had better say something.

"I suppose so."

"You only suppose?"

"Well... Yes... er... what the monkey does is immaterial."

"I see."

The burning bush then asked him some rather more traditional questions about Antony and Cleopatra, to which he gave some rather traditional answers, and the interview came to an end. He had no idea whether or not they would offer him a place, but about a week later a letter arrived saying that if he got three 'A' levels, he would have a place on the general degree course.

Going for the interview at Hull was very different. There was the journey, for instance: it was much longer than he had imagined and it took him to places that until then were mere names. Manchester he had been to before, if only to watch Everton beaten, 4–3, by Bolton in the semi-final of the Cup, when Nat Lofthouse was invincible and Dave Hickson got crocked by Malcolm Barrass within the first ten minutes. Beyond lay the Pennines, Huddersfield and Leeds, where from the train you could see mostly the backs of houses and factories, though in the latter case, at least some were more interesting than the ones at home, because they really did look like t'mills in all the classic illustrations of the Nineteenth Century: rectangular and tall, but elegant in their own way, with several storeys and rows of surprisingly airy windows, and of course, great chimney stacks. Leeds was only the halfway point. You still had to cross the long flat plain of East Yorkshire. When he arrived at Hull Paragon it was raining, but the bus station was next door, and his instructions were clear: he was at the university in time for lunch, which he had in a new, fine-looking red-brick Students' Union, having been met by a second year student, with a wispy beard, a red nose, and a pronounced Sheffield accent. Jimmy ate very little of the lunch because he felt so nervous, but he did relax a little because he shared a table with several other interviewees and the second year students (who showed them round and looked after them), so he was not as apprehensive as when he went to Liverpool University. There, he had been left to his own devices and had had to find his own way to the room for interview through a warren of buildings and corridors. At Hull a student took him, even though the university was much smaller and much more compact.

The first interview was with the Head of the History Department. He was a dapper man in a well-cut suit and a florid, floppy bow tie. He had just come back from a year's exchange at an American University and seemed to be much affected by the experience. He talked a good deal about it, but asked Jimmy very few questions about history. He also seemed keen to let Jimmy know what a splendid place Hull University was, and how much Jimmy would enjoy his three years there. He assumed that Jimmy would accept a place, and even hinted that only two 'A' levels were necessary, if they were appropriate.

The interview in the English Department was formal and Jimmy found himself confronted by a panel of four people: a large man with grey hair who looked like Vaughan Williams, a nondescript woman in a navy blue suit, another woman with a veritable helmet of iron-grey hair, and a young man in a sports jacket who looked little older than Jimmy. Fortunately, as it turned out later, the lady in the helmet asked the first question. It was about courtly love as portrayed in Chaucer's *Knight's Tale*, and this had been discussed only the day before in school: Jimmy was able to talk about it for at least ten minutes. This led to further questions and answers and then to an extended discussion, with the other interviewers chipping in occasionally. However, the young man in the sports coat seemed to be becoming impatient with all this. Very abruptly, rapidly and with a slight stutter, he interjected a question about Tennyson's *In Memoriam*. Even if Jimmy had heard the question properly, he probably would not have understood it, because his efforts to read the work had been feeble. It was so long, tedious and about someone mourning the death of his best pal for ten (or was it twenty – or maybe even thirty?) years. Considering honesty to be the best policy, he confessed that he had read it only skimpily, saying that as yet it had not been dealt with in class. The sports jacket looked as though he doubted this and went on to ask Jimmy what, even with his limited acquaintance with the work, he thought of the style in the poem. Desperately, Jimmy scratched around in his head for an answer and when his comment, "appropriate", was frostily received, he added quickly that he liked the alliteration and the onomatopoeia. Immediately he was asked for examples and his heart sank because the only ones he could think of were from either *Sir Galahad* or *The Lotus Eaters*, which had been studied in the lower forms in school and were the source of his remark in the first place. Just when he was about to give up hope that something significant to say would come into his head, steel helmet came to the rescue, by saying that she thought that Tennyson was a bit of a bore, and she more or less invited Jimmy to agree with her, which he did but, he hoped, with a sufficient show of reluctance. Vaughan Williams then asked him some questions about Shakespeare and the interview ended very amicably, with even the young man smiling. Two days later he was offered a place to study Joint History and English. Prospects began to look bright.

There were other developments that made prospects look brighter. On those odd occasions when he could afford it, he went to the pub with Albie, Freddie and Gordon, an apprentice coach trimmer, whose job had already had such an effect on his physique that he was known as 'the lad with the big strong hands'. One night, they were joined by Ivor O'Connor, who regaled them with stories of his prowess in getting dates with girls, now that he knew how to dance. This seemed like a skill worth acquiring, especially as, if Ivor were to be believed, "You only need the waltz and the quick step, and maybe the foxtrot to get the girls". They all were persuaded to go the next Friday to 'The Edwards School of Dancing' with him.

After a traumatic but mercifully brief introduction, they all began to pick up the skills fairly quickly and in sufficient depth to avoid treading on the toes of their equally inexperienced partners. The school operated very much like a club and the friendly atmosphere meant that they soon began to feel easy with the girls who attended. There were two fairly large rooms and so there could be a beginners' and an advanced class, but in the second half of the evening both groups came together and there was a proper dance, mostly to records of Victor Sylvester. Because there were 'Paul Jones Medleys', where everyone changed partners, and the music changed too, you got to do the different dances with the more experienced girls, and so learned faster. Also, there were plenty of ladies' requests and all the girls were expected to ask someone to dance, so the initial shyness soon evaporated. This was a much better way of getting to know girls than hanging round the Pit.

Yet with this group of local friends, he rarely went dancing, other than on Friday nights. They went to the pub often enough but he could not always join them because of his lack of funds. He sometimes went to the pictures with them, or perhaps to see either Everton or Liverpool play, whichever team happened to be at home. On the other hand, he did meet some of his fellow Sixth Formers at dances and this was because they went to hops in schools usually run by the old boys' or old girls' associations of the particular institutions. There were two advantages to this, the first being that they were cheap. The second was that the girls were usually Sixth Formers too, and for some reason he found these easier to talk to. Perhaps it was because you could ask them which schools they went to and what subjects they did, to break the ice. Also, the girls nearer home were working, had money and very often their boyfriends were older: to their experienced eyes he was still a school kid, a 'college pudd'n'. Many of them were already looking for husbands.

None of these schools was situated in his part of the city, so he had to go on the bus to get to any of them. If the dance finished late he had to walk home. The girls more often than not lived much nearer. He told himself that this was the reason he never asked any of them if he could walk them home, even though this did not make much sense: the truth was he was frightened to ask in case they refused.

Then one night he saw across the dance floor someone he thought he recognised, as she lived, or used to live, a couple of streets away from him. He remembered her as a skinny, rather tall girl, with straw coloured hair who was regarded by the other kids as a bit snooty because she went to grammar school. He could not be sure it was the same person because, though this girl looked like Maureen McCrae, she seemed not so tall and certainly not so skinny. She was not what he thought of as his type, but she was not unattractive, and when she was not dancing, which was not very often, he liked the way she talked animatedly with her friends. Actually going over to a girl and asking her to dance was always nerve-wracking and on this occasion it was even worse, but the old adage, 'nothing ventured nothing gained,' came into his head and he decided he would have to be bold. However, it was not that easy because he did not want to be the first on the floor when the music started, and if he delayed too long some other bloke might ask her. That's what happened at the next number. Then the one after that was a foxtrot in which he never felt comfortable. He nervously sat that one out. The next one was a quick step, which he thought he could do well. It was also a Dixie-land tune: he might even be able to show off a bit. In fact, the floor began to fill up quite quickly and he got to Maureen just in time. When he asked her to dance she looked up and smiled, but she did not seem to recognise him. Just as well, he thought: otherwise she might have refused. She danced very easily. He did a reverse turn halfway down the hall and she followed perfectly. He did a double turn at the corner and she responded so well that he felt they were Fred Astaire and Ginger Rogers. This was going better than he expected, so he ventured, "Are you Maureen McCrae?"

"Yes... I am," She said, looking at him quizzically.

"And do you still live in Abbott Street?"

"What's all this? Am I supposed to know you?"

"Well, you probably won't remember me, but I live in Rupert Grove."

"Rupert Grove? That's only round the corner from us."

"Yes, weren't you friends with the Martin sisters in Priory Grove?"

"But that was ages ago."

"Ar... but do you remember their cousin, Billy Wilkins?"

"Will I ever forget him! He was a terrible nuisance. He always used to say that I was his girlfriend and I hated him and his squint!"

"Oh yes, but he seems to have lost his squint... he and I used to go down Priory Grove on one skate each... It was the only street with proper smooth tarmac."

"Yes, now I remember... Mrs Martin always complained about the rough kids from your street playing down there."

"Well, one of them was me."

"But I can't remember you amongst that scruffy lot."

"Well, can you remember my posh sister, Alice Thompson?"

"Oh. I remember her... she was friends with the Martins too... Then you must be Jimmy Thompson!"

"That's me."

She was obviously surprised and did not know what to say: he was not the same person as the ragged-arsed kid that Mrs Martin complained about. This all made Jimmy feel good, because she appeared to be really interested in him, perhaps even a little intrigued. She asked him what he was doing at this dance without realizing that, like her, he was in a Sixth Form. It was clear that she did not even know he had been at a grammar school for the last six years. Once the penny dropped, and they began to talk about 'A' levels, it turned out they were taking the same subjects, and even the same periods in History and the same books in literature. The particular dance ended and as he walked her off the floor they were still talking and laughing about the kids they used to be and know in the old days (all of five years ago) and it seemed to be the most natural thing in the world for him to stay and continue the conversation. She introduced him casually to the friends she was with, but the next dance began and again it seemed natural that they should dance with each other. In fact, he never went back to his friends from school, but waved to them as he danced by: their grins meant that they thought he was doing all right without them.

It was all so easy: the conversation simply flowed. He did not have to make a special effort to think of topics or to worry about how he spoke. They talked about growing up in Everton; about the funny people who lived round about them like Dick Gaddes, the milkman, whose horse would suddenly take it into its head to go home; and Snow White and her dirty kids; about the eccentricities of their teachers; about the difficulties they experienced in their 'A' level subjects (French in his case, History in hers). And so it continued as they walked home together and even on her front step they went on and on, until she became aware of the neighbour opposite peeping through the curtains at them.

"My goodness! It's half past one!"

"Flippin' 'eck; so it is."

And suddenly they were tongue-tied. Should he try to kiss her? He daren't. He just daren't. Should he ask to see her again? He recalled the agony of waiting for Jenny when she didn't turn up, and for that reason the words would not come out. He could not turn on his heel and walk away. But what should he say, what could he say? He was aware that she expected him to say something, because though she was smiling she had a puzzled, perhaps even a pained, look in her eyes. Then he almost blurted out, "Is there a dance there every Saturday?"

"Oh, yes… every Saturday."

"And do you always go?"

"Nearly always… I'll definitely be going next week."

"Oh… right… OK, I'll see you there then."

"OK… See you there."

And in a flash she had the door open and had disappeared

inside. He stood momentarily; staring at the space she had left behind, came to himself and slowly turned for home.

'You bloody idiot! Why didn't you ask her out? She wanted you to! The pictures – a walk – anything. Oh, you idiot! And the way she disappeared so fast. You've really buggered it up, mate. Aaaaagh! Shite!'

This was the sort of conversation he had with himself all the next week. He also had to put up with the ribbing of his classmates.

"Who was the Judy you walked home on Saturday night?"

"Never you mind."

"Does she jump?"

"What's that supposed to mean?"

"You know what it means. Now, come on. Tell all."

"There's nothing to tell. I just took her home. That's not a crime."

"What you did when you got there might not be criminal, but Holy Mother Church might not approve."

"I didn't do anything!"

"I bet."

One consolation was that the home gang knew nothing about it, but he could imagine what they would have said.

"Maureen McCrae!? That stuck-up long skinnamalink. You mean the toothy one from Abbott Street?"

She was no longer skinny, nor tall, nor toothy, and he kept thinking about her and wondering whether he'd ruined his chances. He'd never seen her around the neighbourhood, so he would have to wait till the weekend to find out.

He began to think of how Saturday might go. If they both got there early and he asked her for the first dance, it would be difficult not to stay with her the whole evening: then everybody would think this was really serious. If he were to hang around a long time before asking her for a dance, she might get upset and then refuse to dance with him, or someone else might monopolise her. In the end he decided that he would not go too early and then when he got there he would play it by ear. Any thoughts he might have about what would happen later, if he walked her home again, he put out of his head, in case they became dangerous.

On Saturday he prepared very carefully and not only pressed his suit, he even went so far as to dab the edges of the cuffs with ink where they were beginning to wear and show white. Though he found it difficult not to jump on the earliest possible bus, he did delay setting off and he arrived at the dance at what seemed to be a reasonable time. At first he could not see her, but then heard peals of laughter from a group of girls in the corner of the hall: there in the middle was Maureen, smiling and lively. Suddenly he felt very shy, because he became aware that it was presumption on his part to imagine that she would be waiting anxiously for him and him alone, when really she was enjoying herself and her obvious popularity. Almost immediately she was invited to dance and took to the floor, with the enthusiasm she had shown the week before when dancing with him. He began to wonder if what had happened then had been briefly significant for her only because of the unexpectedness of meeting someone from her own rather rundown locality in these somewhat more elevated surroundings. He became unsure of himself and did not know quite what to do. The problem was resolved when, as she danced by, she caught sight of him, smiled broadly, half waved to him and mouthed a 'Hi'. Encouraged, he asked her for the next dance and to his surprise, they seemed to carry on where they had left off. Even so, he knew that he should take things steadily and to make no assumptions about her and what she might feel or think.

Again, they walked home together, and this time the conversation ranged far and wide: films; books; the theatre (he had to make it sound as though he went more often than he did); the Foyer Francais at the university, which he did sometimes attend but rarely knew much of what was being talked about. On the other hand, he did make her laugh by imitating the accent of the old man who always introduced the speakers. He puffed out his cheeks and twisted up his mouth seemingly, *"Ce soir nous avons le plaisir d'un discours par M. Poupouliniere au sujet de..."*

When they got to Abbott Street, she said, "Listen, I think I'd better go in the back way. That woman opposite complained to my mum. She said we disturbed her, laughing and talking loudly till all hours of the night."

Somehow, when they got there, neither of them knew what to say. With his heart pounding, he put his hand on her shoulder. She did not object so he said, "May I kiss you goodnight?"

"Yes, please."

At first they kissed rather gently, but then he felt a growing desire to kiss her more intently, and the fierceness of her response took him by surprise. He was the one who actually broke away, but then he stood with his head leaning on her shoulder. He said very quietly, "Am I going to see you during the week?"

The reply was unexpected. "I don't think so."

"You don't think so. Why not?" he asked, pulling back and trying to look into her eyes in the dark.

What she said next surprised him even more. "You see. Well... er... I've got a confession to make. I've got a boyfriend already."

He stepped right away from her, but she pulled him back and went on, "But that doesn't mean I don't like you, and I've really enjoyed your company... And he's away in Germany in the Air Force... and he won't be back for ages."

"I see that but..."

"Well, we can be friends, can't we? And it would be funny if you didn't kiss me goodnight, wouldn't it?"

"Well, yes, but... I mean..."

"And there's no harm in walking home together, is there? We both live in the same place."

By this time he was completely bemused and didn't know what to think. However, he did not feel as upset as he might have done and wondered why. He began to think there might be an advantage in all of this. Or he felt it rather than thought it, because the notion had hardly articulated itself in any clear way. He wanted a girlfriend of some sort but he did not want an entanglement. So, as what she said sank in, he realized that this was why he was not too distressed by the idea. Even so he could not resist the temptation to milk the situation for all the sympathy he could get, so he said, as glumly as he could, "Will you be at the dance next week, then?"

"Oh, yes. I'll be there every week."

Then she kissed him goodnight, and his play for sympathy succeeded better than he expected. They arranged to meet again in the same way next week and from then on there developed between them a rather odd relationship. They only ever met at the dance, and as time went on they did not even dance with each other quite so often, but he always walked her home. Their conversation was something he looked forward to all week, and she obviously enjoyed it too. She also helped him with school work, especially the English and French Literature, because her teachers gave much more direct help and notes that were geared to passing the examinations: she even brought some of them to the dance in her handbag so that he could copy them up and give them back the next week. He helped her too, because sometimes she seemed to get lost in the detail of the History and couldn't see the wood for the trees, whereas he was good at seeing the direction events were taking, more often than not because he had had to work them out for himself.

Though their relationship was not a secret, there was a touch of the clandestine about it, which added a frisson of excitement to the affair. When he asked her whether her school friends knew about her real boyfriend, she said, "Of course they do".

"Well, who do they think I am, then?"

"What you are... somebody I've known for years... with no romantic attachment... like a brother really."

"Oh, is that so?"

"Yes, and it's what my mum thinks too."

"She knows about me too, then!?"

"Yes, but she thinks there are several of you... who all live round about... But she is suspicious about why I always come in the back way on a Saturday."

"And what about David? Does he know about me?"

"In a way... I tell him what I tell my mum."

On the other hand she told Jimmy quite a lot about her boyfriend, David: that she had known him for several years, that they met at the church that all her family attended, that he had a place at Manchester (where she had applied) when he came out of the forces, and that she was definitely going to marry him some-day. She was very serious about this.

And yet at her back door she could be very passionate with Jimmy, so much so that he began to worry about this and wondered if he had gone too far. He even took to going to late Mass on a Sunday morning so that he couldn't be expected to go to Communion: he could say he had broken his fast, which in those days had to be kept from midnight. He also avoided confession, because again he did not want to face the embarrassment of explaining himself, or perhaps having the priest tell him he had definitely committed a mortal sin. The legalistic attitudes that he had learned earlier began to plague him. Was the matter serious? People did much worse things. Yes, but there could be no doubt about his intentions: he went out every Saturday night knowing full well what he and Maureen would do on the way home. Furthermore, he was not being honest with her: he was taking advantage of her situation in order to gratify his own self-ish desires. Yes, but, damn it, she was using him too. They were as bad as each other. Their relationship was just about sex.

But it was not only about what they got up to in the back entry! He liked her and he was sure she liked him. When they were together they laughed a lot. That must mean something. And didn't they help each other too? And he walked her home so that he could protect her. Who was he trying to kid? He walked her home because she let him do things he had been scared to try with Jenny. But how bad were the things they did? He would go nowhere near all the way and anyway, he could be sure she'd put a stop to it long before that. At this point in his worrying he would begin to realize he was going round in circles. He wished he were not a Catholic and then he would not have to worry about what was wrong or by how much it was wrong, or whether he really meant to do what he did. His beliefs were so inconvenient.

Then a truly frightening question crashed into his conscious-ness: was he beginning to lose his faith? The words of several of his Jesuit teachers came to mind. The worst fate that could befall anyone was that he should lose his faith, because that meant he had turned his back on his most precious gift and was on his way to perdition. God had given him this gift and he was reject-ing it, for the sake of a few selfish pleasures. God could do noth-ing to help him because he would not help himself. The punish-ment would be everlasting. He felt lost again. There was nowhere to turn. There was no one he could tell. He was on his own in the air raid shelter and the bombs were falling. He was outside the Black Swan with whitewash on his new mac. He was surrounded by a gang of screaming girls in the playground of his first school and there was nowhere to hide; no bolt-hole to run to.

But if God was going to punish him, and if he were certain of all this, didn't that mean he had not lost his faith? Some conso-lation! So what if he did believe in a vengeful God? It did little to alleviate his misery; and what about all the rest of his faith? How much of the so-called doctrine did he really accept? He had argued at times quite vehemently with friends, some of whom were supposedly Catholic, for the real presence, but now, when he went to Mass and the priest raised the host, he wondered what he was looking at. From his earliest years he had been taught to say, "My Lord and My God": he did no longer know if he really meant it. He wanted to mean it and not only because he was afraid not to.

He thought about simply not seeing Maureen again, but couldn't see a way to do it that was not cowardly. If he did not turn up at the dance ever again what would she think? How would she react? What would she feel? He imagined her saying, "Oh, well, all good things come to an end," and then concentrating on David. On the other hand, she might be very distressed, and she might experience the despair he had felt (briefly) over Jenny. He tried to think about what would happen if they discussed the situa-tion, but every scenario he put forward seemed either impossible or ridiculous: she would probably think him a fool. Perhaps he could demand that she choose once and for all between him and David. But what would he do if she chose him!? He might then have to confront David, whom he had never met but imagined as taller and tougher than he. There was no solution he could think of, so he let things drift.

However, matters were taken out of his hands. The next

Saturday, Maureen was unusually quiet on the way home and when he gently asked her why, she told him that David was coming home on a long leave and that she would not be able to see him for several weeks. Jimmy did his best to look glum, but she went on quickly to suggest that the next day, as a final fling, so to speak, perhaps they could go out somewhere; maybe Ainsdale or Thurstaston. They discussed the idea in a desultory fashion and, she being keener than him, volunteered to make some butties. In a half-hearted way he agreed that if the weather were good (risky as it was still only late spring) they would go to Ainsdale, and if not to Thurstaston. They would meet at the Number Nineteen tram-stop at half past ten.

He thought she might not turn up, but as she did and as it was quite sunny, his spirits rose. There were other people at Exchange Station, but not the crowds there might have been and so the train journey to Ainsdale was very pleasant and their conversation was as good humoured and she as animated as she had been when they first met: she even laughed at his jokes. There were several parties of day-trippers on the first part of the beach and the sand hills, but as they strolled along, they thinned out so that before long they were the only people about. They found a quiet, sheltered spot in the dunes where, once out of the wind which was quite sharp, it felt quite warm. They lay side by side, eyes closed, feeling the sun on their faces and arms.

Maureen said, "Are you going to miss me when David comes home?"

"Yes."

Her next question, typically forthright, shook him. "You're not in love with me, are you?"

He did not know what to say, because he did not know the answer. He found her very attractive, even though at first he'd thought she was not the type of girl he usually became interested in. And at the precise moment he wanted to make love to her. Perhaps it was mere lust. There were times when he thought he had been in love, and that included with Maureen, but now he suddenly realized he did not know what the expression meant. And yet, and yet, with her he felt there was something missing:

he could not say what it was. Maybe it was the fact of David. He was aware that she had moved, and opened his eyes to see that she was leaning on her elbow and looking down at him.

"Well, are you going to answer?"

In the circumstances he felt he could be perfectly honest with her, because there was nothing to lose.

"Honest, Maureen, I don't know."

She continued to look down at him, half smiling, but he did not know whether or not she was upset.

Then she said, "I don't know either, but I do like being with you a lot".

And she snuggled next to him with her head on his shoulder and sighed. He said, "Same here".

They began to kiss... A long time after, they heard kids playing nearby and scrambled up, hurriedly organizing their clothes. It was time to eat the butties. Later still, it began to feel chilly, but neither of them wanted to leave. He said, "Do you still go to church?"

"Yes... Why?"

"Do you believe in sin?"

She did not answer straightaway, then said, "I suppose so".

"Do you think that what we did today was a sin?"

Again she took her time answering, and he knew she could not look at him. He watched her fingers playing in the sand.

"I think... on balance... probably... yes," but then added quickly, "but not a very serious one".

They were both quiet for a while, until she said, "We could have been much, much naughtier than we were, couldn't we?"

"Did you want to be?"

She did not answer, but she looked quite taken aback. She blushed and then more or less threw herself at him, held him very tight and whispered in his ear, "I don't want to think about it. I don't want to talk about it anymore. Let's go home."

They hardly spoke on the train or the tram, but they sat very close to each other all the way, and as so often in the past, he felt that this was the most normal thing to be doing. It was dark when they got there but she said that she did not want him to walk her all the way to her house. He replied by asking her how long David would be home. When she did not reply, he said, "Then when will I see you again?"

She answered, "I don't think you should".

"Ever?"

"Never."

"Why not?"

"Because I'm going to marry David!" And with tears in her eyes, she ran off.

He did not believe it. He turned up Priory Grove and as he went through the short entry to the debris at the bottom of Rupert Street a delicious sense of melancholy swept over him: he saw himself as the rejected lover, who was doing the right thing. He would have to accept the suffering, and the deprivation, and struggle on with his life. But really underlying this melodramatic, almost synthetic, air of sadness, there was a feeling of relief that he was unwilling to tap into yet. He also tried to ignore the tinge of guilt that gave this douce cocktail of emotions a bitter edge. However, an event the next day forced him to pay attention to it.

When he had got home that Sunday evening, he had had to set about finishing a History essay for the Monday morning. Because he had found it so difficult not to think about Maureen, and because he was listening to the American Forces Network at the same time, it was two o'clock before he got to bed. The next morning he woke up late, and rushing about made little difference to the fact that he would be late... unless he borrowed Alan's new bike. This was risky, but he reckoned it would be worth it. As he got it out into the street it began to drizzle and this made the sets on the road treacherously slippery, especially as the bike had very narrow tyres. He knew he would have to be careful. Halfway down St George's Hill, a group of kids ran across the road and having to brake sharply made him skid, but he managed to stay upright. However, having yelled at them, he then had to play the part of the 'serious' cyclist and really set off precipitately, standing up on the pedals as he went. At the bottom he was travelling far faster than was safe and almost before he braked he knew he was going to skid. However, the bike went from under him so sharply that he was still taken by surprise. Unfortunately, he did not stop, but continued to slide into the main road all entangled in the frame of the bike. One of the recently introduced buses was coming along Netherfield Road. The driver jammed on his brakes and luckily did not skid, but the bus did not stop immediately. As though in slow motion, Jimmy saw that he was going straight into the path of the bus and he could do nothing about it. Fear paralysed him and he thought, but could hardly believe, that he was going to die. Yet it was all horribly prolonged. Gradually he came to a halt with the front wheel of the bike between the front wheels of the bus. A crowd gathered round with some people asking if he were hurt, others telling him how lucky he was, and the driver, no doubt in relief, cursing him for being so daft. Apart from cuts on his hands where he had tried to stop himself from sliding, and an aching backside from bumping on the cobbly sets, he was unhurt. However, he was very frightened, even though the bike seemed to be relatively unscathed, because the gear wheels were uppermost in the skid and things like the brake handles could be pushed back easily into place. But it was not Alan's wrath he was afraid of, but God's. This seemed to be a timely warning and he knew he would have to confront his conscience openly and go to confession. Until he did, he knew he would remain frightened and that this sense of impending doom would remain with him. If it were not God telling him, then Life was arbitrary and that seemed worse. The one way out of the impasse was absolution.

On Saturday afternoon he went to St Francis Xavier's church, expecting one of the many priests to be hearing confessions, but the church was empty. He sat in the Lady Chapel for a while and tried to pray, but the only words that came into his head were from a hymn, '...Father, let me call thee Father. 'Tis thy child returns to thee. Jesus, Lord, I ask for mercy. Let me not implore in vain. All my sins I now detest them; never will I sin again...'

He could not be sure he did detest them and all the words seemed to be almost too pious. He began to think this very thought itself was another sin: there seemed to be pitfalls everywhere. He said a Hail Mary and went out. As he turned the corner into Shaw Street he met Father Smythe, who, to Jimmy's surprise, was wearing an open-necked shirt and what looked like a combat jacket.

"Good afternoon, Jimmy, what are you doing down here at this time of the day?"

Jimmy searched desperately for a lie that sounded reasonable, but could only splutter. The priest laughed heartily and said, "OK, Jim, if you don't want to say, you don't have to". Suddenly, Jimmy knew he wanted to tell the truth and so said he had hoped to go to confession.

"Well, I'll hear your confession if you like."

This came as an even greater shock. Talking to an anonymous priest in a dark box was one thing. Talking to someone you knew, and being completely open and truthful, was very different. Smythe laughed again and said, "Never mind, lad. Let's go for a little walk and just chat." At first, Jimmy felt awkward: no priest had ever been so friendly and natural, but he found himself relaxing as they talked about how Everton and Liverpool had done during the season that was just over. After a time, they came to Fusco's.

"Would you like a cup of tea?"

"Err…"

"I would… I've been to visit my old aunt in Everton Brow and her tea's like the proverbial gnat's… never mind. At least here it's strong: you could trot a mouse across it."

The far end of the café was raised higher than the rest and the one table there seemed quite private. It was empty. Smythe made his way there.

"Two teas, luv, when you're ready."

They sat down and the teas were brought.

"OK, Jimmy, what have you been doing with yourself lately? … You and I have hardly come across each other since the time of the football team… Anyway, I heard you had left?"

"I had, but I couldn't get a job and so I decided to come back and try for university."

"Good for you. Do you think you will make it?"

"I think I can, if I get myself sorted out."

"Have you got problems then?"

"Not really, but…"

And soon Jimmy was telling him about Maureen, and his not knowing what was right and what was wrong, and Father Croft and the Polish priest and the lad who said all offences against the sixth and ninth commandment were mortal. Father Smythe listened patiently and never at any time looked stern: he did not seem shocked by what Jimmy had to say and his eyes were as twinkly as usual.

"Well, Jimmy, I thought you'd have enough sense to realize how daft the lad was who said all these sins are mortal. You know as well as I do that it depends how serious the matter is, what your intentions are and what the circumstances are… But you've got to be responsible in these things. An awful lot of girls get into trouble and that can mean a tough life ahead of them, because some hot-blooded fellah like yourself takes matters too far."

"But I don't think I'd do that… "

"Maybe not, but it could begin with a few harmless skirmishes: it's powerful stuff as you well know… but I don't think you've been so awful."

Jimmy stared at the table because he did not know how to respond.

Father Smythe went on, "In all your relationships you have to treat people as people, not objects… you have to be committed to them, and not to your own desires and urges, and it's sometimes difficult to distinguish one from the other. It's different if you're courting seriously, because then the commitment is developing properly. Still, I suppose you young fellahs have got to get to know the girls and so there's bound to be some kissing and cuddling… But I can't say if you have committed a serious sin or not… only you can decide with this sort of thing… only you can say how self-centred you've been."

"Well, I'm not sure myself, really…"

"No, it's not always easy to tell… and, remember, you should always give yourself the benefit of the doubt… But she seems a sensible girl… it's a pity you've chucked her: she's got more sense than you."

"Whaa... I didn't chuck her. She..."

"Are you sure?" And he laughed again. "Well, that's enough of that... how are things with your family?"

Jimmy told him about how grumpy he had been at times and how he had begun to wonder whether he was fair to the others, and gradually the conversation got round to how lazy he felt he had been.

"Now, that's something that's easily sorted, isn't it? ... But, listen, Jimmy... Why don't you make a silent act of contrition and I'll do the same with the words of absolution so you can stop worrying about it. Then, I'll have to go."

They walked back to the house in silence. Jimmy felt he ought to say something to express his gratitude, but could not discover an appropriate formula. They said goodbye and Father Smythe said to keep in touch. As he walked home, Jimmy's throat felt tight several times. But he knew he felt reconciled and calm and grateful. Now he could begin again.

However, he still felt uncomfortable about something, but was not sure what it was. Gradually, over the coming weeks, it emerged: What was Maureen thinking? What was the state of her soul? Had he corrupted her? Was she happy with her David? Dare he try to find out? Or would she become an occasion of sin? This did not seem to be a very worthy thought. He was beginning to slide into the slough again.

Chapter VIII

A LEVEL WAS APPROACHING. He began to work, but mostly on the History and the English, because in these he thought he might stand a chance. At French he seemed to get worse: he couldn't remember the vocabulary and got confused over the constructions he should use. The harder he tried, the worse the situation became. Some wag in the Sixth Form wrote *'Decem Dies Ire'* on the board. This was changed every day... *'Novem'*... *'Octo'*... until *'Dies Irae'*; the Day of Wrath arrived. As they went into the first exam, which was the Chaucer paper, Dave Preston asked him, in a panic, "How do you spell Boccaccio?"

"B... o... souble d... a... souble d... i... o."

"There are no ds in Boccaccio!"

He found that in none of the examinations did he ever fail to find something to write and yet he knew that his marks would be far from outstanding: he became very aware of the schooling he had missed and of how much he only half knew. On the other hand, there was never any risk of him being overwhelmed by the detail and so he was able to concentrate on making his answers convincing, not to say forceful.

When it was all over and there was nothing he could do but wait, he felt calmer than he expected, though this seemed to have something to do with the air of unreality that surrounded him. What was he doing taking 'A' levels, which might result in him, Jimmy Thompson, from scruffy Rupert Grove, going to university? The sense of strangeness was enhanced by the fact that there was no need to go to school and there was nothing that had to be done: there was no homework and no revision. Even in the days when he had neglected his work, it was always there in the background, nagging at him. Now he was at a loss without it. Even the weather seemed to be odd. It was neither one thing nor the other. It did not rain and it was not cold, and yet the sun did not shine because the clouds never rolled away as they were supposed to in the song.

One day, for something to do, he decided to go to New Brighton and back on the ferry. The ships in the river reminded him of the time he had thought of going to sea as a career, and he became aware of how fortunate he was not to have followed that particular inclination because he realized that the possibilities now open to him, should he get to university, were extensive. Briefly, he was tempted to feel confident about the future, but then suddenly felt afraid. What if he failed his 'A' levels? Or what if they were not good enough? What would happen to him? He would have to go off straight away and do his National Service – and in the army too. He would have to face the bullying sergeants and corporals his friends had told him about. He would also have to live in a barrack-room where there would be no privacy. And what would his companions be like? Might they too be bullies? He recalled having read in the paper about a lad who was so terrorised by his fellow recruits that he had committed suicide: it had happened at the notorious army camp at Catterick.

A sensation of hopelessness engulfed him: he was once again a feeble, helpless thing. He remembered an occasion when he was a kid, playing in the street: somebody had brought out boxing gloves. In fact, they were training gloves and so big that you could cover yourself almost completely with them. On the other hand it was very difficult to hit your opponent a really clean blow, so you ended up mauling each other like playful kittens. Then a lad from the next street came by who had some real experience of boxing, and asked if he could have a go. Jimmy was slow to get the gloves off and the result was that he had to fight the expert. Suddenly it was as though the gloves had shrunk to half their size because the punches rained in on him from all angles and even when he saw them coming, they still broke through his defence, so powerful were they. He felt puny and weak, unable to defend himself because there was no way he could see of avoiding the ruthlessly efficient onslaught, and to hit back was out of the question, so desperate was he to block or avoid the ceaselessly pumping fists of his opponent. Whereas five minutes before he had felt as strong as the other kids, now his strength had drained away. Though, in the excitement, he was not aware of any serious pain, he knew he was being hurt and was very frightened. There was no opportunity to run away and the shame would have been worse than the beating: he had to continue until a blow to his nose resulted in gushes of blood and an adult stopped the fight. What remained uppermost in his memory of this incident was the sense of weakness and, as a result of that, helplessness.

The same sensation gripped him as the ferry approached the landing stage at the Pier Head. So awful did he feel that he decided that he would walk home in the hope that he could shake off the notion that he had no control over his own destiny: he could even hear in his head the words from a popular song, 'Like a leaf caught in the draught'. He knew there was a short-cut through Bevington Bush, which was in quite an old part of the city and interesting because the name (if not the buildings) smacked of those more romantic-seeming times before the War that his mother and aunts and uncles talked about so enthusias-tically. Gradually the gloom lifted as he thought about the adults he knew: despite their stories of the halcyon days of the twenties and thirties, he really did not envy them. He had opportunities that they could not have thought possible.

He began to enjoy the experience of walking and then he started to take notice of what was around him. This area had been badly hit during the War and there were several large pieces of waste ground that had been bomb sites. One of these ended in a very tall, windowless wall, on which was written in large, unpunctuated, capital letters, 'NO TIPPING CALTHROPS'. What on earth could calthrops be? They must be things, but the name sounded more like a disease suffered by big animals. Could there perhaps be hides infected with calthrops which disreputable tanners dropped off at the dead of night on the poor unsuspecting citizens of Bevington Bush? Or were they complicated entangle-ments of wrought iron, which were designed to be useful pieces of equipment but had somehow gone wrong in the making, and were now so embarrassingly unrecoverable that they had to be disposed of secretly? No, an animal disease seemed much more likely. Well, whatever they were, there was no trace of them, so either they had been swiftly cleared away, because they were a threat to public health, or, more probably, the stern admonition on the wall had succeeded. Then, the rest of the building to which the wall belonged, appeared and on its front it bore the proud sign, 'H. Calthrop and Sons, Builder's Merchants'. Though this was a disappointment, he was cheered to discover that the local populace was not going to catch calthrops, which, he had felt sure, would result in hideous deaths, where bodies would be blackened and bloated so badly that they could not be buried but would have to be cremated.

At this point in his musings he found himself outside the door of Holy Cross church. He felt he should not simply pass by so he went inside. It was cool and quiet and peaceful and the sanctuary light glowed comfortingly. Prayers of a lifetime passed mechanically through his head without meaning anything very much, so he tried very hard to say them again devoutly, but this was not easy and he kept losing concentration. He wondered why he was praying. It came to him that he wanted a miracle: that somehow God would make his 'A' level papers good enough for him to get into university. There was something wrong here because if it were his own fault that he should fail his examinations, there was no reason for God to help him out: that would be unfair to all those who had worked hard and deserved success. Perhaps he deserved a little bit of success. He had made some effort, hadn't he – towards the end? And it was not as if he were stupid. After a while it occurred to him that little profit was to be got from all this, so he decided that he would just sit there quietly: he relaxed and began to feel at ease. His mind wandered in what seemed to him to be no particular direction. Gradually he became aware that he was thinking again the thoughts he had had on the ferry, but now they were not frightening, nor even mildly disturbing. Why shouldn't he go to university? What was to stop him making a success of it if he did go? And if he failed 'A' level and had to go in the army, so what? Others had done it before him. Maybe they would teach him to drive: a lad up the street had learned in the Service Corps. It dawned on him that for once he was not afraid, that he had support, and that that support had something to do with being in the church. Was it Jesus in the tabernacle talking to him? It did not feel as though it were, and he could not hear anything except his own thoughts. Suddenly he knew what he had to pray for: it was that he would be able to deal with whatever it was might happen to him; that if he were to go to university he would buckle down to the work required; that if he had to go in the army, he would be able to take the discipline and the bullying and living in a barracks. And he knew that if he asked for help and not for a miracle, his prayers were much more likely to be answered. When he went out into the street, he felt more confident than he had for a long time. How long would the euphoria last?

Not very, if he did not find a way to endure the waiting for results. He looked for a job, but all he could find at first was pea-picking, which was hard on the back, tedious and poorly paid. However, a woman who worked in the school canteen with his mother suggested that he should write to Tillotson's, a cardboard box company, where her two daughters worked, because they seemed to take students on temporarily every summer. In fact, he decided to phone first to enquire whether this were so and was told that if he presented himself at the office the next day there would be a job and that it would last about six weeks.

It turned out that two German fitters were about to arrive to install a new multi-colour printer, and three unskilled labourers were needed to assist them. The machinery had already arrived and was standing in crates in the yard, waiting to be lifted into the factory. Jimmy was put to work immediately with two other newcomers, neither of whom was a student. One was a tall, portly man of about fifty, who Jimmy mistook at first for a boss, because he was wearing a striped suit! Apparently he had no more appropriate clothing, because he had worked all his life as a waiter and his last job had been as the major-domo in a posh city restaurant, which he had left because he had had a disagreement with its new owners. The other was a short, wiry man in his middle thirties, who had got fed up with the seasonal nature of his job as an upholsterer, and had been told that Tillotson's was a good firm to work for, and that, because the factory was doing so well, temporary workers generally were offered permanent jobs there, that is, if they did not do something hideous, and showed that they were willing. Jimmy liked him from the start. He was quiet and unassuming, unlike the waiter.

Clearly these three stooges had to be supervised, and here lay a problem. The company had many engineers and fitters, because there were so many machines to treat the card in various ways: to cut it, print it, crease and fold it, and even to glue some parts of it. But they all had their own specific tasks. Moreover, there was a hierarchy, the intricacies of which Jimmy could never quite follow. Apparently, having anything to do with the installation of the German machine was seen as a come down: those associated with it might be seen as lackeys. Consequently, no one wanted to supervise the three unskilled labourers bringing in the machinery – that is, until towards the end of the first day, when everyone became keen to help.

Even so, during that first morning, life was confusing, because sometimes one person and sometimes another came and gave Jimmy and his new colleagues peremptory, but usually conflicting, instructions. The situation was dangerous because all the crates were heavy, some weighing maybe a couple of tons, and had to be lifted by means of a hoist that projected from the very top of the building. They then had to be swung into the third storey and put on rollers so that they could be manoeuvred to the place where the Germans, when they arrived, would assemble the new machine. Fortunately, Arthur, the former upholsterer, was far from stupid, and because he had served in the Navy, knew about ropes and knots. Billy the waiter and Jimmy went on to the top floor to work the hoist. This meant that they pulled on a circular chain, which could not run back on itself and which turned a set of pulleys in a block so that a reasonable amount of effort lifted the heavy crates. Arthur would tie a thick rope around a crate and Billy and Jimmy would lower the huge hook down for him to put through it. He also attached a second rope, which hung down from the third storey. When the crate had been lifted just off the ground and had settled itself into a position that Arthur considered secure, he then went up to the third floor and called to the others to 'haul away'. When the crate was high enough to be swung into the third floor, he called to them to stop. One of them, usually Jimmy, went down to join Arthur to help him pull the crate into the building, while the one up top now lowered the crate very slowly, by pulling on a second chain, which ran backwards but only one link at a time. Once the crate was in, all three of them levered it up with crowbars, and slipped rollers underneath it. With much pulling and shoving, and changing direction (a difficult manoeuvre on rollers) and with much stopping and starting, they got the machinery to the appointed place. It soon became obvious that this part of the job would take at least a couple of days.

Sometimes they got help from engineers, fitters and their mates, but often they were left to their own devices until, that is, about half past three in the afternoon, when Jimmy noticed something which Billy soon broadcast in the fitters-mates' place to which the three newcomers had been assigned for breaks. Tillotson's consisted of two buildings with the yard between the two. From the top floor as you worked the hoist you could see into the rooms of the other building. Nothing happened there all day until, at half past three, Jimmy saw several girls come into a room at one of the lower levels, undress and start to take showers. They were, it seems, girls who worked on what were called bronzing machines, which printed the gold lettering on certain packets and in which the ink was, in fact, very fine dust: they were allowed two bottles of milk a day(!), a shower and a complete change of clothes before they went home. Once the fitters knew this, you could not get near the hoist and people were prepared to do any of the other work too, in the hope that they could get a turn on the hoist later. Arthur, Billy and Jimmy had nothing to do. The next morning, of course, they were left to get on with it by themselves, but by three o'clock they were being pushed out again. However, this time the help remained only briefly. At half past three the young women duly entered the shower room, but then, to the surprise of the lecherous watchers, they lined up along the double window, pulled tongues at the men and drew makeshift curtains across.

Working in this man's world was a revelation to Jimmy. He was used to expletives, but not the extent to which they were used in the factory, where every second word was some variation of 'fuck', the incidence of which, however, dropped considerably if the men were in areas where women were to be found. Nevertheless, given the hierarchy of engineers, fitters, engineers' mates and fitters' mates, the language did have a democratising effect as it created an atmosphere of 'all lads together'. Conversations, during short breaks that were taken in one of three rooms portioned off from the extensive engineering / fitting shop, were to do with sport, smut or jeering at the doings of politicians or celebrities as reported in the popular press – usually the *Mirror* or the *Herald*, but sometimes the *Mail* or the *Express* or even the *Chronicle*. The most elevated paper Jimmy ever saw there was *The Liverpool Daily Post*, which at that time still considered itself a rival to *The Manchester Guardian*. It was read regularly by a young engineer who had aspirations, but who was regarded as something of an oddity by the others, even though they had respect for his engineering skills and knowledge. Jimmy was impressed with the skills and knowledge of all of them.

At lunchtime, Jimmy went to the canteen, because not only was the food good and wholesome, it was also very cheap and as a junior Jimmy got it even cheaper, so that he had each day a three course meal for about 1/6d. There was only one canteen, but hierarchy prevailed there too. The top administrative and secretarial staff had an exclusive area clearly defined by the provision of table cloths. The supervisory staff in their white coats had formica-topped tables, whereas the rest had to make do with plain wood. No one ever complained. In fact they rarely, if ever, criticised the firm and all agreed it was one of the best to work for: wages were good; management was even-handed; the general conditions of work were very acceptable; and everywhere was clean. The social and sports clubs were well provided for and used extensively. On reflection, Jimmy wondered if the company had some sort of non-conformist connection originally, because the culture of the engineering shop was not that common in the rest of the factory, and several of the foremen and women he met later were proclaimed church-goers, though not Anglican. Also, he had pointed out to him once or twice, workers noted for their convictions, usually to do with commitment to giving a fair day's labour for a fair day's pay, and to keeping the Sabbath.

However, his first six weeks at Tillotson's were dominated by the Germans. These were the first he had ever met and in the early days he looked on them with awe. During so much of his childhood Germans had been referred to in terms of hatred, fear or contempt: they were scarcely human. Yet an article that he had seen in *Picture Post* not too long after the War had drawn attention to the plight of ordinary Germans, and he had felt a certain sympathy for them. Both these fitters in their own way were engaging. The senior and elder of the two was of medium height, fairish, though balding, with a sallow complexion and a slightly Asiatic look about him, and this was enhanced by his slimness. His English was excellent. The other was tall, very well-built and very lively with a boisterous sense of humour. He could have been taken as English; that is, until he spoke, because though his command of the language was reasonable, his accent was pronounced.

Hans, the elder, was a good diplomat. He never told you what to do but always requested Billy, Arthur or Jimmy politely but firmly to do this or that. He got on well with the English fitters, who were early convinced of his know-how. He was also a good ambassador for his country and made use of the growing aware-ness of the Cold War in its rehabilitation. He had been a prisoner of the Russians, but was one of the lucky ones to have made it home. He never openly condemned his captors, but in stories about his experiences of fighting against them, he made them seem less than human. For instance, at break one day, he told Jimmy how he had come across bodies of German soldiers, standing up in the road in a solid block of ice: they had been tied together and had had water thrown at them until they froze to death. On another occasion, when he was talking about his days as a prisoner working alongside Russian peasants, he made it appear that they were primitive. One day a woman, who normally finished work a little before the others to prepare food for them, left the field even earlier. She was heavily pregnant. When they got back for their meal, she had had the baby and was busily cooking. The baby was lying on the floor and when Hans suggested she should pick it up, she said that if it were tough it would survive, and if it were not, it would be better if it died. For a long time after, Jimmy accepted this story as true.

Heinrich never mentioned the War. In fact, except when he was working, he seemed to take nothing very seriously: he joked, he sang, he talked about drinking beer and chasing after girls. However, there were no women in the large room in which they were constructing the machine, so Jimmy was never able to see Heinrich's technique with females because the Germans did not use the canteen either. Jimmy was suspicious of him, and used to wonder if he had been in the Hitler Youth. He was the right sort of age and, Jimmy thought, shape.

The building of the printing machine went along fairly easily and in the early stages the most unpleasant task was the washing of all the parts with paraffin to remove the grease they had been covered in to protect them while in transit. The laying down of the base of the machine seemed interminable. Hans explained that it had to be dead level and virtually immovable, because the heavy, high-speed rollers that would be working above it required great stability. The base was followed by two heavy, carefully-machined sides. Heinrich got very excited and worried at this stage because, he said; a colleague had been killed doing this. The team raising it, by hand, had panicked and run away, leaving the German fitter to his fate. What seemed more frightening to Jimmy was that only one side was fixed firmly: the other had to be left loose so that the rollers could be slotted in by moving it each time. However, the fitters were very careful with the rollers, which were finely-finished stainless steel. They wrapped yards of cloth around them before they put them in a chain sling to lift them into place, which they did by means of a block and tackle attached to an overhead girder.

Once the job was completed, Jimmy was given work elsewhere, as promised, and told that he could stay as long as he liked. He was put in a room full of women. They were known as the knockers-out and they were very intimidating, the few men in the place being their fetchers and carriers and definitely an inferior species. The name was appropriate, not because the girls were particularly large or strapping, but because they were self-confident, vigorous, on piece-work, in a hurry, and very well paid. Their job was, indeed, knocking-out, and for it they used wooden mallets. They would take maybe fifty sheets of card (each about a square yard in size), which had been printed, creased and partly cut in the shapes of boxes, and literally knock them out, ready to go to other machines to be glued. They could be for soap powder, jellies, cigarettes or almost anything. There were different rates of pay for different boxes, with the smaller ones being the better paid. This meant that if the girls, who worked in pairs, were given something like Oxydol, for which the rate was poor, they would work very fast in order to get on to something more profitable as soon as possible. The men had to see to whatever they needed immediately, so Jimmy had to make sure that they were well provided with card, that the flat boxes when stacked were cleared away promptly, and most especially, that the waste material, which gathered round the girls' feet, was removed regularly. It had to be pushed down a trapdoor underneath the work bench, where it was carried away on a conveyor belt and then deposited into a crate over which a press was situated.

Periodically, the press descended to squash the waste card down into a hard bale. One youngster working near Jimmy was not only dilatory in this part of the job; he was also fond of cheeking the girls. They kept warning him but always seemed to be in too much of a hurry to do anything about it, until one day they grabbed him and shoved him down the hole. Jimmy could hear him screaming as he was carried along by the conveyor belt and tipped into the crate. Fortunately, the men working down there got him out before the press came down. He, and Jimmy, worked assiduously from then on.

The work was not particularly heavy but it was unremitting, because Jimmy was responsible for four tables. These were very big and the girls worked a pair at each end, so he had sixteen of them to cater for. Fortunately, on his very first day in the knocking-out shop, John, who worked the next set of tables, suggested that they worked together until Jimmy knew the routine. However, they got on so well together that they continued to cooperate right up until Jimmy left. John had just finished his National Service and was working in the knocking-out shop only until Tillotson's found him a better job. He seemed to have much more common sense than the other lads, most of whom were about Jimmy's age: they took nothing seriously. John, on the other hand, wanted to talk about everything under the sun, and claimed that this was the result of his experiences in the army in Germany. At first he had been like most of the other squaddies: he had skived, complained, got drunk and made himself obnoxious to the natives. He would never volunteer for anything and spent most of his time lying in his bunk, reading nothing more elevated than 'Reveille'. Then he had moved camp and had found himself alongside two characters who were older than the general run of soldier, as they had been deferred while they qualified as industrial chemists. First they introduced him to jazz and particularly the records of George Shearing, and then to American big bands like Stan Kenton, but their interests went much wider, and this was what made such an impression on him. However, he was still surprised that they volunteered for almost everything that was on offer, because, they said, it got you out and about. He discovered that they were right and he followed their example. He did finish up with some bum jobs, but mostly this was not the case and as a result, he not only saw most of Germany, he also did lots of interesting things: he even played cricket and went skiing. However, what was really important was that he met very interesting people, and realized that what made them so different from the majority of squaddies was that they read – and everything they could lay their hands on. He followed suit – at first with some difficulty and much impatience and then with ever greater facility. It dawned on him that he had

had no real education, which was why he was attending night school and taking 'O' levels, though he already had Maths, which he had taken in the army. He was scathing about the secondary modern school he had attended because it had done so little for most of his contemporaries. Only the handful that had wanted to stay on were given any useful tuition. On the other hand, he had to admit that, like all the other kids, he had jeered at the keenoes, who were regarded as hardly human. He regretted this and was determined to make up the lost ground. So it was that he and Jimmy spent a good deal of time talking about history, politics, social conditions and even philosophy. However, their favourite topic of conversation was the records that they heard on the American Forces Network. Admittedly, you got the popular stuff like Guy Mitchell, but you could also hear Les Brown and his Band of Renown, Duke Ellington and even the Sauter-Finnegan Orchestra, with arrangements of songs like *April in Paris,* which left most popular music back among the nursery rhymes.

The extra four weeks that Jimmy did at Tillotson's passed very quickly and pleasantly. He got to know the girls quite well and learned to take their banter in his stride, but he was still very wary of them and they obviously regarded him and, to some extent, John, as oddities. Then on the very last day that he worked in the factory, Jimmy met a girl who knocked him sideways, she was so staggeringly beautiful.

Because he was finishing, he had to go to the office at four o'clock so that he could get his P45, the pay for the week he had had to work in hand, and whatever holiday pay he might be entitled to. She was already there, sitting on a bench, waiting, because she was leaving too, in order to take a job nearer home, her parents having moved to a new housing estate. She had the face of an Italian Madonna: brown eyes below delicately-arched brows, a well-proportioned nose and lips that were neither thin nor heavy, and when she smiled, which she did often, she showed just enough of her even white teeth. However, her outstanding feature was her skin: white would be too harsh a description, and creamy excessive. Her dark hair was pulled back but not too tightly and tied in an elegant bun. Her white blouse with its simple collar set against the deep blue of her overall added to her air of innocence.

She smiled shyly at Jimmy and moved up on the bench to let him sit down too. She spoke first.

"Are you leaving today too?"

"Yeh. I've come to have my wages made up."

"So have I."

"Why are you leaving? Don't you like it here?"

"Oh, yes, I do and I've got lots of mates here, but we've moved to Cantril Farm and I have to get a bus and a tram to get here. It takes ages, so I've got a job in the Automatic instead."

Her Liverpool accent was strong, and did not quite fit the character that Jimmy had created for her in the split second when she had smiled up at him from the bench, but he was so entranced that he was convinced of nothing so much as her innocence, and even her name, Maria, proclaimed her origins, which he imagined were in the bosom of an old fashioned Italian family – only her father could be English, which would explain the name, Stephenson. He could find out the details later. They sat for at least ten minutes, chatting easily and amiably. She asked him if he were going to the dance at the social club that night and he said he was, even though he had told John that he would not. She seemed to be very pleased at this and he could not help but think that this was the beginning of a meaningful relationship. Then she was called into the finance office. Jimmy felt elated. And as he sat there almost in a daze, he realized that for once he could be sure he was happy. When she came out she flashed him a smile so open as to be almost beatific and said, "Gorra dash or I'll miss me bus. See ya tonight, Jim. Tarra, well!"

With two weeks' wages and his holiday pay, and all his income tax back, he had more money than he had ever had in his life before. He could even buy a dark grey suit with a subtle red over-check like Albie's: what a pity he could not do it straight-away so that he could look really smart at the social club. And he imagined himself dancing with Maria, him in his dark suit and her in the sort of dress that might be worn by Pier Angeli or maybe Teresa Wright.

But when he arrived home he was faced brutally with reality: there was a letter from school and everyone knew it contained his 'A' level results. He paused before he opened it. Would it mean that his sins had found him out? That he had failed abjectly because of all the time he had wasted? There flashed across his mind a picture of himself sitting at one o'clock in the morning with his feet up on the hob by a dying fire, smoking a woodbine stolen from his indulgent big sister, and listening to AFN, literature unread, essays not done. It symbolised his unwillingness to help himself, his besetting lethargy. He felt his energy drain away, but the ring of anxious faces around him demanded that he opened the letter, though what he wanted to do was run away and hide, so that he did not have to face up to the consequences of his own feebleness.

At first, what he read when he did open it meant nothing to him. Then he saw that he had got French at 'O' level, and thought that was all he had achieved. It was as though he really had been hit by that bus at the bottom of St George's Hill: the numbness that he remembered as the initial sensation when struck by a ferula, a split second before the pain arrived, he felt over his whole body. He sat down involuntarily. He looked at his family. Their distress was palpable. He looked at the letter again. There were numerical marks (no grades back in the dark ages of the fifties). Gradually it became clear to him that he had got 60 in history and 56 in English: he had two 'A' levels. He was speechless. Jane could stand the strain no longer and took the letter from his weak grasp, but even she at first seemed incapable of understanding its meaning. Then her face broke into a wide grin and she said, "Ooer, he's got two 'A' levels and French at 'O' level!"

Suddenly, everyone was jumping up and down, shouting. Next, quite out of character, they were all hugging each other and nobody was making any sense. They were not especially good results, but they were better than anyone had expected even six months ago.

His mother said, "But what does all this mean for going to university?"

"Oh, yeh," said Jimmy, and he tried to focus on the problem.

Liverpool he knew immediately was out of the question. Hull had not said that he needed three 'A' levels, but simply that his results had to be satisfactory and the History professor had hinted that two would be good enough as long as one of them were History. He explained all this to the family, even though they all knew it already.

"I'll have to phone on Monday, won't I?"

"Aye, lad, tha' will," said Alan in a mock Yorkshire accent, as though the acceptance at Hull was a foregone conclusion. Jimmy felt a surge of optimism too and immediately remembered Maria. In his head he could hear the voice of Howard Keel singing 'Everything's goin' my way'.

In his new interview sports jacket and the smartest shirt he could find, with a tie stolen from Alan and just a suggestion of Brylcreem on his hair, he set off for Tillotson's social club, feeling much more confident than usual. He tried to time it right so that he would be there not too early but not too late either, because he suspected that it would get crowded when the bar shut and he might have difficulty locating Maria. He looked in the dance hall first. It was already fairly busy, but still empty enough to take in at a quick glance who was there. There was no sign of Maria, but over in the far corner there was a very rowdy group where the girls were all heavily made up, and the lads were wearing those midnight or powder blue suits (forerunners of the Teddy boy style), which the tougher sorts all seemed to wear at that time. He went to the bar and found that it was not too crowded either. There was John, pint in hand, standing talking to the barman.

"Hello there, Jimmy. I thought you said you weren't coming."

"I changed me mind."

"Ah well, I'm glad you're here, 'cos I got some good news today, just after you'd gone. Next week I'm getting a printing machine: the one left by the fellah who's moving on to that German machine that you put in."

"Eh, that's great. I'm really glad. Congratulations!" There was a pause as they grinned at each other. Then, as though shocked, Jimmy said, "Eh listen. I've got some great news too. Fancy forgetting – I got two 'A' levels and it might mean I can go to university!"

"Wow, that really is good news… I'm feeling envious already… Congratulations, kid. Give this fella a pint, will you Sammy?" and he shook Jimmy's hand vigorously. They talked excitedly for a while and had several pints before Jimmy remembered why he had come. By now his inhibitions had all gone and he confided in John, saying that he was sure he could get something going with this fabulous girl. When he suggested they should go into the dance, however, John said he was not much of a dancer, and so Jimmy went by himself. Maria was not immediately apparent, so he slowly moved around the hall, eyeing the girls surreptitiously. When he got opposite the rowdy gang, he became aware that someone was shouting to him.

"Eh, Jimmy, Jimmy come over here."

He was taken aback, because the girl making all the noise was more heavily made up than all of the others: she positively glowed, and even from across the room he could see that it was caked on her face. To his horror he saw that she was coming across the room to him and that everyone was looking at them. When she arrived, all smiles, and he looked closely at her, he was thunderstruck to see that under all the almost orange paint was Maria. She put her arm in his and more or less dragged him across the room saying, "Come and meet the gang".

To his amazement he actually knew some of the so-called gang from his early days running round the Pit. One of them, Allie Morrissey, he'd known from when they were kids. He came from a street off Mere Lane where the tough lads came from.

"Hello, Jimmy, la. What's you doin' here?" he said.

"I've been workin' at Tillotson's until today, like," he replied, thickening up his accent.

Despite his sports jacket, which clearly distinguished him from the others, they seemed not to notice, and for the most part ignored him. Maria, however, did not, and said, "Aren't you goin' to ask me to dance, then?"

He could hardly refuse, even though it was a foxtrot, in which he was never too confident about where his feet should be. So they danced, and in a very smoochy way. She had even less idea than he about the authentic steps but they moved together to the rhythm of the music in a more than satisfactory way: she clung to him and he was sure that she was pressing even harder against him than was necessary, which was exciting, but the dream of her as the innocent young ingénue in need of his manly protection was rapidly fading. Furthermore, because she was shorter than him, her attempt to dance cheek to cheek resulted in her pressing her face into his jacket, and he realized that he was beginning to feel annoyed that her awful make up was coming off on it. This was not turning out anything like he expected: he wanted to leave, but could not think of a way to escape. Fortunately, Maria's exuberance gave him the opportunity, because when they got back to the group, she began to laugh and joke with the other girls: she never stood still but jumped about all over the place. He was both fascinated and horrified at the same time. He could still just about see the Madonna under the paint, but her cackle was almost maniacal. Carefully he worked his way to the edge of the group and then slipped out to the toilet, where he made vain attempts to get the make up off his coat. As he was sneaking out the front door he met John, who (and this was the biggest surprise of a surprising evening) was leaving with one of the knockers-out. She was not caked in make up, and looked quite different out of her overalls. She was not only as beautiful as the Maria he had met outside the finance office but also quiet and well-groomed. As they walked along to the bus stop together, John quizzed him about the 'vision of loveliness', as he put it, that Jimmy had been chasing. When Elaine, who, it now transpired, John had taken out several times, found out who they were talking about, she said, "Oh her! I'm surprised two smart chaps like you didn't know about her already."

"What's that supposed to mean?" said John.

"She's a man-eater. That's what!"

At that point they reached their bus stop, though Jimmy had to walk further on to his.

"So its goodbye then, Jimmy lad. Listen; let us know how you get on. You can always pop into the social on a Saturday. Elaine and I will probably be there, won't we, love? ... And Maria will be too busy gobbling up the men in the Automatic." Even Jimmy laughed. Then Elaine suddenly kissed him on the cheek, and said, "That's from the girls in the knocking-out shop. Several of them had designs on you, y'know. I hope you do well at university, and they'll all be pleased to know you're going."

Jimmy felt like saying that he was not completely sure yet that he would be going, but decided not to. Instead he mumbled a 'Thank you' just as their bus came. He had time only to shake John's hand and they were gone.

He decided to walk home. It was not far and as he went he reflected on how little he knew about people, how he had misjudged Maria and Elaine. He also realized how lucky John was to have such a girlfriend, but he knew too that they were both lucky. But, as he strolled, he couldn't help feeling that he had turned a corner in his life.

CHAPTER IX

O N MONDAY HE PHONED both universities: the outcome was the one he had hoped for. He was going to Hull. There were problems; however, because, not having been sure what would happen, but also because no one had told him what to do, and because he was dilatory anyway, he was late applying for a grant. This was not too serious: he had what seemed to him the small fortune he had earned in Tillotson's. He needed it because there were all sorts of things to be bought – from a suit to socks; from a trunk to a new (respectable) briefcase. The university informed him too that he would need a gown: it was compulsory for lectures. As usual he depended on his mother and sisters to organize things for him, though he got fed up hearing one or other of them say that they did not know what would become of him when he was completely responsible for himself. Everything was got ready in time, and he even acquired his dark grey suit with the subtle red over-check.

On the day he left, with a small suitcase for his immediate needs, his trunk having been sent in advance, and a new mackintosh over his arm, he felt that he had become an adult at last, and this was even though his mother insisted on accompanying him to the station. It was only when they were on the bus that he realized how upset she was at his going, and the significance of his being the youngest of her children occurred to him. She sat next to him with a very solemn face and said nothing. He stole a sidelong glance at her and was certain that before he actually got on the train she would cry. His immediate reaction to this thought was that he would be embarrassed. The next was how meanspirited he was. He began to reflect on their relationship, and on how much he had depended on her in the past. There came to mind the memory of running home from school on Friday lunchtimes during that period when she was recovering from serious illness, when no one could be certain that she would not become ill again. The last lesson before lunch was singing and they always ended with Mr Wade's favourite, *Danny Boy,* and at the words 'and all my grave will warmer, sweeter be,' Jimmy used to get such a lump in his throat that he had to stop singing. Then he would race home, using all the shortcuts to make certain she was all right. He thought of her present situation. He was not the only one to be leaving: his brother was about to take up a promotion that would mean moving to London; Jane would soon get married; and Alice was at Training College (albeit in Liverpool). But because he was the last and had always been regarded as 'the baby' (a term of which merely the thought usually made him cringe, though not today), his mother was obviously even more upset. He wanted to put his arm around her and say, "Never mind. I'll be OK. You don't have to worry about me," but none of them in the family was that demonstrative, so he sat quietly next to her, and hoped that if she did cry he wouldn't too. He thought about how she had had to struggle to bring them up, and even to survive in the early days. He remembered too how much Jane had helped his mother and all of them for that matter: she too must be upset at his going. Then he consoled himself with the thought that his mother and Jane were very proud of him, especially as he was off to do something that nobody in their entire family had ever done before.

At the station, to his surprise, there were two others from his school. One was Tim Bridges who, it turned out, was the Ferens Scholar and on an enhanced grant. The other was Phil Speirs, who had left school two years earlier but was being sent to university by his company. Jimmy's mother seemed to be comforted by the knowledge that he would be with people he knew, and Tim's aged father said they were three lads together and they'd be all right: no doubt he needed to be consoled too. She did cry, but not very openly, and Jimmy put his arms around her because for once it seemed the appropriate thing to do. She then whispered something that he realized only in retrospect was to be of supreme importance to the rest of his life, through university and beyond:

"Whatever you do, son, keep going to Mass."

"Sure, Mam, I will. Don't worry."

He kissed her gently on the cheek and got on the train.

The weather was fine throughout the first couple of weeks at university (which is in a pleasant part of the city). Everything looked good, even the disused army camp in which they found themselves, because the hall of residence they had been promised was still far from completion. Jimmy did not mind: he had something he had never had before – a room of his own, even if it were in a Nissen hut. And the village of Cottingham was a big improvement on Everton. The temporary residence contrasted with the rest of the university, which was very new. However, its traditional design in a red brick of quite a dark hue, gave it a spurious appearance of age: the university was trying hard to develop a sense of permanence. Moreover, in the fifties, universities could direct the lives of their students much more than they can now, and saw it as their duty to introduce their lower middle and working class students into the ways and the manners of their social superiors who were, of course, to be found in more elite institutions, on which they were modelled. Hence, the dinner for freshers in the first week was a very formal meal and hence too the wearing of gowns on every possible occasion. Attendance at dinner in the evenings was compulsory in all halls of residence (even old army camps), and to be late was an offence that required miscreants to apologise to top table with a subservient bow, whilst gentlemen students (anyone not a freshman) banged on the tables in mock annoyance with their spoons, as they cried, "Sit down" or even "Will you sit down – immediately", all the time trying their best not to let the poor unfortunate do just that.

Jimmy realized that he had an opportunity to begin all over again: nobody in the university had any pre-conceived ideas about him. Tim and Phil were taking Classics and Physics respectively and he hardly ever saw them except in hall. He was also an unknown quantity to his lecturers. Yet he did run into difficulties in the first two weeks. He had not realized that Joint History and

English required him to take an ancillary subject and the only one on the approved list for him as far as he could see was French. He was appalled to discover that the course was way beyond 'A' level and that some of the lectures were in French. Furthermore, in English he had to do Old English and the lecturer, Dr Mimms, on the first day told them that when he had had to learn Chinese and Japanese in a hurry working for Intelligence during the War, the technique used had been to throw students in the deep end. He intended to use the same method. He finished his first lecture after ten minutes and as he went out said, "Buy yourselves Sweet's *Anglo-Saxon Grammar* and translate the first thirty lines of *'Othere's Travels'* for next week".

Jimmy did manage to do this but it took ages because words change in the middle according to their grammatical function, so you have to start working out the syntax before you can even look up the meaning of a word. He also had an essay to do in History, another in English, a French prose and an unseen. It was not that he was not prepared to work but simply that there were too many things to do, some of which (besides the Anglo-Saxon; the French, for instance) took him an inordinately long time to complete if he were to reach the standard that he imagined was expected of him in a university.

He began to feel afraid again: it was just like he felt when he decided he had to work for 'A' level: there seemed to be far too much ground to cover, for someone of his low intelligence masquerading as a serious student. He wanted to run away again and he felt so much on his own. There was no one he could tell. What if he went home and told them all it had been a mistake? The effect of that would be truly unthinkable: everyone would be disappointed, his mother and Jane especially, and there were all the things that had been bought – especially the smart suit. Then the thought hit him – 'Ar, you silly bugger, what are you doing worrying about a bloody suit!? ... No. We've got to think about this... Stop and think constructively... That's the very thing we never seem able to do!'

Then he remembered the day on the ferry when he had panicked at the thought of the difficulties he might face as a student. He thought back over it again and he remembered Calthrops – perhaps he was suffering from them now. He smiled to himself and thought, 'Let's go and sit quietly in church – and then see what happens'.

He walked to the Marist church and sat in the back row. He prayed for a while, again not for a miracle, but so that he would have the courage and perseverance to go on. 'My God, how I need perseverance.' Then he just sat, and when he felt calm, he ambled back to the university. He went into the queue for morning coffee and, just in front of him, he recognised a student from the next hut who seemed to be on the same courses as him.

"Hi. How are you finding things?"

"Bloody real." (He later discovered that 'real' was the Barrow-in-Furness equivalent of the Liverpudlian 'gear'.)

"Yeh, but what about all that Anglo-Saxon? Doesn't that bother you?"

"Not anymore."

"Why not? Did you find a cog?"

"No. I just changed my courses."

"You changed your courses... why? Can you do that?"

"Look, there was just too much to do... So I went and saw the Dean and told him. And he said lots of people move about in the first term and that it did not matter because usually everything balances out in the end."

"So, what are you doing now?"

"Special History and Ancil. English."

"Is that all? ... No French?"

"No... and there's no Anglo-Saxon in Ancil. – it's just like a year of 'A' level literature. I've even done some of the books already at school."

"Where will I find this Dean?"

"He's on the top floor of the Arts Block."

"Listen. Don't save my place. I'm going to see him straightaway!"

He was still very apprehensive when he knocked on the Dean's door, but inside he met a benign silver-haired gentleman, not unlike Mr Holmes whom he had met in the Liver Buildings.

"Well, young man, have you got a problem? What can I do for you then?"

Within half an hour, Jimmy had switched to Special History and Ancil. English. However, although he felt that many of his problems had been solved he was still wary of what might happen if he did not work steadily. So he went straight off to work on his History essay. Immediately he learned a lesson, though this was followed by another that was just as important. The first was that once a booklist is given for an essay, all the relevant textbooks disappear from the library; all the up-to-date ones that is. He found just a few old mouldering texts that hardly mentioned attitudes to property rights between 1789 and 1815 in France, which was what the essay was about. He also discovered that very few places were left unoccupied at the library tables. He had to go to a temporary hut-type building, grandly referred to as 'The Reading Room', to find a place. There he trawled through the books he did have and did find some information but he came to the conclusion that without better texts he would not be able to do the subject justice. After about an hour and a half, he felt he needed to stretch himself. However, it was raining heavily outside so he wandered around the shelves that occupied the bottom half of the hut. Here he learned the second lesson. The shelves contained journals, and many of them were history or economic and social history journals. He flicked through one or two of them and to his great surprise found an article about the very topic he was engaged on. What's more, it referred to an earlier article on the same subject with which the author begged to differ. Following this up, he discovered that there were several articles recently published on the same area. None of these were mentioned in the booklist. He set to work with an eagerness he had rarely felt about academic work.

Some three weeks later he went to get the essay back from the tutor concerned, Mr Spender, of whom everybody spoke in very respectful tones. Two other students were in there too and Mr Spender dealt with them first. He said he wanted to deal with Jimmy's separately. Jimmy felt himself go cold, like he did on the day when he went to the Plumpton Street School Dental Centre as a child. He was left till the last and while he was sitting there in increasing apprehension, the dentist called to the nurse to ask how many more patients there were and she replied, "Only one and he's the special case".

Jimmy had almost run out he was so frightened, except that he was riveted to the spot. In the event, the dentist was very nice and told him he had good teeth and that was why he wanted to give him some special fillings.

"These are good, son. You look after them and clean them regularly." Jimmy did. However, on this occasion, Jimmy became even more apprehensive, because Spender was quite rough with both the students, accusing them of falling into the same trap. Jimmy was not even sure he knew what they were talking about. They left. It was his turn.

"Now then, Mr Thompson, what have we here?"

Jimmy smiled his face-aching smile.

"You did not fall into the trap, but that might be because you avoided it, or it might mean you didn't even see it."

Jimmy tried to speak but he was not sure that he could say anything that made much sense, but Spender went on, "Still, I'm not going to be churlish about this because, on the whole, your essay is quite good. You have developed a good argument, based on recent research, and it's not badly written. However, it relies too much on certain articles. Now, that's no bad thing, but I would have liked a little more from the standard texts, just to show you are acquainted with them. Why did you use them so sparingly?"

"I couldn't get them until just before the handing-in date."

"Ah, there you are, Mr Thompson. It's dog-eat-dog out there. Still, that's not bad for a first attempt and it is a difficult topic. Keep it up."

As Jimmy stood up to leave, Spender asked him which school he went to and when Jimmy told him, he said, "Ah. That explains it, then. You will have had Dr Grisedale as your teacher. Good afternoon."

When Jimmy looked at the mark, he discovered he had got a B+. The way Spender had spoken he had thought he might get an

A of some kind. Second year students later assured him that any kind of B from Spender was good.

This should have given a boost to his confidence, and it certainly came at the right time. From that point on he should never have seriously doubted his own ability: with care and attention, he could cope with any of the difficulties the university courses might throw at him. And yet, he still had serious worries about his competence and worth. The Ancillary examination at the end of the first year, he had been told, really was like another 'A' level, but it caused him grave concern because there were difficult texts, such as Milton's *Areopagitica* and obscure ones like *Hooker's Laws of Ecclesiastical Polity*, to deal with. At first he did not know that these could be avoided in the exam. He spent too much time trying to come to grips with them until he discovered that the examination was broken into sections and you did not have to provide answers for all of them: he realized he could get by on Marlowe's *Faustus* and *The Sonnets of John Donne*. Ancillary subjects lasted only three terms but they had to be passed, so Jimmy worked hard in the summer term to make sure he did not fail.

There were to be times over the three years when his marks were not so good, but they were never critical, and were due to lack of work or lack of interest, and yet he could never quite see it that way. His worst mark in an examination came during a fallow period in the second year and was partly due to bad luck. It was in a general course, English Economic History. As he was also taking a special course in Tudor and Stuart Economic and Social History, he calculated that at least two questions on the general paper would come from the special area. Consequently, he prepared only one answer in any depth. It did come up, but there was nothing on the Tudor or Stuart periods: he did well to get even the 22% he was awarded. The tutor, Mr Davis, who taught both courses, was obviously annoyed, and even more so when Jimmy tried to explain how it happened. However, this setback had a positive side to it because Davis told him that he did not expect his more competent students to play such silly and dangerous games. Jimmy still found it a little difficult to believe that Davis's opinion was valid.

Even when everything seemed to be going well, he always had an uncomfortable feeling, real even if slight, that disaster might hit at any time: you were never completely safe. Furthermore, he never felt worthy of the moderate successes that he did have. There could be no doubt that to some extent this was the result of his early experiences during the War when his very life had been threatened almost nightly. And bombs are indiscriminate: righteousness is no safeguard against them. However, his religious upbringing and schooling had only served to make matters worse because the threat of hell and damnation was never very far beneath the surface of the teaching even of a doctrine such as 'God is love'. The attitudes engendered were pharisaical: you had to keep the rules, no matter how pernickety, otherwise you would be struck down, and this could be in the midst of your sin. Even if you kept the rules, you were not necessarily safe, as the almost indiscriminate use of the ferula had shown.

The stress of carrying the internal contradictions in the teachings of the Church at a time in one's life – adolescence and early adulthood, when the moral code preached on sexual activity was inconvenient – was too much for some of the Catholics, especially among the men, and they fell away. Firstly they would stop going to confession and then to Mass. Indeed, for some this had already happened. But Jimmy could not do this. His sense of foreboding was too strong, as was his fear of the consequences of rejecting God, who might not be there but very probably was.

Intellectually also, Jimmy had to deal with contradictions. As his historical understanding developed, he became aware of the extent of the corruption in the Church, which led to the Reformation, of its antiquated attitude to science in its quarrel with Galileo, and of the generally conservative stand (pace 'Rerum Novarum' and the like) which it took in politics in the Nineteenth and Twentieth Centuries, even to the extent of supporting fascists like Franco and Dolfuss. All the writings of Marx were rejected because he was an atheist. The teaching that he had received in the Sixth Form had not prepared him for this, concerned as it was almost solely with apologetics. He could put forward metaphysical arguments to justify articles of faith, and often did, with athe-ists, agnostics and members of other Christian denominations, but he could never satisfy his own fear that what he believed was a sham: science seemed to contradict so much of it, and in the fifties we had not yet learned to mistrust science.

He continued to go to Mass, and not only because his mother had asked him to, though her request, the manner in which it was made and the circumstances in which it had occurred, remained a powerful influence on him. He went to confession and commun-ion, despite the fact that when he looked at the host, he was no longer absolutely certain that this was the body of Christ. Instead of being a source of strength, it was another contributory factor in his abiding sense of insecurity, in the feeling that there was no sure place in which to stand.

In the very first week of the first term he had joined the Catholic Society and he went to one or two meetings: he was not impressed. Rightly or wrongly, he came to think that it was dominated by the sort of Catholics who tried to give the impres-sion that they were intimate friends of the bishop; that they knew personally the Vicar General of the Jesuit order, or had been to Ampleforth, and that probably meant both the former. He had joined other clubs at the same time – the History Society, whose meetings he was hardly ever to attend, and more importantly, the Soccer Club. He took part in the trials and got himself a place in the second eleven. He then discovered that there were several Liverpudlians playing football, and so he felt at home.

On Saturdays the teams played in various divisions of the East Yorkshire League. The away venues were varied. One day you could be playing in the city itself, for example at the Metal Box Company sports ground, where, according to the mythology, if you were winning at half time, your opponents' buddies inside the factory would make sure that the pitch was deluged with acrid brown fumes, which they were used to, but on which you choked. Or you might be out in the countryside playing a village team such as the one at South Cave. The name was apt: all the players were short but stocky, an impression enhanced by their overlong football knickers. They were also swarthy and believed in rough physical contact. They were troglodytes! Even the pitch was pre-historic. It sloped not only from end to end but also from side to side: if you over-hit a corner kick, there was a danger that it might end up at the diagonally opposite corner-flag.

On Wednesdays they played other universities, and almost every other week this meant away trips to Leeds or Sheffield, Durham or Leicester. It also meant heavy drinking, usually in Bawtry, along with teams of every description from these other institutions who were also making their way back. Behaviour was riotous, but very rarely resulted in fighting. Everyone seemed to be more interested in singing the crudest songs Jimmy had ever heard: *The Ball of Kerrymuir; Cathusalem, the Harlot of Jerusalem; The Virgin Sturgeon;* and many others, which he found very funny at first, but later seemed to have very little point other than vulgarity for its own sake.

Jimmy, like his team mates, drank a lot of beer, but in those early days he never made himself ill, even though he might wake up with a bit of a headache the next day. Other students drank themselves footless every Wednesday, and one vomited so much he damaged the lining of his stomach, which resulted in him being put permanently on a diet, as though he had an ulcer. On another occasion, during the Suez Crisis, they had to have an old petrol bus because diesel was scarce. The trouble was that it was difficult to start, and if it stopped the engine stopped too. After the usual visit to Bawtry, students kept demanding stops by singing raucously, 'We want a piss parade' to the tune of Santa Lucia. To get the bus going again, the soccer players constituted themselves as a rugby team, formed a double, or maybe even a treble, scrum behind this decrepit coach and pushed. Once it started, everyone then had to run and jump on the bus. This was extremely dangerous, despite the fact that they were crossing a fairly thinly populated part of Lincolnshire. Even worse, one character, Albert Blackley, was so drunk that when the scrum collapsed he fell on to the road and promptly went to sleep. Only when the bus had gone on a couple of miles did anyone notice he was missing. Turning round to go back to fetch him was so hazardous that the bus driver threatened to strand them all. He refused to stop the bus again until they reached Hull. However, by that time Blackley had started to puke – seriously – and the only way to deal with the problem was to stick his head out of the door, which was then held firmly against his neck so that he could not fall out. The rest of the party then counted up the number of times he was sick – according to the splashes on the rear windows, which fortunately were kept closed, the weather being inclement. Though he never got as drunk as Blackley did on that particular night, drinking became a problem for Jimmy in the more relaxed atmosphere that followed the first year.

The Head of the History Department informed second year students at the beginning of the autumn term that there would be, as he put it, "no life-threatening exams" in that academic year. His reasons were firstly, the very practical one, that students suffer from what he called 'second year-itis', when they can become a little complacent, and secondly that he wanted them to enjoy the History course and not have to worry unduly about the loss of grant through examination failure. The final year would be the time to get down to serious work, so there was no Part One in the second year. He was true to his word. Moreover, the Department laid on regular trips to places of historical interest: to Anglo-Saxon and Norman churches in Yorkshire; to Durham Cathedral; to Beverley Minster; to Scarborough Castle; and to York for a whole week when every style of British architecture could be studied, from a Roman tower to a Twentieth Century factory.

One day, during York week, they were all standing outside a pub looking at the building opposite, which, according to Booker, their ancient lecturer in Medieval History, was a good example of Tudor architecture. Tony McCann, a friend from Liverpool, was just behind Jimmy, with his back to the pub door. He grabbed Jimmy's arm and pulled him into the bar, which was so small that they had merely to turn round to be face to face with the barmaid from whom Tony promptly ordered "Two pints of bitter, please". They swiftly downed them and stepped back into the street, only to find that the building they had been in was also a gem of Tudor architecture, and that the group was now on the other side of the street looking across at them – everyone, that is, except Booker, who fortunately was gazing at the roof tiles and enthusing about their quality. This incident gave Tony and Jimmy a reputation as drinkers which, in the silliness of youth, they felt they must live up to. Back at the university, they took to going out each lunchtime to the Gardiner's Arms on Cottingham Road, there being no bar in the student's union at that time. At first they had only one pint each time, but then it was two and even three. They went out more often in the evening too, and slowly their capacity increased: they were joined by others, usually old boys of Jimmy's school or of Tony McCann's – their reasons for being at Hull were the same as his. On occasions they got very drunk, perhaps celebrating a twenty-first birthday, or the promotion of Everton back into the first division of the football league. Once, at the soccer club dinner, Jimmy drank so much that when he was tipped off the coach that had been hired specially for the purpose, he could not walk straight, no matter how hard he tried. As he approached Ferens Hall (now completed) he found that, instead of remaining on the drive, he was walking on the lawn, and that the desired destination was getting further away. After several attempts to rectify this he decided to follow his nose, as he put it to himself. He ended up back at the main gate, where he found two characters in a state similar to his own. They were the notorious Fritz and Pinkerton.

Pinkerton had graduated from Hull a couple of years before, but had found life in the real world very dull, so he had persuaded Fritz, who had graduated from Liverpool at about the same time, to come to Hull where they could take the PGCE course, and so become students again. That evening, besides the soccer club dinner, Fritz, who was a ladies' man, had also been invited to a Christmas Ball at one of the women's halls of residence. He intended, even at this late hour, to keep the appointment, but found himself encumbered by a footless Pinkerton. Just as Jimmy arrived on the scene, and even through the drunken haze, he was amazed to see Fritz push Pinkerton into the ditch. He was just about capable of remonstrating with Fritz, but knew that if he got down in the ditch to help Pinkerton, he would never get out again.

"Look, Jimmy, he'll be all right. He's gone to sleep. Let's make him comfortable." And he began to kick leaves down on to his unfortunate friend.

Jimmy said, "Are you sure now? He'll be all right?"

"Yerss ... He's safer down there than wandering around on the road in that state, is'n 'e?"

Jimmy helped with the leaves and then wandered off back towards the hall, the incident having served to sober him up enough to walk straight at least some of the time.

The next day he was very ill. He did not think his head could hurt so much: when he first woke up he was certain that there was a huge nail through his skull, fastening him to the bed head. He took some aspirin and was promptly sick. He lay down again and groaned, but that made his head worse. An hour later he got up again, pulled on a jersey and jeans over his pyjamas, which he was surprised to find he was wearing, and walked very gingerly to the village, ignoring the stares of the passers-by. He bought some Alka-Seltzer, thinking it would settle his stomach as well as reduce his headache, but five minutes after he had taken it he was sick again. There was nothing for it but to lie there and suffer. He slept again, and sometime in the afternoon felt sufficiently recovered to try another Alka-Seltzer. This time he managed to keep it down. In the evening he was able to get out of bed and sit in the armchair, but he still could not eat. Nor could he the next day either. It was a week before he felt normal again. In the meantime he told Tony that he must cut down on the amount he drank and he made his grant the excuse. To some extent this was true: he was running short of money and could not possibly write home for help.

However, he was very dissatisfied with life at that time and not only because of the fear that he might become, if not an alcoholic who drinks to live, then a boozer who lives to drink. He did not know where such an expression came from, but it kept coming back into his head time and again. The paradox was that though the professor had made sure that the pressure was taken off so that they could enjoy life, the reverse seemed to have happened to Jimmy. His work had suffered: it was always done, but never quite as thoroughly as in the first year – and this was the time he had taken the chance with the Economic History exam. He got up late; he missed lectures; he returned to hall early, saying he was going to work but lay on his bed and more often than not fell asleep. He began to fear that he would become as lethargic as he had been during long periods at school, but instead of doing something about it he sank lower, almost wallowing in his misery.

His intellectual difficulties got worse: he could not square the religious beliefs he was too afraid to drop with his developing understanding of political and social movements and institutions as his ideas moved further left, influenced as they were by books such as Edmund Wilson's *To the Finland Station*. His thinking was affected too by the debates in the students' union; that is when he could muster the energy to attend them. Speakers like Roy Hattersley and Bob Cryer were clever and persuasive, but they were not the only ones. Harold Silver was prominent when he came to Hull for his PGCE year. This is not to say that the agnostic/atheist camp had all their own way because, besides being the President of the Debating Society, Kevin MacNamara was also a leading member of the Catholic Society. Moreover the religious contingent at Hull was strong in the fifties, the membership of all religious societies being high.

Jimmy got on fairly well with the girls in the various overlapping groups to which he belonged: the History students; the friends he made in English in the first year; even some of those in the Catholic Society, but they were not the ones he dated. Soon after he arrived in Hull he got in touch with Kathleen O'Brien, who was at the Training College. He knew her from the Sixth Form dances in Liverpool, but nothing much came from this, partly because he handled the relationship in an inept way but also because she had a boyfriend back in Liverpool, and she left at the end of his first year anyway.

However, her younger sister arrived the following autumn and he went to the pictures with her one Saturday. Though she was a nice girl and not unattractive, he did not want this relationship to develop any further because, probably quite wrongly, he felt that he was being passed on from one member of the O'Brien family to the next. He did not know how to go about ending it and so did it in a ham-fisted way, which was quite out of character. He arranged to meet her in the university Saturday dance and then did not turn up but went to the pub instead. When she phoned during the week, he told the student who came to tell him there was a call for him to tell her he was not in, without even checking it was her. They did meet later at a dance and he was casual in the extreme even though he could see that she was upset. She got annoyed and told him he was the most arrogant person she had ever met, turned around and left. At first he felt smug about this, but the more he thought about it, the more ashamed he became. He could not see a way to repair the damage and he doubted if she would ever accept an apology, so in his usual way he did nothing, but the affair did his ego no good, given his other problems at that time.

Then one Saturday early in the summer term, he danced several times with a girl who looked too young to be a student. It turned out that Brenda was in the upper sixth of a local girls' grammar school and was taking an open scholarship and hoped to go to Oxford. She lived in Cottingham, so he walked her home. Just as they got to the front door it opened and her mother appeared. He immediately thought that she must be worried about who her daughter might be consorting with, so he put on his best air of respectability and trustworthiness: it worked because he was invited in to supper. He behaved impeccably and got on well with the family, to his relief, especially with her father, who was keen on football. To his astonishment, father and mother went to bed, leaving him and Brenda alone, sitting together on the settee. It was obvious even to him that she wanted to be kissed. However, her reaction took him completely by surprise, because she opened her mouth immediately and writhed and squirmed so much in his arms that they almost fell on the floor. Very quickly matters went further than he intended, but he was being carried willingly along. Just when he was beginning to feel completely engulfed, her father shouted from upstairs, "Isn't it time that lad went home?"

They sprang apart and when they had got their breath back, he made the feeble excuse that he was playing football in the morning and so would have to go, because it had already gone one o'clock. She looked at him as though she knew this was an excuse. He said, "Are you doing..."

"I never go anywhere during the week," she cut in. "I'm working for my scholarship."

"Do you..."

"I go out only at weekends."

"Shall we..."

"You could take me to the pictures on Saturday... if you want to, that is."

He got up to leave and she went with him to the front door. They kissed politely and he said, "See you next week".

As he walked back to Ferens, his mind was in a whirl. 'Wow! That was really something... Blimey, it's goin' to be like it was with Maureen all over again! ... What am I gonna do? ... See her again? ... No... She's an occasion of sin... I don't care, she's great... How serious was what we did? ... I didn't go all the way, did I? ... And some fellahs would... Don't try to slide out of it... You took selfish pleasure from... Oh! Shut up... Hitler murdered six million Jews... do I end up the same place as him? ... Oh why, oh why do I always have to get off with girls like Brenda and Maureen who are more experienced than me and know their own minds?'

Yet he fell asleep as soon as he got to bed. When he woke up he felt vaguely disturbed. As it was Sunday, he began to get ready for Mass, and it was only when he looked in the mirror to shave that he remembered what had happened the night before. Then he felt quite weak and almost slumped over the washbasin: he was facing a dilemma again and did not know what to do. For the present, he said to himself, he had just better get on with it. He went to Mass but found it hard to concentrate on what it all meant because he had great difficulty keeping thoughts of Brenda out of his head.

The next week was miserable. He got no work done at all. Mostly, he sat and smoked and the more he sat the worse he felt. He was a failure in every way, he told himself, and this all stemmed from the fact that he was steeped in sin and was too weak to free himself from it. He was too wishy-washy to actually go out and do the things he wanted to do, to commit some really full-blooded sins – with Brenda or any other girl. He should have been looking forward to seeing her, and in a way he was, but he was also fearful. The situation was crazy and hopeless. Then, in the middle of the week, he realized he had a sore throat: he put it down to all the cigarettes. However, it got worse and by Thursday night he had a streaming cold, which even prevented him from going to the pub with Tony. He tried to convince himself that it would clear up by Saturday, but it did not. He had to phone her. Her mother answered.

"Hello, it's Jimmy. May I speak to Brenda, please?"

"Oh, just a minute. I'll call her… It's that other young chap for you."

As she waited for her daughter to come, she said, "You sound rough. Have you got a cold?"

"Yes, I'm afraid so," he said, and he could hear her saying as she handed over the phone, "It's that student, and he sounds dreadful, poor chap".

"Hello, Jimmy. Are you OK?"

"No. Not really. I've got this awful cold. I don't think it would be sensible to see you today."

"Oh dear. That's a pity… and it's a film I want to see… *Friendly Persuasion.*"

"Sorry… will it still be on next week?"

"No. I don't think so… but, look, don't worry. I can go with… er… some friends from school."

"Oh… OK… then will I see you next week?"

"Well, let's see… why don't you phone me when your cold is better."

"Er… right… OK… I'll phone then… er… bye."

"Bye, then. Thanks for letting me know. Bye."

"Bye."

He came out of the telephone cubicle into the hall common room and sneezed. Then he coughed: it hurt his chest even when he blew his nose. Then he realized that he was angry.

'She doesn't bloody well care... I've been worrying meself sick all week about her and she doesn't bloody care! ... What an idiot... aaarr, Shite! ... And didn't her mother say 'other chap'? ... Which other bloody chap? ... She had me for a sucker... don't be so bloody daft... you took her home once and now you imagine there was a big romance... well, sod her ...'

He felt even more annoyed, but with himself, and especially because he had sat and moped and neglected everything, when the one thing he had promised himself was that never again would he sit and stare into space as he had when at school. And he decided that, cold or no cold, he would set to work on that essay for Political Theory that he was so afraid of... 'We'll sort that bugger Locke out once and for all.'

As he was making his way up to his room, he met Geoff Hambleton, a big chap from Blackburn who sang in the SCM/Catholic Society choir.

"Ah, there you are, Jimmy. I've been looking for you."

"Oh, aye."

"Don't you play soccer?"

"Yes, but it's the summer, and there are no games, and I've got this terrible cold."

Geoff held up his hand as though to ward off Jimmy and his germs. He moved several stairs away and said, "Oh, I am sorry... Listen, there's going to be a massive invasion by the Hull Catholic Society of Leeds Catholic Society in a fortnight's time, when exams finish. We are going to play them at as many games as we can. It was supposed to be summer games, but their mad Scousers say they can only play football, so I'm trying to get a team together. Will you play?"

"Sure I will. This cold should be better by then and I've got no exams anyway."

"Right, then. Great. I'll put you down for it. Look, I must dash. I've got others to see. I'll give you details later."

He started to run down the stairs but then stopped and called back, "Oh, by the way, do you go to the Catholic Society Mass on a Saturday morning?"

"Er… no…"

"Well it's just that we have a continental breakfast afterwards: lots of people come. It's good fun, really. And next Saturday we'll be sorting out the details of this Leeds trip. If you come you can find out all about it."

"Oh… OK… I'll try to be there."

That evening he went to confession. The priest probed him about this girl. Would he be seeing her again? Jimmy said he thought not.

The next Saturday he went to the Catholic Society Mass.

Chapter X

THERE WERE MANY MORE people than he expected at the Saturday morning Mass. Who they were also surprised him: lads he thought didn't even go to Church anymore and people from other denominations. One reason for the latter, he soon discovered, was the choir, which must have numbered sixteen or so, half of whom were from the SCM: it sang very well, in four parts – even the responses. Everyone seemed to go to breakfast – in a pleasant dining room, which was part of the Marist house. Most people he did in fact know, even if only slightly in some cases; and several of them went out of their way to speak to him, so he did not feel too much out of place. Two things struck him in particular. The first was that the old guard, the ones he had thought of as the 'aristocratic' Catholics, had disappeared and had been replaced by people from much more heterogeneous backgrounds. In consequence, the atmosphere was more democratic, less inward-looking than he had remembered from the first year. The second was how cheerful everybody was. They laughed and even joked with each other, but in a kindly way, quite unlike the soccer club, where humour seemed to consist largely of jeering at one another, or turning what others said into double entendres or innuendoes. He even liked the food, though it was simply rolls, butter, marmalade and jam, coffee or tea.

When it came to getting sorted out for the trip to Leeds the following week, Geoff asked the men to come to one end of the dining room, and a History student, Mary Calvert, from the same year as Jimmy, looked after the women. It was only a question of finding out who was doing what, and of persuading the undecided, who claimed they couldn't play anything, to fill up gaps: none of the games were meant to be taken seriously, though the whist group said they would 'moider the bums!'

Jimmy had seen Mary Calvert about the place even from the very first day, but she was so very quiet and unassuming. She never ever stood out among the History students, always seemed to take a back seat, to be only on the edge of things as though not wanting to be noticed. Yet here she was taking a leading part in organizing the women's teams and even raising her voice in order to be heard over the din. He found it very difficult not to keep looking at her. She was much prettier than he had remembered, but also he noticed, probably because she had to speak more loudly than usual, that her voice was that of a mature woman and that it was beautiful: he kept listening to her and not to Geoff. During the following week too, he always looked around the lecture rooms to see if she were there, and then if he could, would sit behind her and to one side so that he could glance at her now and then. There was no danger that she would catch him looking at her because she looked to the front all the time. He thought that her self control must be marvellous, and this put him even more in awe of her. Walking across from the arts block to the students' union one day, he found himself walking just behind her and considered the possibility of catching her up and talking to her, but then felt suddenly awkward, even gauche, and every sentence he tried to formulate as an opening gambit seemed either banal or incoherent.

The next Saturday he went to Mass again because the coaches were leaving for Leeds straight after breakfast in the Marist house. Everything was very much like the week before, except that there were even more people. By chance, on the bus he found himself sitting next to Jeremy Burns, who came from Liverpool, but was not someone he had ever talked to very much: he hadn't been to one of the usual Catholic grammar schools because, until he came up to university, he had been in a seminary. As Jimmy expected, Jeremy attended Catholic Society meetings and functions regularly. Jimmy commented on how the composition and the atmosphere had changed since their first year and Jerry said this was because Mary was the Secretary and Danny Bennett was the President. Jimmy did not know who Danny was but

Jerry pointed him out: he was sitting in the front with his wife, someone else Jimmy did not know. They were mature students, several years older than the general run of undergraduate, and Jimmy had not seen them the week before because they had been away. It transpired that Danny too had been training to become a priest, but had met Bridget when on holiday in Ireland, and though not far off ordination at the time, he decided that, having met her, his vocation had changed. They both intended to teach.

"He was the one who introduced the study groups on Sunday evenings."

"Oh, and what are they?"

"Just that. You study the scriptures, Catholic doctrine and social teaching and so on."

"It sounds awful."

"Oh, but it isn't. It's marvellous, and it's mostly down to Danny."

"Are you kidding me?"

"No. Listen, mate. You don't think that after six years in a bloody seminary, you'd get me in there otherwise."

This was said with such vehemence that Jimmy could not help but be impressed. Then he added, "But see for yourself. Come down to Thwaite Hall tomorrow evening at eight o'clock. You'll never be the same again."

Jimmy laughed disparagingly, but Jeremy went on to tell him about the discussions, which were incredibly progressive for Catholics, and ranged far and wide over philosophy, politics, science and so on.

"Have you ever heard of Teilhard de Chardin?"

"Can't say I have."

"Well, there you are, you see. He's a Jesuit palaeontologist who squares Christian notions of creation with evolution. I'd never heard of him either until I met Danny."

Now Jimmy was interested, because this was one of the problems he had tried to ponder for himself, but with little success. He was certainly tempted to go to Thwaite, and Mary was sure to be there too.

The day at Leeds went well: each Catholic Society won some

and lost some and the games, but not the Whist, were played in good humour and not too seriously. In fact, Jimmy's soccer team had four Leeds students playing for them because they were short. Afterwards, food was laid on and this was followed by a barn dance, which turned out to be much more enjoyable than he had expected because the band was good and so were the callers. Everybody joined in because the steps were easily learned and the chaos that ensued when they got them wrong was part of the fun. At one point he found himself dancing with Mary in one of the progressive pieces: he decided that he would definitely go to the study group on Sunday.

The process used by the study groups – so many students turned up that they had to run two, but they always reassembled for a plenary session and coffee at the end – was based on booklets developed in the States, where concern that young adults were falling away from the Church was expressed earlier and more openly than in Europe. In one sense they were traditional in that they focused on doctrine and morals, as taught by the Catholic Church, but what made the approach different was that these were considered in the light of carefully chosen passages from the New Testament (with occasional forays into the Old) which students were expected to interpret for themselves, albeit in a collective way, the importance of discussion being stressed. Furthermore, the human situations used as case studies were ones in which young people actually found themselves. But what was important, which Jimmy was to recognise more and more as time went on, was that the scriptures were interpreted with very deep sympathy for, and understanding of, the actual human condition as experienced by people just like him. This grew naturally out of what, for Jimmy, was a different approach to the relationship between God and each individual, which for the first time in his life enabled him to see what was so fundamentally new about Christ's message. There was no Damascus Road experience. He was not suddenly transformed by a shaft of light like John Wesley, but change did take place and it began in a small way on that first night.

He was glad to see that he was in the same group as Mary, but

Danny, who he still had to meet, was in the other one. Leaders of the discussions had been chosen the week before, and everyone was expected to take a turn. The leader of Jimmy's group was Jeremy Burns. The text was the one about the Prodigal Son, which in the light of how Jimmy had felt about his life a fortnight ago (and still did to some extent) was appropriate. Somebody read the passage and then Jeremy asked them what they thought about it. Lots of people spoke and had the sort of opinions you would expect of Catholics: this was about remorse, about someone realizing the error of his ways, about returning to the fold and being forgiven. Mary asked what the group thought about the attitude of the older son and then there was considerable disagreement. Most people seemed sympathetic to his attitude: he had remained faithful; he hadn't frittered away a fortune on women and high living; he'd not asked for anything; and so on. Others said that it was the same message as the labourers in the vineyard, when those who worked all day got the same as those who worked for only an hour: it was God's vineyard and couldn't He do what He liked with it? This was accepted by some, but others kept raising the issue of fairness, so much so that they hardly looked at the case studies, which were discussed only in a very perfunctory way.

When they went out for the plenary session and were milling about getting coffee and tea, members of the other group started to tell them about Danny's Irish version of the Prodigal Son, saying that they must get him to do it for them, and so when everyone had settled down, that's what happened, though Danny said he would shorten it a bit, and apologised to Bridget for his stage Irish accent.

"I'll not do the first part, but remember this young fellah is a real bastard: he doesn't want to do any work, he just wants to have fun, like the rest of us do so often. Let's go on to the part where he has spent all his money and he's living in squalor. Just imagine such a character. Try to think what he's thinking. Wouldn't it be something like this? ... 'What a stupid git I am... if I wasn't such an ejit, I could still be living in comfort in the Da's house... this is bloody awful... I hate pigs... and me an orthodox

George Timmons

Jew too... I'm that hungry I could almost eat that slosh they're grubbing in... what if I went home? ... Arr, I couldn't! ... The ould fellah would kill me! ... Or if he didn't do that he'd go on about it forever more... just supposing I did go home, how could I get round him? ... What if I admitted the awful things I've done? ... I could say, "Father, I have sinned against you.".... no... no, say, "I have sinned against Heaven and against you.".... That would get him. He might fall for that.'

He paused. Then went on:

"Anyway, you can do the rest yourself: you can see what he's like and what he is after. And he expects to be punished and he thinks he might have to be a servant. And he's got all his speech prepared. But what happens when he gets home?"

The other group kept quiet. There was a short silence and then a girl from Jimmy's group said, "The father doesn't give him a chance to make his excuses, he's so overjoyed that he is safe and has come back. He doesn't care what the son has done. What is important is that he is home."

The discussion which followed was quite animated and Danny persuaded those who were not sure about his interpretation to look again at the text and especially at the sections about the father, and how he is consumed with love for his children. Then someone said, "But what about the elder son and his raw deal?"

"Well, what about him?" said Danny.

The sorts of argument that they'd had before followed, until Danny asked, "Why is he in the story at all? He doesn't have to be... not if it is about remorse and then forgiveness. Why is he there? Why did Jesus put him in?"

The argument became very noisy, till somebody said, "OK, Danny, you tell us why he's there".

Danny said, "Well, you know I don't like doing that, but we are going to be here all night, if we don't get on... look, we call this the Prodigal Son, but it ought to be called 'The Prodigal Father,' and what he is prodigal with is his love for us, and, you see, we, on the other hand, are like the elder son – when we see someone getting the things we think only we deserve, we say it's not fair. But remember what the elder son got and what the labourers who had worked all day in the vineyard got was this precious love of God and eternal life with Him. It's infinite and of that you can't have more or less of it. And when we stray, God wants nothing more than to forgive us and He doesn't tell us to 'Say three Hail Marys' or 'Go on a pilgrimage to Rome in your bare feet' or 'Flagellate yourself and then you will be forgiven'. He says, 'Oh son, I've been worried about you, come in and sit down. Put your feet up and have a cup o' tea.' That's the sort of father Jesus knew and that's why he called him Abba, which, remember, is like calling him 'Dad' or even 'Pop'. He wanted to shock people into realizing how much God loves us – all of us, without exception, and how he will forgive us everything. On the other hand, the elder son is like us – we find it difficult to forgive. God the Father doesn't."

They had overstayed their time and so left in some confusion, but Jimmy could hear Danny and Mary arranging next week's discussion leaders: nobody refused and that seemed typical of the good will he had found. As he walked back to his room, he reflected on the night's experience: it was certainly different from anything he had experienced as a Catholic before. If he had understood what Danny was getting at, and if it were Catholic teaching, then he would have to review his ideas. Perhaps too he should make an effort to read the New Testament.

Life seemed to go on very much as before and yet everything was different because Jimmy felt that, though he had no more answers than earlier, there were answers to be had even if, as yet, he did not know what they were. Occasionally he had a feeling that could be regarded, if he did not think about it too much, as contentment, but he was afraid to really savour it in case it disappeared: that old habitual sensation of incipient threat was too familiar to drop all at once. Often in the past he had found that just when everything seemed to be proceeding well, something would happen to turn hope into disappointment. Nevertheless, somehow he sensed that he was on firm ground. From here he could take stock and then if he moved carefully and thoughtfully he might be able to see where he was going, and if he went one step at a time, he might get somewhere. When he thought of where this might be, he realized that he did not know, but again he told himself that the best solution to this particular dilemma was to attend to the things that needed to be attended to. The most important of these might be to find out who this new Jesus was but another was certainly academic work: after all, that was what he was at the university for.

For the first time in his life he decided that he was not going to be blown about willy-nilly by events that were going on around him, but that he was going to assert a measure of control over them. Lying in his pit, blowing smoke rings at the ceiling, would get him nowhere, so he tidied his room, put all his books and papers in order, sat at his desk and began to read for his essay. After half an hour he wanted to lie down and have a smoke: the thought came over him that he had not changed at all. Then he remembered that he had promised himself that he would go a step at a time, 'So… right… don't roll a cigarette for another half an hour… back to the books!' In this way he got through a whole morning, that is, until about eleven o'clock when he had to set off for a lecture – one that he did not always attend.

Afterwards, he met Tony and they went to the refectory together instead of going to the pub: Jimmy said he had this work to do and was relieved to hear that Tony had had a change of heart too. Jimmy said, "Tell you what, why don't we go to the Bluebell in Cottingham at about nine o'clock this evening, and then we can both get lots of work done and still look forward to a pint".

"OK. Sounds like a good idea. I'll see you then."

Later when they were in the pub, Tony said, "You know, I don't think I want to go drinking at lunchtime anymore," and he went on before Jimmy could interrupt, "I get what I'm beginning to think of as the four o'clock gloom: it descends on me every time. I enjoy the drink and the company, but it's just not worth it, because when the effect of the alcohol wears off I sometimes feel I could cut me throat."

Jimmy said he knew the feeling and there and then they agreed that they would avoid the expeditions to the Gardiner's:

their second year was nearly over and next year they would have to work harder than either of them had done so far. However, when Jimmy told him about the study groups, Tony was not keen on the idea, so the following Sunday Jimmy went by himself, as he would every week till the end of term, though he realized that his motives were mixed: he wanted to get to know Mary Calvert as much as he wanted to know Jesus. He found that gradually he became better acquainted with both.

Several times the discussions at the end of that summer term centred on prayer, which Jimmy had always found problematic because he saw it as a chore made especially difficult because his attention wandered. Usually this happened when he felt that concentration was essential, for instance when he went to confession. His attitude, when he was at his most pharisaical, was that he had to be completely conscious of the meaning of every word and phrase, otherwise saying his penance would be worse than useless. Moreover, when he made his act of contrition he had to really mean what he said. However, the words came out just as words: he felt they meant nothing though he said them over and over again. So he was gratified to hear Danny say that prayer was simply talking to Jesus or the Father or perhaps the Holy Spirit, or even merely putting yourself in their presence.

"Sit comfortably in a chair, close your eyes, and imagine that Jesus is standing next to you. Just be with him. Perhaps think of his hand on your head."

At first when he tried this, nothing much seemed to happen: in fact sometimes he just drifted off into sleep. However, as time went on, he found he could stay awake. Then, gradually, he began to feel that he really was with someone. Whoever it was never spoke to him, at least not in a way he could hear, but on some occasions he realized afterwards that he had ideas in his head which, though not answers to prayers exactly, gave him a sense of direction: they were possibilities, starting points, alternatives.

He also began to read the New Testament, but in a new way: he wanted to know who Jesus was and he tried to think of him as a man, not as God-made-man, even though he thought he believed that Jesus was the Son of God. He began to find that certain passages were very moving, for example when Jesus wept as he walked towards the tomb of Lazarus. For the first time he realized the poignancy of the fact that both Martha and Mary said that, had Christ been there, their brother would not have died. Yet earlier, Jesus seemed to have taken a decision not to visit the dying man, and he tells his disciples that they will wait and from this situation God will be glorified. What moved Jesus so much was the grief he had caused Martha and Mary by his deliberate delay, and Jimmy began to understand dimly that so often when Jesus helped people he did so because he understood their unhappiness and wanted to relieve them of their burdens, which is why he kept telling people to keep secret the fact that he had cured them. He did not want to demonstrate that he was the Son of God; he wanted to help those he felt sorry for. So he did not condemn the woman taken in adultery and when the young man who came to visit Jesus in the night could not give up his riches and follow him, it says, *"and Jesus looked on him and loved him"*. (Mark X, 21.)

He was also struck by the ordinariness of some passages. When John's disciples come to seek him out, Jesus says, "Come and see where I live". Now why should he do that, other than that's what young men do? And when he goes off to pray early in the morning when he's staying with Peter's mother (or is it his mother-in-law?), she is concerned about him and sends Peter out to look for him. Jimmy imagined a Liverpool mam saying, "You'll have to go and look for him. You never know what might have happened to him, wandering around in a place that's strange to him."

And Peter saying, "But, Mam, he often does that. He's gone out to say his prayers somewhere quiet. He can look after himself."

But she replies, "That's as maybe. I don't care. The poor fellah's had no breakfast! Now go and find him!"

You could also almost imagine that at the marriage at Cana, and Jesus was there with 'the lads'. When his mother asks him to help with the problem, he reacts like many a young man and says, "What's that got to do with me?" But as a typical mum who knows her son well, she says to the servants, "It'll be all right. Just do whatever he tells you."

Jimmy found that seemingly less important passages like these led him to worry less and less about the historical authenticity of the New Testament. What mattered much more was that he felt he was meeting Christ.

Nevertheless, he knew his motivations were not so pure as they might have appeared. He wanted to impress Mary and he knew this was not going to be easy because he was sure she saw him as a loud Liverpool lout who drank and smoked too much. However, he could think of no other way to get close to her, especially as it began to dawn on him that all the girls he had known intimately had gone more than halfway to meet him. He had never really made the running with any of them. When he thought about this he came to the conclusion that he needed formal situations in which to approach girls, even if this was only where one asked them for a dance: there was a social formula one could put into operation. Casual approaches were different: he feared rejection and this made him timid.

Then, one lunchtime when he went to the refectory quite late, he found it nearly empty. As usual he looked around to see if there was anybody he knew to eat with and found himself looking straight at Mary. He did not know whether the fact that she was looking at him was accidental or not, but she half smiled in recognition, if nothing else. The most natural thing seemed to be to sit with her.

"Hello, do you mind if I join you?"

"No, of course you can."

He took his things off his tray and carefully assembled his knife and fork and spoon. He tried desperately to think of something engaging to say, but only commonplaces came into his head. He heard himself saying, "There aren't many people in here today".

"No, there never are after about half past one."

"Oh, do you come in often at this time?"

"Well, not often, but sometimes – when I don't think I can stand the noise and clatter when it's busy."

"Oh, yes. I suppose it is noisy."

He realized he had never even thought about it because usually he would be making as much row as anybody else. There was quite a long pause – again, because he could think of nothing significant to say, and she seemed content to get on with her lunch which, he was pleased to notice, she must have only just started before he came in. Once more the words seemed to come out as though he were a ventriloquist's dummy.

"I'm later than usual because I've got to finish that Political Theory essay: the deadline is the last day of term so there are only two days left. I seem to have been working on it forever. Have you done yours?"

"Yes, I handed it in last Friday, because I wanted to have the last week free to clear up some Catholic Society work, and to have some time just reading – all the things I want to read just for fun."

"Well, I've been struggling with it. Do you find that stuff easy?"

"Not really, but I went to listen to Green's lectures on Marx, because I was interested after reading that book that Spender recommended."

Jimmy was quite surprised, almost confused, by her answer: there were so many questions he wanted to ask. Who was Green? What was a nice Catholic girl doing writing about Marx? What was the book? Was it *To the Finland Station*? He did not know which to ask first, until it came to him that to discuss the book might make him appear intellectual, perhaps even a good student of history.

"Would that be *To the Finland Station*?"

"Yes. Have you read it?" she asked, assuming he had. "Isn't it marvellous?"

"Oh, yes…"

"What I liked was that just when the philosophy is getting heavy, Wilson breaks off to give you the historical context or an absorbing anecdote. And I think I understand Marxism now that I can see its philosophical and historical antecedents, don't you?"

"I think so… but tell me, why did you decide to write on Marx?"

"Er… lots of reasons really. Why do you ask?"

"Well. I just wondered... the Index and all that."

"Does that matter so much anymore... and aren't we as students free to read what is required?"

"I suppose so. Who is Green, by the way?"

"Oh, don't you know? He lectures in the Sociology Department and I heard he was very good: he certainly made it all clear to me."

"I wish I'd known, but it's too late now."

They were both silent for a while and concentrated on the food, but Jimmy was thinking furiously about what he ought to say next. He was still intrigued by the fact that someone like her would want to write about Marx.

"What do you think of Marx now you've written the essay?"

"I think I'm quite impressed really. Setting aside his atheism, he makes a lot of sense... not so much with all that Hegel stuff about thesis and antithesis, but with the analysis of capitalism, and after reading the Wilson, don't you think he understood Nineteenth Century conditions better than his contemporaries?"

Jimmy was thrown by this. He was sure there was a smart answer but he couldn't think of it. He began to feel hot. He was supposed to be impressing her but things were the other way about. He never imagined someone so apparently timid could be so forthcoming. Just as he was about to stammer out some nonsense, he was saved by a music student he knew vaguely who he had half noticed going round the few people remaining in the dining room. Jimmy knew him as an extravert.

"Greetings my good children... allow me to break into this no doubt intellectually stimulating conversation, or are you, gallant young man, whispering sweet nothings in her shell-like?"

Raising his hand ostentatiously, he continued, "No need to answer that young sir".

Then he sat down very close to Mary and said confidentially, "Listen, love, wouldn't you like to introduce this Liverpudlian git to some real live culture... Yes, of course you would, so now's your chance to persuade him to take you to the City Hall on Saturday to hear the Hull Philharmonic play Rossini, Bach and Dvorak."

"Well, er…"

Mary and Jimmy looked at each other but she did not seem at all sure about this, so he thought he should ask a diverting question.

"What's this all for, Frank? You don't usually sell tickets like this."

"No, but so many people in the orchestra are from the music department here that someone thought it would be a good idea to sell tickets on the campus. They've been advertised in Crush and round and about but the bloody philistines in this place haven't responded."

"I don't know really," began Mary, but Frank went on, "It'll finish by half past nine, so if you go in your best bib and tucker you can be in time to get back here for the end of the going-down dance. And the proceeds go to charity."

To Jimmy this was an opportunity too good to miss. The thought of sitting in a concert with her and going to the dance afterwards was a much better prospect than he could have hoped for. He decided to be bold.

"Shall we, then? You did say this week was for doing things you enjoyed."

He realized that the presence of Frank made it just that bit more difficult for her to refuse, but he found himself gripping the edge of the table in suspense. He looked at Mary and hoped that he didn't look too much like a faithful dog pleading to be taken out for a walk. Her lips were smiling but her eyes showed tension. Then she broke into a deep throated chuckle and said, "Very well, then, but I'm not sure I can afford it. How much are the tickets?"

"To you two love birds the special rate of one pound sterling – each."

Inwardly, Jimmy breathed a sigh of relief: he had just drawn his last four pounds out of his account. He quickly took out his wallet and gave Frank two pound notes, and Frank handed the tickets (over-printed, student rate: £1) to him. Mary said she'd have to give it to Jimmy later, but he had no intention of taking the money from her. He wondered whether to give her a ticket but knew that if he held on to it she would have to accompany him. To prevent anything going wrong, he got up quickly and said, "I must go back to the library or I'll never get this essay finished".

Then, as he stacked his dishes on his tray, he continued, "Where shall we meet on Saturday?" and without giving her a chance to reply, went on, "Shall we say seven o'clock on the City Hall steps?"

Trying to appear as though time now mattered, he hurried away before she could change her mind. When he got to his essay it took him a long time to settle back to work. He kept thinking about his lunch break, of how different Mary seemed from the character he'd imagined her to be, of whether the things he had said were foolish, but mostly of how lucky he had been that Frank had been selling those tickets. Fortunately, after a while Locke took over. He finished the essay and handed it in. He also managed to keep busy during what was left of the term and so did not think too much about the coming visit to the concert with Mary. In his now habitual way he refused to let himself expect too much in order to avoid disappointment.

Though he had already bought his rail ticket there was still plenty to do, because he was not going straight home. He had arranged to stay several weeks with his aunt and uncle in Shropshire, so that he could work in the tile factory where his uncle, having left farming, was now a charge-hand. However, because no one was certain of a room in hall next academic year, he had to pack all his stuff in his trunk and arrange for it to be collected to go in advance on Saturday as he was travelling on Sunday. This was all easy enough, but he needed to take his bike with him: it could not go in advance as he needed it for the last part of the journey, because though there were trains he could catch, they ran none too often and he did not want to rely on them. This meant he would have to cycle the last fifteen miles in his best suit and mac! He also had to think about how he could load his bike, because it was by no means certain that his trunk would arrive before him. How could he tie on working clothes and shoes? And what about his dirty washing and his briefcase and whatever books might still be in it? He borrowed an army knapsack and stuffed as much as he could into it even though, in his trial run, it wobbled on his back because it was not flat. His briefcase he found could be attached to the cross bar by means of the flap and its buckles. The rest would have to be fastened on to the handle bars or secured behind the seat by means of brown paper and bits of string. He chose not to experiment with the details of all this and concentrated instead on washing his best shirt and pressing his trousers and his tie in preparation for the concert.

As he travelled into Hull on the bus he continued to try not to think about how the evening with Mary might go, but certain possibilities kept entering his consciousness and one that he was prepared to entertain was that the hall might be nearly empty. Would this be so embarrassing that he would feel even more self-conscious than he did already? How full would it have to be before he could feel comfortable? Who else might be there? Would acquaintances think it odd that he was with Mary, who to his recollection never seemed to have had a boyfriend? When he arrived on the steps five minutes early he was surprised to discover her there already. Moreover, he was almost taken aback by how attractive she looked: she was wearing a suggestion of make up and her hair was loose, whereas it was usually tied up severely. He could not help but think that she had gone to a good deal of trouble for his sake: he felt elated and really rather proud as they went in together. He was glad his creases were sharp and his shoes were polished.

Their student-rate tickets were not for expensive seats so they had lots of stairs to climb, but as nowhere in the City Hall could be described as poky, their seats were comfortable and there was plenty of legroom, so they were not thrown too close to each other. The conversation went easily: the programme was the first topic and as it suited both their preferences, Jimmy felt that he could say something relevant about all the pieces and appear as least as knowledgeable as Mary.

Gradually they got round to the study groups, because she was interested in his reaction to them. He was careful not to appear over-enthusiastic in case he aroused her suspicions about his motivation for attending. On the other hand, he could be perfectly honest about them because they had made him think seriously about what he believed. He said nothing about the new sense of direction that he knew they had given his life. As yet this was too personal and too private to discuss with anyone. Thus the half hour that they had to wait passed quickly enough and it was only as the leader came out that Jimmy realized that his fears about the size of the audience were unfounded.

The concert itself was very enjoyable, even though the irrepressible Frank himself blew a false note in his trumpet introduction to the final movement of the Dvorak, at which even Mary almost laughed out loud. In fact, when they got outside and Jimmy mentioned it, she did break out into a delighted and delightful peal of laughter, so that he felt he could also remind her that the same Frank had suggested that they should go to the going-down dance after the concert. She looked surprised and said that she had assumed that they would. On the bus to the Students' Union, Mary talked much more animatedly than he expected and about all sorts of things, so that he began to wonder if she felt as excited as he did about this evening: maybe she was interested in him in the same way as he was in her. His hopes began to rise and when they got to the dance he was not disappointed. She wanted to dance every dance and even agreed to go to the bar in the second interval, and to his amazement asked for a pint of bitter, saying that it was something she always wanted to try. Perhaps this was her night for kicking over the traces, though he noticed that she did not finish it – after all, beer was an acquired taste. As they returned to the dance they became aware of the fact that there was a jazz band in the men's common room. Mary's eyes opened wide and she asked Jimmy if he could jive, which he admitted he could in a limited way. She positively pleaded with him to teach her. This was not easy. She did not have Maureen's sense of rhythm and it felt rather like dealing with a handcart. When he pushed her away from him as the jive conventions required, she strayed too far, performing what he took to be folk dance steps as she went. However, the amazing thing was that she seemed to think that she was performing really well. Jimmy, for his part, was so pleased that he was doing something for her, that he persevered.

The dance ended after midnight and that meant a long walk home – doubly long for Jimmy as he would have to take Mary home first. However, he was happy just to be with her, especially as she was excited, almost high, seemingly as a result of the evening with him. He began to wonder about what might happen when he got to her front doorstep, but that was a good way ahead.

"When will you be going home – tomorrow?" he asked.

"Oh no, I'm staying here for a few weeks to get some work done."

"Do you mean so that you can earn some money?"

"No, I mean things like the reading I should have done – and maybe some for next year. And I'm going to take my landlady on a couple of outings. She's a bit crabby, but she's a poor old thing and on her own too, so…"

"Won't you see your family, then?"

"Well, not for about a month. But no one will be at home until well into July, anyway."

He did not pursue this any further but told her instead about how he would stay with Aunt Agnes and Uncle Fred and work in the tile factory as he had last year. He told her about how boring the work could be, though things would improve when other students arrived from the College of Art, but their term did not finish until at least a fortnight after the university. There would be little to do, he said, and this gave him the opportunity to ask if he could write to her. She did not answer immediately. Then she said, "I suppose you could… here."

He wanted to ask her why not at home too, but because something seemed amiss he decided it would be better not to. She gave him the address and then went silent: the excitement, almost joy that she had shown earlier had vanished, and she became the very serious, quiet person she had always appeared to be over most of the last two years. He still wondered if he should kiss her goodnight when they got to her digs: the prospect of this seemed less and less likely as they approached the house. He could think of nothing to say until they arrived at the garden gate, but as he was about to thank her for an enjoyable evening, just as on another very different occasion, the front door opened but this time a rather scruffy old woman peered out at them.

"Is that you, Mary?"

"Yes, Mrs Baggulley, it's me. Everything's all right."

"No it isn't! What time is this to be coming home?"

Mary turned towards Jimmy to say goodnight but by then the old lady had scuttled down the path to scrutinise him.

"Who's this fellah? Why's he here? Have you been with him all night? What have you been doing with him?"

"Nothing, Mrs Baggulley. He's a fellow student from the university, and we've been to a concert and to a dance, and that's all."

"I hope that's all. I don't want to have to report you to the lodgings officer, you know."

Jimmy wanted to say, 'Don't be so ridiculous, you silly old bat,' but knew that this would upset Mary too, and probably make things even more difficult for her, so he merely smiled his most obsequious smile. Mary, instead of getting annoyed, seemed very solicitous of the old girl and said, "Never mind now, Mrs Baggulley, we are late only because we missed the last bus and Mr Thompson kindly brought me home because he was worried about me walking through Hull by myself."

And she turned to Jimmy and continued, "Goodnight, Mr Thompson, and thank you very much".

"Goodnight, Miss Calvert," he replied as ironically as he could. "I'll probably see you next term. Goodnight, Mrs Baggulley. Nice to have met you."

He turned and walked down the street, thinking, 'Stupid old cow!'

He had gone at least a mile before the incongruousness of the situation registered fully. How could this old woman be so rude to a girl as patently innocent as Mary? And if she is so awful, as Mary herself hinted, why does she stay there? And who the hell is the lodgings officer? What century does that old bat think

we're in? The only way in which he could make any sense out
of this was to believe that Mary was so good and so caring of
others that she stayed in the digs because the old lady needed the
money or perhaps the company, probably both.

He had plenty of time to think on the way back to the hall.
Somehow the last hour had taken the sheen off the evening,
because whereas his relationship with Mary had seemed to be on
an upward curve until well after they had left the dance, it had
dipped severely once he asked if he could write to her. Why this
should be so was a mystery to him. Was it that there was something odd about her family? That could be a cause for concern,
but it would not be a reason for him to get depressed about the
relationship: in a flight of juvenile fancy he saw himself taking
her 'away from all that'. Almost immediately he recognised that
for the ridiculous notion it was, and anyway, she had not seemed
certain about him writing to her at all – not even in Hull. Why
could that be? Maybe she had a boyfriend already and Jimmy
was only second fiddle, as he had been for Maureen and Kathleen
O'Brien? Somehow that did not seem likely. Then the thought that
he had been avoiding loomed large: for some reason she did not
want the relationship to go any further. Indeed, it could be that
she now considered that it had gone too far already. His habitual
pessimism began to assert itself. Yes, that was the real reason for
her change in attitude, and Mrs Baggulley's sudden appearance
on the doorstep had saved Mary from an even greater embarrassment. As he grew sadder he became aware of how tired he
felt – and his feet ached because he was wearing his 'best' shoes,
which were still reasonably new.

He thought about hitching a lift. There were still one or two
cars about. Almost immediately he heard one approach and
without even looking he stuck his thumb out. As it began to slow
down, he turned and looked at it carefully and realized to his
horror that it was Albert Blackley in his ancient, battered Austin
Seven. Moreover, it looked full already. He thought about waving
it on but it was too late; Blackley and one of the other occupants
had recognised him.

"Come head, Jimmy lad, gerrin!"

"Where? There's no room."

Albert struggled in his low slung seat to turn and address the two in the rear. "Ay. Ay. You two – bloody shove over and let my mate, Jimmy, in. Gerrover!"

The car was so small that there was barely room for the pair already there. Also, all of them were so very drunk because they were returning from a dinner night at the local RAF headquarters, because they were members of the university OTC.

"Who, who is it?"

"It's my pal, Jim, and it's my car so you just bloody let him in."

"Jim who?"

"Jimmy Thompson."

"Oh, that Scouse git. What's he doin' 'ere?"

Jimmy got in at last but his backside was only partly on the seat and mostly against the side of the car so that he was perched over the others with his head touching the roof, which fortunately was made of some kind of treated canvas and so was not as hard as it might have been. The stink of stale beer and cigarettes was overpowering but as the car started to move the smell improved because all the windows were open. Only Blackley made much sense.

"Well, what you doin' out on your own at this hour o' the night, Jim?"

"I went to the going-down dance."

"Till two in the mornin'?"

"I took a girl home."

The rest of them then became interested.

"Anyone we know?"

"Did you get your bone home, eh, eh?"

"Does she jump?"

Jimmy ignored all of this, not so much because there was no point in replying to any of it, but because he was becoming aware of the erratic and rather alarming behaviour of the car. Every slight shift in the positions of the drunken passengers resulted in a sway on the part of the vehicle. The body seemed to be independent of the chassis. But this was not all. Albert Blackley insisted in looking over his shoulder to talk to Jimmy whom he seemed to think, probably not without reason, was the only occupant capable of coherent conversation. This meant that the car wandered on the road – on which Jimmy's eyes now became fixed. Then he noticed that the car always veered in the same direction and that was, fortunately, towards the pavement. He thought that this must be due to some particular propensity of Blackley's driving – until it became clear that even when he kept the steering wheel straight, the car still drifted to the left.

"Albert, tell me, why does this car veer to the left, no matter what you do with the wheel?"

"Ar, now that's an interesting question... I'll tell ya, Jimmy... I'll tell ya...'cos it's too full... too full."

"What do you mean, too full?"

"It's 'cos of you and him," he said, giving the occupant of the front passenger seat a mighty thump, and shaking him out of his slumber, "and them two drunken buggers in the back with you," looking round in disgust at them so that the car ran almost on to the pavement before he righted it.

"I still don't understand..."

"It's the distiboo — the distrrriboo — the weight's all wrong."

"How do you mean?"

"Err...err...who knows what I mean! All I know is that when I'm in the car by myself I don't have any of this trouble... you see it's when all you buggers are in it, it sort of slips down the camber... it's the camber, that's what it is, me old mate."

"Tell him about the crown wheel." This from the now aroused front passenger.

"You shut your face and go back to sleep."

"Tell him about the crown wheel!" This very loudly and insistently.

Jimmy hoped they wouldn't start to fight. They might never get home.

"OK... OK... I'll tell him, buggerlugs... well, you see Jimmy, it's like this... when you start this car, you have to put it into reverse first, otherwise it won't go forward... now the theory is... the theory is... and it's only a theory, mind. The theory is that the teeth on the crown wheel are so old that they are all bent in the direction of forward drive. So you have to put it into reverse to straighten them up enough to engage in... engage in forward... forward... whatsit. Do you see, Jimmy, do you see?"

"Yes, I see."

But what Jimmy saw to his great relief was the gateway of Ferens looming up. They got through without hitting anything and down the drive without running on to the lawn. They all fell out and one of them, Alan, from the back seat next to Jimmy, could not get up again. Jimmy had to support him to his room, open the door for him and direct him so that he fell on to his bed. When he got to his own room he was too tired to worry about Mary, but he did remember to put on his alarm.

When it went off he had no idea where he was but soon became aware of the fact that he needed more sleep. He considered staying where he was, but despite his new found notion of the goodness of God the Father, he knew he could not miss Mass, and especially not on a day when he had to make what might prove to be a difficult journey. He told himself this was mere superstition, but it made no difference: he had to get up. Once on his bike, he felt better and in church he seemed to see everything as charged with a new significance. He tried to pray the Mass, and at the Offertory tried to offer himself and his worries and wants. He thought of Mary and then when he found himself praying that the relationship would prosper, he saw that he was doing again what he'd done when praying for success in exams. He was expecting the Holy Spirit to wave a magic wand. He saw himself as obsequious: bowing and scraping to God so that he could have his way. This was unworthy of his new idea of God and unworthy even of himself. He prayed instead that, whatever happened, he would be sensible, he would be strong – strong enough to accept that the relationship would develop, stay as it was, or even end. During the Consecration, at the words, 'Hic est enim corpus meum,' he thought of himself as being at the Last Supper and that Jesus was offering himself to him, Jimmy, plausible rascal (Father Burden's description of him) from Rupert Grove.

For the first time in many years, perhaps for the first time ever, the significance of that fact occurred to him in all its splendour. At the Consecration of the Blood, he thought hard about the meaning of the words, *'Hic est enim calix sanguinis mei, novi et aeterni testamenti: mysterium fidei: qui pro vobis et pro multis effundetur in remissionem pecatorum'*. The blood of Christ spilt for him – he thought of himself as being on Calvary, witnessing the loss of that blood for the salvation of all men and women. This seemed to be so real that whatever doubts he may have had about his beliefs simply disappeared. He knew life would never be the same again.

Chapter XI

RRANGING HIS TATTY PARCELS on the bike was not easy, and even when he was satisfied that nothing could fall off, he found that it was quite difficult to get on the wretched machine: he had to tip it sideways, slip his leg through the only gap above the crossbar and then gradually, a step at a time, manoeuvre it into an upright position. He did not feel secure, especially as his stuffed knapsack wobbled about on his back, but he set off for Paragon station in good heart, because the sun was shining, and because he had actually got everything attached either to himself or the bike, when earlier it had seemed that something would have to be left behind. People smiled as he went by, which meant that he was conspicuous: he did not mind this too much but he hoped he would not meet the police. Before long he began to feel very hot because he was wearing a suit and a mackintosh, all the pockets of which were stuffed with oddments and, though the road was flat, he had to struggle quite hard to keep the bike going at a reasonable pace as it was so overloaded. There was, however, only one really tricky moment, and that was when he had to stop at one of Hull's many level crossings. He found it difficult to stay upright without putting two feet down on the road and then when he set off again, he was decidedly unsteady, much to the annoyance of the motorists behind him.

He did get there in time to catch the train and, it being Sunday, he was able to find a seat in a compartment next to the guards' van, so that he could keep nipping out to make sure that no one was taking his precious belongings off his bike. He relaxed. This was the easy bit. Once he got to Stalybridge, life became difficult because he had to change trains and at a station to which he had never been before. He clattered out of the guards' van and realized that he would have to go to the main entrance to find out which platform he needed for the next stage of the journey. Inevitably, he had to carry the bike up a flight of stairs and down another, only to discover that the train to Marple left from the platform he had arrived at in the first place. Moreover, he had to wait an hour for his connection. When at last it came, it was the most ancient and decrepit train he had ever seen: it did have a guards' van, but no corridor. It was also surprisingly busy and he could not get a place near the van. The journey was only short in distance but the train stopped at every tin-pot suburb of outer Manchester and at each station Jimmy had to jump out to watch what came out of the van. Marple turned out to be a repeat of Stalybridge: a dash up one staircase and a struggle down another, only to have to return to where he started from. Then his luck changed, because on the next train there was a guard in the van, even though it was Sunday. He asked Jimmy where he was going and said, "Don't worry, lad. I'll see you don't get off without it and I hope you're in time for the carnival".

"The carnival?"

"Aye, the carnival... you have entered it, haven't you?"

"Entered it? What?"

"This 'ere... for the best decorated bike competition. Tell you what though, lad... you'll never win with that. It's ingenious, but there's not enough colour. That's what the judges like: colour."

There were several parcels and trunks and things in the van so Jimmy asked the guard if he could stay there and sit on one of the more solid-looking boxes. The guard agreed: he seemed to be glad of the company and he proved to be a shrewd conversationalist. It was not long before he had Jimmy describing his life as a student. Just before they got to Wellington, the guard said, "Well, there seem to be some daft buggers there, lad. I hope you are not going to waste the opportunity you have been given. It's me and those like me as is paying for it, remember."

Both were quiet for a while and then he asked Jimmy what he would do when he finished. He had no real answer to this and remained silent, but the guard continued to look at him in an expectant way, so he said, "I'm not sure but" (out of the blue) "I suppose I might teach".

"Oh, aye, and what will you teach?"

"History, I guess."

"Whose history?"

"What do you mean 'Whose history?' – Just history!"

"Well, if I'm paying for it I don't want it to be about bloody kings and queens. I want it to be about real people like you and me."

Before Jimmy could protest, he went on. "Look, lad, we all voted Labour in 1945 and now look what we've done? We've put the old lot back in again. Now why is that do you think?"

He did not want an answer, but went on, "I'll bloody tell you why. Because we've forgotten our history... or probably never knew it in the first place. You go and teach the kids about Tom Mann and Joseph Arch and Keir Hardy... tell 'em about the Chartists and..." he paused and Jimmy was able to get in. "You mean about Fergus O'Connor and physical force ...?"

"There you go... that's what they teach kids, isn't it... about the mad ones – the dangerous ones. But what about William Lovett and Chartist Halls and Sunday Schools and the working classes trying to educate themselves? They don't teach that, do they?"

The train was drawing into Wellington station. The conversation would have to end, but the guard kept on and as he helped Jimmy out with the loaded bike he said, "Listen, you go into them schools and teach the kids the other side of the story. Make 'em see where their real interests lie... and you look after yourself too... but think on... it's my money, remember."

They even shook hands and Jimmy felt a sudden wave of affection for this supposedly ordinary working man, for he realized that he was not in the least ordinary: he was not likely to forget the guard. What he did forget, at first, was to worry about the struggle to get the bike out of the station. He was still wondering why he knew about Fergus O'Connor and not about the Halls and the Sunday Schools – and anyway, what were they? If he were a historian, he would make it his business to find out.

However, the luxury of pondering such notions soon evaporated as he was forced to deal with the more immediate difficulties of cycling uphill virtually all the way to Dawley. He got off the bike quite often and at one point even took off his coat and lay on the verge in the shade of a tree. It was Sunday teatime and nobody was about: everyone would be at home enjoying their ham with nicely crisp cos lettuce and fat juicy tomatoes. He became aware of his thirst and looked around for a hawthorn tree, knowing that he could chew its leaves as he had when a child; they tasted better than most of the others, which on the whole were bitter. After Dawley it was downhill all the way and with his coat flying in the wind, and despite the banging he had to take from the miscellaneous objects in his pockets, he free-wheeled almost all the way to Blesses Hill (which the cognoscenti now call Blists Hill). His aunt looked sternly at him when he arrived, with his face all red and his hair stuck to his head as the sweat had dried out in the wind.

"My God! Have you come all the way from Hull like that? What would your mother say if she could see you, I don't know."

"Why? What's the matter?"

"Well, you're all bundled up in all those clothes and the sun's been cracking the flags all day."

Despite having lived in the countryside for more than fifteen years, she still used big city metaphors. They often sounded inappropriate, but somehow they went with the oddness of her accent, which was a disconcerting mixture of Salop and Scouse, and made Jimmy smile at most of what she had to say – that is until he got used to it again. It was one of the many things that endeared her to him, though the most important was that, unlike his mother, she spoilt him.

"Come in, come in and take that lot off. You must be roasting. And just look at that bike! Is it safe with all that piled on it?"

"Well, I'm here, aren't I?"

"Yes, but only by the grace of God and the skin of your teeth by the looks of things." Jimmy got out of his coats. His suit jacket was soaked and he knew it would have to be cleaned, if it were not to smell. He took off his shirt too, and went outside again, this time to the tap, which fortunately stood outside his aunt's house, there being no water in any of the houses in the row. No one would find it in the least odd that he should be having a good swill in public and he did not mind that his best trousers took a soaking too. Once he was in tomorrow's working shirt, though it was crumpled from being in a parcel tied on his bike, and sitting at Aunt Agnes's table, he felt much better. And, sure enough, there was cos lettuce and ham and tomatoes, and strong tea – so you could trot a mouse across it, as his aunt (like Father Smythe) might put it.

Uncle Fred did not arrive till nearly midnight because he was working the afternoon shift, three till eleven, but he was his usual cheerful self and obviously pleased to see Jimmy, one of his favourite nephews, he said, but that meant all of them in fact.

"And have I got a job tomorrow then?"

"Oh, yes. I saw Mr Whitmore on Friday and he said he was expecting you. Ar, he said he's relying on you and John Astley and his friends from the college, because there's such a lot of work on, and they want to get a conveyor built to be ready after the July fortnight. And Mossop says they're short-handed on the yard."

'On the yard' meant all the odd jobs about the place that had little to do with direct production, but had to be done – like unloading the fondu cement that went into the backs of the fire-places the factory made, or providing extra labour when needed by the fitters or the plumber or the carpenter. It might be that a job arose suddenly – because there were extra orders of tiles to be got ready or maybe someone was away sick or at a funeral. During the factory annual holiday, several people were needed to keep certain operations and processes running, and there were always repair jobs or minor works that could only be done when the operatives were away. In fact, one that nobody liked was to help the plumber to service the ladies' lavatories. This was because the other workers who were around made all kinds of smart smutty remarks about what you might be doing in there.

Despite this, Jimmy, when his turn came to do this, found it quite surprising. There was much more pornographic graffiti on the walls and doors than in the men's and it was much more neatly written and drawn. There seemed to be remarks about most of the men in the place. Perhaps this was why chaps did not like going in there: they were afraid of what the women thought about them, their proclivities and their sexual prowess.

At a quarter past seven the next morning, Jimmy, hardly awake yet, free-wheeled down Dabley Lane (elevated to Coalport Road now), remembered to brake when he got to the bottom, clattered across the Memorial Bridge – how sensible of the people of Jackfield to construct it (to replace a ferry) in memory of the dead of the First World War – and into Maw's Tile Factory. There were not many people about because most began work at eight o'clock, but George Benning, foreman of the yard, was there already dishing out work. His eyes lit up when he saw Jimmy – not out of friendship, but because extra hands made it easier for him to make sure everything got done.

"Mornin', Jimmy. How bist?"

"Mornin', George. How bist yourself?"

George did not reply but went on telling people what to do and reorganizing them now that Jimmy was here.

"Watty, you don't have to help Gordon with the faience mix – Jimmy can do that. He's done it before. You can take the broken saggers down to the crusher."

Jimmy was glad to hear this, because working with Gordon, a sort of second cousin of his, meant he would be able to catch up on the doings, the comings and the goings of the Quint family, i.e. all the brothers, sisters, nieces and nephews of Uncle Fred that Agnes had not chatted about the night before. Also, the job was marginally less boring than wheeling saggers down the yard. When taking saggers last year, he discovered that he could load the barrow, wheel it to the crusher – a huge mill wheel rolling round a giant pan and controlled by an incredibly old man also called George – unload and be back again for another lot in four minutes. He had had to find a way to extend this to six minutes, which meant that he would complete ten trips an hour. So he placed the saggers on the barrow in a particularly painstaking way, marched slowly and with great solemnity down the yard, as though he were a soldier at a royal funeral, stacked the cracked and crumbling saggers with as much care as would have been required for the Great Wall of China, and then ceremoniously slow-marched back again. Even then, Tommy Caulfield, the old chap who normally did the job, told him he was going too fast and spoiling it for him. What usually happened of course was that every time Tommy arrived at the wheel he and George both stopped to have a chat and probably a smoke.

Part of George Benning's problem that morning was that Tommy was away at a wedding. Normally, he and Gordon would set everything up and start the faience mixer and then Tommy would go wheeling saggers. Today, however, George wanted all the routine jobs done early so that he could get as many hands as possible, and as soon as possible, digging a trench for a new water-pipe on what was known as the top road. This in turn had to be done quickly because the new conveyor would have to go out over that road and the management did not want both jobs going on at the same time.

As Jimmy and Gordon got the tubs of dust (a greenish clay that had been ground, ready to be pressed into tiles) and those of grout (the crushed saggers, the rough muggen box-like containers in which the unbaked tiles are placed to go in the kiln) and the buckets of water, Gordon talked about the family so much that they nearly forgot to count how many they were tipping into the blunge-pot, but they must have been correct because there were no complaints from the moulders later that day. Whereas tiles, even those six by ten, can be pressed into shape, larger pieces of ceramic have to be moulded or they will have too many faults. This rougher, heavier mixture had to be made first thing every day, so that the big sections of fireplace surrounds could be made later that day.

When they had finished, they set off for the top road – but by a roundabout way. This was not only because Gordon was naturally gregarious, but also because he assumed that Jimmy wanted to renew the old acquaintances of last year. Jimmy did, but always felt acutely embarrassed by this and said he thought they should go straight to the trench: Gordon would not hear of it, so they went through the gloss and dipping departments, then through the bisque-sorting and the press shops, shouting 'hello' to everyone as they went and being greeted all the way by smiles and shouts of recognition. However, halfway down the press shop they caught a glimpse of Whitmore, the managing director, striding towards them in his usual way with his white coat flying, so they dodged out and between the kilns, stumbling over heaps of coal, and being cursed cheerfully by yet another George (one of the many Astons) for kicking up the dust. When they got to the trench they found that some of the younger men had their shirts off because it was so hot already. Everyone was complaining. The job was more difficult than anyone expected. The first foot and a half was easy enough because it was only dusty cinder compressed into place over generations, but the next foot and a half was foundry ash, admittedly only in pieces as big as golf balls, but these had been jammed together over at least a hundred years and had formed a mass nearly as tough as concrete, just like the blocks that lined the banks of the river. At this early stage, they were trying to work merely with crowbars, picks and shovels. Then somebody realized that there was clay under the foundry ash and so they developed another technique, which was to tunnel through the clay and then smash the foundry ash with the crowbars. Someone went to fetch a sledgehammer. The work was still gruelling and not helped by the fact that they were being constantly visited by Whitmore or Mossop, the works manager, or Benning. Jimmy had hoped for lighter work on his first day and at one point reflected on a debate back in the Sixth Form when his arrogant confreres had castigated lazy British workmen, blaming them for all our so-called economic problems. What he was thinking as he smashed the crowbar down, spraining his wrists, was that if his present colleagues did not behave like stereotypical workers and stop to lean on their shovels, then he would soon collapse into the trench. It was a long, hot morning and lunch of only half an hour did not give him sufficient time to recover, especially as by then his hands were well and truly blistered. But as usual at Maw's, other work cropped up and in the afternoon he and Gordon were delegated to go and clear a rubbish shoot that was blocked. This was dangerous because you might easily slip down it into the lorry out in the road below, but it was not grinding work. Nevertheless, when he got home that first day, he fell asleep on the sofa while his aunt was cooking his meal and before he had even had a wash.

The first two weeks at Maw's were full of hard graft and most evenings he did little more than read his uncle's paperback novels – cowboy yarns or detective stories, like *Simon Templar, The Saint*, but he soon discovered that there were few variations in the plots. However, he began to feel less tired in the evenings and so sometimes he would walk across to the All Nations pub where he usually went with Fred who, when he was on mornings, was free in the evening to go for a drink and to play dominoes – his favourite fives and threes. Without Fred, Jimmy would sit in the garden, where there were usually one or two people talking quietly. The beer was very good, home-brewed and as light in colour as bitter, but it was mild.

One particularly pleasant evening he decided to walk along the side of the canal first. This had lost its industrial aspect because it had been many years since coal had been carried along it to be dropped in barges down the 'Incline' and into the canal next to the Severn. The blast furnaces that had been near it were now overgrown ruins, and the foundries had all but disappeared. In fact, with the evening sun shining dazzlingly through the hawthorns, nothing could be seen of the last vestiges of the evidence of those activities that had made this place the cradle of the Industrial Revolution. Jimmy had to cut a stick to chop down the nettles that barred his way, but he got to what remained of the old building which had housed the engine, which had been responsible for lowering the full barges into the canal below and pulling up the empty ones. He went beyond into the fields beneath the Hay Farm, which were known as the banks, and sat down to watch, in the setting sun, the valley below where he used to live. There were people gossiping on the Memorial Bridge, and sitting outside the Boat Inn. He could see too the Duke of Wellington, the former huge pub where so many of Fred's relations still lived. Beyond it was that odd hamlet called the Tuckies, and Robert's Farm. Towards the Coalport Bridge-end of Jackfield, the cottage his family had lived in during the War could just be made out though it was falling down and nettles were beginning to take over. He thought about the best part of his childhood, which had been in that valley before he lost whatever innocence he may have had. He thought too of how far he had come since then, yet he felt disappointed. Had he wasted even the limited talent he knew he must have because he had always been afraid? He never really trusted anyone or anything, least of all his own abilities.

He was overtaken by a feeling that he could not put a name to or understand. It was a kind of sadness and at the same time a longing, but for he knew not what. Yet he was not unhappy and there seemed to be a hint of promise in what he was experiencing – he had a future, and one that had clear possibilities. Suddenly he found himself reflecting on the thoughts that had passed through his mind almost unconsciously as he had cut his way along the canal: he had almost been seduced by the pleasant way of life which he saw all around him. At Maw's he did not have to think. He simply did as he was told, and the work was never really that hard when you got used to it, and he could even see the funny side of his having to unload single-handedly six tons of cement because everyone else was working on the trench. And people here were so pleasant and such good friends, unlike several of those he had worked with at Tillotson's. He realized that he had been toying with the idea of getting a permanent job at Maw's. Then he thought about the boredom, the repetition, the sameness, day in and day out. He had worked one day on what was called the glider. It was a large wooden tray suspended on a runner so that it could literally glide along an overhead bar from the sorting shop to the dipping shop. Two men loaded it up with bisque tiles and pushed them to be dipped. They went backwards and forwards all day. Because one of them was missing for an afternoon, Jimmy had been asked to stand in. The elderly man he helped was invariably and, finally, annoyingly cheerful. It dawned on Jimmy that this poor old chap at some time in the past must have realized how awful his daily life was, but must have decided to make the best of it. Cheerfulness was his antidote to ennui. Jimmy did not want to settle for that, even if Maw's seemed to offer him the safety and security he always felt he needed.

What should he do with his life? He had heard third year students talking about going on the 'milk round' and at first he thought it was only Science undergraduates who did this, but so did the others. He heard mention of Shell, and the Midland Bank, and Lever Brothers – all sorts of companies. He tried to consider what he might find himself doing, and wondered if in the long run he might finish up like Mossop or Whitmore. Somehow, this did not seem right for him. He could not imagine himself taking on the kind of responsibility they must have, and he certainly could not see his present fellow workers taking much notice of any orders he might have to give. Then he remembered his conversation with the guard, when, off the top of his head, he had said he might teach. If he did, it would have to be history – because he felt comfortable with it, and it did seem to be important, and after that conversation, perhaps more important than he had first imagined. But he had disliked school so much! Could he stand being back there? What would it be like to control a class of unruly boys? He recalled at least two teachers, who, even in the strict ferula-ridden ethos of his old school, had had difficulty in asserting their authority. He had also heard that the reason the dreaded Father Burden was such a disciplinarian was because, when he had been a scholastic, boys had played him up: poor sod! He too must have been afraid. If that explained his attitudes and behaviour then Jimmy felt some sympathy for him. But why be like him? What if you could be like Dr Grisedale and make kids laugh? Now, there was a prospect worth considering – if you knew the history – there was the rub – Jimmy felt he did not know very much history really. Then bloody learn it, you soft sod! Yes, that's it! Learn it. But there's so much of it! And you might make a mess of it! And it can be complex and difficult to understand: too difficult for someone as stupid as little Jimmy from Rupert Grove. How could *he* teach in a grammar school? ... But what else could he do? At this point he looked at his hands and was surprised to discover he was tying them in knots. He also became aware that his whole body was tense and that rivulets of cold sweat were running down his sides. Shock at how he was reacting to his own anguish made him feel very afraid: he was being overwhelmed, trapped in the Anderson shelter, and surrounded by the furies in the playground. There was no bolt-hole to run to. 'Jesus, mercy. Mary, help,' came into his head, he knew not from where. He clung to this in desperation, and even repeated it *sotto voce*. He began to recall what he had learned in recent months. Suddenly, he had an image of the prodigal father putting his arms around his errant son. And he remembered Danny's advice: he thought of the hand of Jesus on his head. He prayed, 'Jesus be with me and stay with me,' over and over again. Gradually, he calmed down.

As he walked back along the canal, he realized that he had prayed hardly at all since arriving in Shropshire and his firm intention to read the New Testament had been forgotten. He knew he must make some time every day when he could rectify this and he must develop the habit over the next week, because soon the other students would arrive from Shrewsbury and then he would probably be out in the evenings with them.

Suddenly he stopped and stood still in the evening sunlight. Wasn't he in danger of going full circle, back to the tit-for-tat religion of his childhood, where if you don't pray every day, you can't expect God to love you and help you? Wasn't he returning to superstition and magic formulae? Say the correct spell, all would be well. No, he would not go back to that. He was near a wooden bridge that crossed the canal and led off to a path to the Hay Farm, known as the Rock hole. It was always shaded just there so he went and stood on the bridge and thought again of Jesus' hand on his head. Again he became calm and, instead of rattling off prayers, he closed his eyes and listened. He heard nothing. That did not matter, because, in the silence, he felt very aware – of what? He did not know, but somehow he knew that this was where he ought to be. Furthermore, he discovered that he had a new notion in his head, one that seemed worth contemplating.

Did he love Mary, and, if he did, what did that expression mean? Suppose she loved him. Could he then exploit that situation and use her for his own pleasure? He realized that loving someone meant not wanting to hurt them, or offend them, or use them. It's the reverse of all those things: you want to please the one you love, protect them, be at one with them. And here was the crucial point: wasn't his relationship with Jesus the same? It was not a question of asking the person you love for the things you want, which was so often how he had seen prayer in the past. It was wanting to be with a person, of talking to them and listening to them: just as it had been when he had sat on the banks and worried. His friend, Jesus, had been there with him. And on the bridge, he had heard nothing, but hadn't Christ spoken to him through his own thoughts? Seeing prayer as talking to Jesus, not as a daily chore to be got through, was the message he had received.

He wanted to be with Mary too. He wanted to talk to her. Yet he had put off writing to her, not because it was a chore, but because he knew he would find it difficult. He decided that instead of going to the pub he would start a letter and simply tell her what he'd been doing. So, he went home and wrote: mostly it was about life at Maw's but he tried to make it as funny as possible. He also told her of how pleasant the countryside around was, and in describing how the worst effects of the Industrial Revolution were now hidden, he was able to discuss some history with her. He said he hoped she was enjoying her excursions with Mrs Baggulley, and that she was not working too hard. He posted it the next morning on his way to work.

All the next week he hurried home each day expecting a reply: none came. He began to despair, but he tried not to pray about it in the old way. He simply asked Jesus to be with him. By the following week, the art students had arrived and life became quite tolerable because, no matter how tough the work might be, the chatter never ceased and was often very funny. In the evenings, there were excursions down to the Severn to swim, dashes on bicycles to pubs – one evening they tried cycling to Bridgenorth, stopping at every pub on the way for a half of bitter. Surprisingly, they did not get drunk: they must have pedalled off the effects of the drink between stops. On the other hand, they never got to Bridgenorth. They got fed up with the cycling long before then and went back to the Cuckoo Oak instead, and there they did get drunk.

The trench was finished, but the yard men were responsible for only half of it. John Astley, one of the Shrewsbury students, had worked in the small drawing office at Maw's before he went to do his National Service. He did not return but went to a College of Art instead. However, because he knew the management from the inside he had a certain amount of pull with Whitmore. He persuaded him to hire a digger, having convinced him that it would be cheaper in the long run. So now they started on the conveyor. At first, only Jimmy was involved. A Welsh fitter arrived just after all the parts had been delivered and Jimmy found himself cleaning them all down as he had the printer at Tillotson's. Then he and the fitter built the sections that were inside the factory, with Jimmy working mostly on the block and tackle. They began in the bisque-sorting shop, because the conveyor was to take scrap tile from there up on to the top road where it would be tipped into a lorry and sold for use as hardcore. The job looked difficult but the conveyor went up much more easily than Jimmy expected, because the fitter was a genius at finding ways and means to get the job done safely, even though this meant that sometimes roof supports, from which the conveyor was suspended, had to be strengthened.

The really difficult part of the construction was that which went out over the road, because it had to be high enough for a lorry to go underneath. This meant that a huge frame of very large girders had to be built first. The rest of the yard men and two of the factory's own fitters got on with this, while Jimmy worked inside. A crane was hired for the purpose, but there was still much mauling work to be done: making concrete bases for the uprights, for instance. Jimmy and the Welsh fitter finished the inside only as the finishing touches were being put to the steel frame. It was merely a matter of tightening up nuts and bolts. By now the younger members of the yard gang were confident and competent enough to climb and crawl all over the structure. Jimmy felt diffident and inept. He was told not to use a ladder, because it might slip on the metal, but to go up the girder 'knee over knee': you grip the other side of the girder with both hands, jam one knee slantwise into the channel, put your other knee over the top of the first – you discover that you are in a remarkably secure position, so you can then shimmy up the girder. However, he found that with a very large spanner to control too he did not feel safe, so he got one of the several ladders that had had to be used in earlier stages of the job. At the top of this, tightening up a large nut, he felt quite safe, that is until the spanner slipped just when he was pulling particularly hard on it. He and the ladder came away from the girder – just to the point of balance, where they seemed to remain for an eternity – then they crashed back on to the steel. Jimmy grabbed the girder and clung to it. He went cold all over with the shock. He heard the Welsh fitter's voice calling him from the other end of the frame.

"Jimmy, bring your spanner over here for a minute, will you?"

Almost in a dream, he climbed up the rest of the ladder and stepped on to the steel beam. Without looking down, he walked across. The Welshman beckoned him to come close and then in a very firm but whispered voice, he all but spat at Jimmy, "Now, my lad, because you had the nerve to cross over to me, I'll let you stay on this job, but you go back now, take that ladder away, and in future, do as you are fucking told!"

Jimmy was even more shocked by this because the fitter was usually a very kindly man. He retraced his steps and this time did as he had been told. As he recovered his composure and thought back over the incident, it occurred to him that no one else was aware of what had happened. At lunchtime he made sure he sat near the fitter and when nobody else was around he thanked him for his concern and from keeping it from the others.

"That's all right, boyo, but I was serious about turning you off the job. If you had stayed paralysed with fear you could be a danger to others. It's sensible to be afraid in a job like this, but fear is a bad master – always remember that, Jimmy." He was beginning to realize this anyway.

That evening, Jimmy made an excuse not to go out with the others, because he needed to think things through. He went and sat on the banks again. At first, he could think of nothing: he was not even sure why he had come, but looking once more at the valley below, he remembered the feeling of regret and yet longing that he had experienced and how in some way it was tied into his future life. Then it became quite clear to him that his problem was fear. Really, he had always known this, but somehow the incident on the conveyor frame had crystallised it. Fear is essential, but it can paralyse us, prevent us living fruitful lives. What the fitter had said encapsulated this. Jimmy needed a way of dealing with it, so that he did not feel like running away in search of a hiding place. There were no hiding places. But how could he cope with that awful thought? As the sense of anguish built up, he reflected on that too. He remembered that in Gethsemane, Jesus was so engulfed in it that he had sweated blood. Jimmy expected Jesus to stand by him, but who had stood by Jesus? He thought he would follow the story through, imagining that he was the young man who lost his shirt and ran away naked.

Earlier that evening, they had all been so firm. Anything Jesus wanted them to do, they were certain they would have the courage to achieve. If he suffered, they would suffer too. But then in the garden, he felt so tired: he'd had a long hard day. He looked towards Jesus where he knelt alone, praying. It's all right for him. He's used to it and he never seems to want any sleep. He thought, I'll just close my eyes for a while, to give them a little rest. I won't go to sleep. Later, he slowly became aware, through half-open eyes, that something was happening. He could just make out in the flickering light of the dying torch that Jesus was bending over, speaking to Peter, who was raised up on one elbow. Were they arguing? He couldn't tell. He drifted off into sleep again. The next time he awoke it was with a start and at first he was not sure of where he was because, even though there were more torches now, it was very dark, the middle of the night. It was only when he heard Jesus' voice saying, 'Why have you come with swords and staves to arrest me as though I were a thief,' that he became fully conscious of what was happening. Suddenly he felt very afraid. He pressed close to the others in a vain effort to give himself some sort of protection, but they were as afraid as he and he sensed their mounting panic: his fear became all but unbearable. There was a scuffle and in the dim light he thought he saw the flash of a sword. Briefly the assailants stood back and Jesus stepped forward and touched one of them, saying something as he did so. There was a moment of silence and stillness: nobody seemed to know what to do. All at once the soldiers leapt forward and grabbed Jesus. Then they began to try to take the others. Someone clutched at his shirt and in horror he pulled away: his shirt came off, but he sensed that he was free. Down through the trees he went, through the nettles, with the brambles snagging at him, down to the town. But where could he go, where could he hide? And he was naked! He could not go home. His mother had despaired of him when he had taken up with Jesus who she thought was mad. His father thought he was a subversive. By chance, he found himself near the place where Ruth lived. She was someone from the past, the drunken and debauched time before he had met Jesus. She would help him, that is if she did not have some man with her. Her door was not barred. It opened to his push. As quietly as he could he called to her, but his voice had become a hoarse croak before she answered him. She struck a light and peered at him.

"Joseph! What do you want? It's the middle of the bloody night... My God, you're naked. Where are your clothes?"

"Ruth, I'm in terrible trouble. I've nearly been arrested. That's how I lost my shirt. Have you got something I can put on?"

"I bet it's that Jesus isn't it? I told you that fellah spelt trouble."

"Yes. I was with him. He's been arrested, so can I stay here?"

"You've got a bloody cheek... I don't hear from you for months... and then you turn up naked... and you're all scratched too... Look at your legs!"

He sensed a note of sympathy in her voice, and said, "Please, please, Ruth, help me. You're the only one I can depend on... and have you got something I can put on?"

She turned and picked up what appeared to be a cloak from her bed.

"Oh, here. You'd better put this on... And I'll look at those cuts."

He sat down on a stool and she got a cloth and water from a large pot. She began to wipe his legs clear of blood. His scratches were not as bad as they had seemed at first. She looked at him and her face softened into a smile.

"I'm going back to bed... Are you coming?"

In the morning, when he awoke next to Ruth, he thought he was back in his former life and a great surge of regret and disappointment passed over him. Then he remembered why he was there and disappointment became despair. He looked down at her. She was beautiful, especially in gentle sleep, with her face smooth and untroubled. But what had he lost! He leapt out of bed so violently that she awoke with a start.

"What's the matter!? What's happened?"

"Oh Ruth! What have I done? What have I done?"

She stared at him in amazement. And he went on, "I've lost the greatest prize I ever had, and all because of abject fear and cowardice."

"What do you mean? What prize?"

"I deserted Jesus, when I should have defended him."

"Don't be silly. How could you have defended him against the might of the Temple and the Sanhedrin?"

"I could have stood by him. I should have been arrested with him so that I could die with him."

"Now I know you're mad!"

"I'll have to go and find out what has happened to him."

Now she jumped out of bed and held his arms.

"Look, you can't go out like that and if what you told me about last night is true, then it could still be dangerous. You stay here and have something to eat and I'll go out and get you some clothes and see if I can find out what's going on."

While she was out, he paced up and down her small room wringing his hands, not knowing what to do in his anguish. He could not eat the food she had left him. He felt sick and all the time he tried to imagine what had happened to Jesus and the others. She was a long time and he was almost prostrate with worry by the time she came back.

"What's happened to him?"

"Well, it's difficult to tell. People are saying all sorts of things but he's been taken backwards and forwards in the night – from Caiaphas to Annas to Herod and back and now he's with Pilate, they say. They want him executed and the Temple people are out stirring up trouble for him."

"How do you mean?"

"They're saying he's a blasphemer, and a Sabbath breaker, and a rebel: they want the Romans to crucify him."

"Crucify him! Oh, that's a ghastly end! Oh, what shall I do?"

"Do nothing, Stay here."

"No, no. I can't. I'll have to go and see."

"Don't be so soft. You can't."

"I must!"

"Then, if you're going, I'm coming with you... if it's only to make sure you don't do anything daft. Put these on."

Ruth made sure they stayed away from the main thoroughfares as far as possible, but even in the by-ways everyone was talking about what was happening. And gradually it became clear that he had been condemned and that he was being taken to Golgotha. They approached the route through a narrow alley and as they got to the end they could see the crowd milling about and could tell that Jesus was nearby. Ruth pushed him forward and he found himself looking straight into the eyes of Jesus. It was only just possible to tell it was him: he was covered in blood: blood flowing on already matted blood, with the cruel crown of thorns oozing more. His hair and beard were caked with gore and dirt where he had fallen. The long robe he wore was also covered in dirt and blood, with signs of the scourging showing through. His mouth was half open and drooping and he was already having to fight for his breath. Joseph thought that Jesus could never forgive him for deserting him in such a cowardly way but as he looked into those eyes what he saw was pity, not pity for himself but for him, Joseph, and he knew that despite his worthlessness, Jesus had forgiven him. Completely overwhelmed, he collapsed, only to be kicked aside by the soldiers and trampled by the mob. He did not care. He sobbed and Ruth crouched beside him and put her arms about his shoulders.

He was surprised that he had thought this through without being distracted, but it was as though the plot had carried him onwards by itself. Did it mean anything? What should he make it mean? 'Think! think!' he told himself. Then what he knew already became clear to him. In the eyes of the Father, the Son and the Holy Spirit, he was not worthless, no matter what he had done, no matter how often he had imagined he had rejected them. Like the prodigal son, he merely had to go back to them: put himself in their presence. They would always be with him. Did he really believe this? The shadow of a doubt flickered across his mind. What if all this should ever be put to the test?

Chapter XII

T HE NEXT DAY THERE was a letter from Mary. It was not very different from the one he had sent her. Certain pleasantries were followed by the expected banalities: how much work she had done, accounts of the places she had visited with Mrs Baggulley. There was even a clichéd description of the waves at Scarborough being like white horses. Then, at the very end, almost as a postscript, came two sentences that had almost the same effect on him as the spanner slipping off the nut.

"I met a third year student in the library and we've had lunch together once or twice. His name is John Webster and he seems very nice."

What shook him was not that he had a rival but who that rival was. Johnny Webster had a bad reputation as a womaniser. Jimmy immediately imputed to him all the seducing skills of a Don Juan. Someone as innocent as Mary, who did not know the ways of the world, might easily fall victim to him, especially as she was unfailingly nice to people: look at her attitude to that old bat, Baggulley! And if Webster realized how holy, yes, holy, Mary was, he would see her as a really great conquest. But the worst aspect of the anxiety that he now felt was that he could do little about it because she was so far away.

He was not his usual self at work and the others began to suspect something was wrong. However, he could not bring himself to discuss Mary with any of them, not even with John Astley to whom he was closest. He tried to act as normally as possible, but it was very difficult: he felt that all he said sounded false and there were times when he was so jumpy that the wrong words came out. Fortunately, people thought he was trying to be funny. Because it was Friday and they would be paid, everyone wanted to go to the Half Moon pub at lunchtime – just for one pint, as usual, so Jimmy was sure no one would come with him when he went to the post office instead. It was a fair walk down a road that had once been straight but was now all twisted and humpy because of landslips – the railway nearby had had to close. The journey suited his mood, especially because it was heavily wooded with many of the trees now at strange angles. He had to try to think things through again and he began by praying. At first he went through all the prayers of his childhood: the Our Father, the Hail Mary, the Glory Be, and so on. Then he tried to imagine himself with Christ, with the hand of Jesus on his head. The first thought that struck him was that he was imagining that Mary had no will of her own, and the second was that if Jesus was with him then he most certainly was with Mary too. She was well protected and he could pray that she remained so. It was not as though she were being bombed! He felt comforted by these notions, but there was still a niggling doubt. What was it Cromwell had said: 'Trust in God *and* keep your powder dry.' Then something his mother often said also occurred to him: 'The Lord helps those who help themselves.' He could not stop the next thought coming into his head, no matter how inappropriate it might be because she had always followed with: 'And the Lord help those found helping themselves.' He smiled to himself. He had decided in that instant what his course of action should be. He would do what he could do and would leave the rest to Providence. He would write her another letter, warning her, in as careful a way as possible, about Webster, and – here was the bold part – inviting her to come and stay with Aunt Agnes and Uncle Fred for a short holiday. That way he could be sure she was well away from danger.

Writing the letter was not easy. Every phrase he could think of to describe John Webster was either too mild or wildly overstated the case, and always sounded presumptuous. Finally, he settled for expressing surprise that she should become friendly with someone like him, because, he said, thinking about Webster made him look for the beam in his own eye. The invitation to come and stay with Agnes and Fred he preceded with a restate-

ment of the delights of the countryside and of its historical importance – not only to the Industrial Revolution, but also to medieval architecture because of the abbeys at Buildwas and Much
Wenlock. Linked with the latter, he also mentioned, perhaps only
half consciously, to mark the difference between himself and
Webster, the Catholic Church in Madeley, which was surprisingly
old. Actually composing the letter made him think again about
his relationship with Mary: he did seem to be presuming too
much. He did not really know very much about her, except that
she did have a family and came from London. How large or small
the family might be and where in London it was to be found he
had no idea. He wondered too if perhaps he had misjudged her
character: she appeared to be quiet and gentle; she was obviously
intelligent, with wide interests; and her religious conviction was
clearly apparent. But at the dance she had behaved out of character, and even seemed a bit wild. Then on the way home, when
she became silent, he had sensed that she could be stubborn.
Perhaps, he thought, he was becoming obsessed with an ideal of
gentleness, which he had created during the time when he had
observed her from a distance and had been afraid to approach
her. Momentarily, he considered not posting the letter, but then
nothing would be resolved. He had to push matters forward: he
sent it.

He did not expect an immediate reply and he knew there was
a chance that it would not reach Hull before she left, but he tried
not to worry too much. In fact, life in the factory, now that the
conveyor was completed, returned to normal, that is for a factory
holiday period. However, it was not such good fun because
more often than not the gang of students had to be split up so
that all the various repair and maintenance jobs could be done.
One Monday, he found himself working with George Aston,
who normally fired kilns: he was working his holiday. George
resented students a little, but Jimmy more especially because so
far he had 'got out of' National Service while George's sons had
had to do it. During their morning break, George was complaining that he had a headache as a result of drinking too much beer.
He then asked Jimmy what he had done on Sunday. Jimmy told

him about going down the river to Swinney for a swim with John Astley and how they had got involved with a game of cricket.

"Cricket! On a Sunday? It shouldn't be allowed."

"Why not?"

"It's the Lord's Day. Don't they teach you students anything?"

There was no way of answering this so Jimmy said nothing. George was a kindly man really and did not want to pursue the matter further. But Jimmy felt riled. A little later he said, "Did you go to church yesterday, George?"

"No."

"I did... and I didn't go to the pub and get drunk."

It was George's turn not to respond but the look he gave Jimmy meant that he had better be careful. They were working in a very confined space – inside a blunge pot in which fresh clay was mixed with water and stirred and agitated at great speed. The agitators, called legs, were simply flat bars that ran down the middle of the pot and turned outwards at right angles just above the floor. They had iron shoes attached to them to make them more efficient. Every year these had to be inspected and replaced if they were badly worn. Occasionally, legs too had to be replaced and this was not easy because, not only were they heavy, it was also difficult to slot them into place because they had to be a tight fit. Both men had to get bars underneath the leg and lift at the same time as each other. Then, one of them had to put the first bolt through while the other got ready with a nut. They had just done this. In fact they'd got the second bolt in. They could relax a little, but they were very hot, sweaty and breathing heavily, and George no doubt was suffering more than Jimmy, who was no longer paying attention. His spanner was down by his side and the nut where it should have been was turning with the bolt. George realized what was happening.

"Put that theeah."

"What where?"

"That theeah!"

"What where?"

"Put thy bloody spanner on the soddin' nut!"

"Well, why didn't you say that?"

George Timmons

George was now very angry, because this smart-arsed student was showing up his lack of education, and had he been asked, Jimmy would have had to own up that he had something of the sort in mind.

"For two pins I'd…"

He raised his spanner very close to Jimmy's nose, their heads already being only a foot apart, because of the confined space. Jimmy realized too late the full effect of what he had implied and was now rather scared. He knew he had to brazen it out. He raised his spanner and said in his strongest Liverpool accent, "George, I'm a younger man than you and much fitter…"

They glared at each other with wide, staring eyes. Fortunately for both of them, working near them helping to strip down an engine on another pot was Billy Hughes, who heard all this but could see only their heads emerging from the top of the pot. He began to laugh almost uncontrollably, but so infectiously that the spell was broken and they both began to smile, George perhaps less willingly than Jimmy.

So the days went by with plenty to do and that meant weekends too, because there were never enough men to cope with all that needed to be done. Jimmy was glad, and not only because it kept him occupied, but also because on Sundays you got double time: his wage packets were particularly big.

The letter came earlier than expected. It had a London postmark, and for some reason that he could not explain, Jimmy felt depressed when he saw it. It had no address to which he could reply.

London, Wednesday.

Dear Jimmy,

Thank you for your letter. It arrived just before I left Hull, but as you can see I am now at home with my family. Thank you for your kind invitation to stay with your aunt and uncle, but I'm afraid that is impossible and I'm not sure it would be wise. Thank you yet again – for your concern about my moral character! You seemed to be implying that it was in danger, but your letter was rather vague. I think that is what you

234

meant but it was difficult to tell. However, I am perhaps more aware of what is going on than you think. I do know about John Webster's reputation, but I had lunch with him and that is all and he is charming and rather more civilised than some other men at Hull – particularly the sporty ones.

I'm going to find the rest of this letter difficult to write but remember that if it is painful for you, it is painful for me too. I do like you and I enjoy your company. I want to thank you (yet again!) for that wonderful evening at the end of term. I had had a particularly trying time over the weeks before, not only because of essays and Catholic Society work but also because of worries about my family. So the concert and then especially the dance were just what I needed. The result may have been that I gave you the wrong impression. If so I am sorry.

What I have to say is that I do not want a serious relationship – not with you, nor anyone else. At least not in the foreseeable future. It is very unlikely that marriage will ever be my vocation. In case you think I'm off to a nunnery, I don't know yet what my vocation is, but I feel certain that it will involve me fully and would be unfair to a husband and even more to children. I'm not sure quite what line to follow: it may be social work, or work with children or maybe I will go abroad, perhaps with the United Nations, maybe UNESCO. I don't want to upset you but if I don't tell you now, the hurt could be worse later for both of us.

I'm sure we can be friends and I hope this does not put you off coming to Catholic Society. I hope too that some day you can find a nice girl-friend who can respond better to you than I can. Thank you for your friendship. May God bless you.

Yours Sincerely,

Mary.

He was surprised that he remained calm. He put the letter down on the table. Aunt Agnes came in from the kitchen.
    "Not bad news, is it?"

"No... it's just a letter from a friend at Hull."

"You look very pale... Are you all right?"

"Yes, I'm OK... I've been working for Jack today, painting still-lage pipes" (which was true), "and I think the paint has got on my stomach."

"Oh, I see." But she did not believe him, He pushed the letter into his pocket and said, "I'm just going down the garden".

This was a euphemism for going to the toilet, because that is where it was and he could think of nowhere else to be by himself without raising questions. It was like a small house but consisted inside of a low brick wall and a long wooden seat with two holes in it: a large one for adults and a small one for children. He lit a cigarette because the smell in there took some getting used to, even though, unlike many of the toilets round about, this one was flushed – by a stream about ten feet below, which ran from the canal behind the house to another larger stream, which flowed in turn into the Severn. He felt a sense of loss, of promise dashed. Then he began to feel annoyed – with himself. How presump-tuous of him to expect her to come and stay with them. How presumptuous of him to warn her about John Webster. She could well know as much about him as she did about Jimmy, whom she had been out with only once and he had always half suspected that she saw him as part of the yobbish sporty fraternity. But the loss struck him again. He had begun to consider it possible that he and she had some sort of future together, and the person he had assumed she was in the days when he had watched her from afar was so attractive in her gentleness. Now gone. He was begin-ning to sound like something out of a fairy story: he thought of Emilie, pined over by Palamon and Arcite in the *Knight's Tale*, and for no other reason than the Chaucer connection, patient Griselda came into his head and he had never been able to take her seriously: stupid cow! Suddenly he felt ridiculous. Could he ever look her in the eye again? He felt confused because these thoughts were in no way consoling, nor did they reduce the feel-ing of grief. He wondered about saying a prayer, but the setting seemed inappropriate. He walked back through the garden, felt the warm evening sun on his back and resented it. What right had it got to be so normal?

With great difficulty he managed to eat most of the meal his aunt had prepared for him and for this he was glad because this meant that she would not ask him any further questions about the letter, and had probably believed his story about the paint. He was trying very hard to act as normally as possible, so he had got washed and changed as he did every evening. John arrived and asked if Jimmy would like to visit some friends of his. For the sake of the charade he was playing, and to avoid the possibility of further interrogation from Agnes, he agreed to go. As they travelled by bike there was no need to talk and Jimmy rode behind so that John could not see how morose he was, nor that he was saying over to himself, 'Jesus Christ, Son of the living God, have mercy on us'.

The friends lived in an unbelievably small cottage in Madeley Wood, but this did not bother them because they had just got married. On discovering this, Jimmy almost set off back home again: the last thing he wanted to see was this vision of domestic bliss. However, this situation actually turned out to be helpful. Despite the dreamlike quality of his existence and what seemed to him to be the falsity of his conversation, the evening was very pleasant and the Barnetts in love with each other without being gooey about it. Because they were old school friends of John, everything was very relaxed and Jimmy was accepted as though he had been to school with them too. Gradually he unwound and on one occasion even laughed. This was at a story she told from a child in the primary school where she taught.

"A and B were sitting on a fence and A fell off. What did B say?"

"Don't know," came the chorus.

"Never mind A!"

Only Jimmy laughed. The other two groaned. The effect was more therapeutic than could be imagined because, not only did the laugh relax him, it also took him back to the Pit and Jenny. It was not how he felt at the time when she had disappeared to Coventry that came back to him, but how quickly he had got over the disappointment. Moreover, charming though the Barnetts were, and idyllic though their situation might be, he came to the conclusion that he did not envy them. He, no more than Mary, was ready to commit himself. He went home in an easier frame of mind than he could have hoped for. Nevertheless, reading the letter again by candlelight in the privacy of his own bedroom, he suddenly felt engulfed again by a surge of disappointment and regret. Then, he prayed, but not that Mary would change her mind: he asked for the mental strength to get over it, to see things from her point of view. Re-reading certain parts of her letter, he saw how brave she was and how sensible. Yet he still needed to know that Christ was there with him, consoling him.

As the days went by, he found that he felt less angry and less often. He was still sad, but the stretches of time when he did not think of Mary got longer and longer, and he began to enjoy the company of the other students and workers in the factory. Some evenings he went along the canal again: he was sure Jesus was with him on the little bridge and the message seemed to be that a lesson had been learned. It was that he was now older and wiser; that in the future he should not let romantic expectations blind him to the realities of life; that he should be more circumspect with other people and not put demands on them. Sometimes, sitting on the banks and looking down at Jackfield and Coalport, he became aware of a new sense of calm: it was not that he was no longer afraid, but that he could cope with the fear.

On the evening of the final day in the factory, he and John had agreed to go swimming at Swinney, but at the last minute, John cried off and Jimmy decided to go by himself. There were usually other people there so it was safe. Also, Jimmy's healthy appetite had returned: he had eaten rather too much sausage and mash, but as he strolled slowly down past Coalport Bridge and along the shady path, bordered as it was with luscious high summer greenery, he felt more content than he had since the carefree days of childhood. The evening was warm, a little heavy in fact, and clouds of gnats chased each other in the slanting sun. However, when he arrived at the swimming spot, no one was there. He felt a little unsure of himself and decided not to go in immediately: some others might come later. Perhaps he was a little early and it was pleasant just to sit and watch the river making its slow progress at this wide shallow point.

After about half an hour a slight breeze blew up and there was still nobody but Jimmy there. Recklessly, he made up his mind to go in before it got any colder, though it was still quite warm. The water felt good: it was just at the right temperature and he swam leisurely and easily in the shallows. However, he realized that this was not very exciting without others there to enjoy it with you. About forty yards further on, the river narrowed. There was a short stretch where it pulled you relentlessly if you got in it. It was smooth and powerful, then it broke into a series of quite high waves for a hundred yards before they petered out in another wide section. It was surprisingly easy to cope with all this and nowhere was it very deep. Jimmy always enjoyed being pulled by the water as it surged through the narrow gap and if you then swam over-arm in the waves you could flash down the river at incredible speed. He had never done this by himself before but he could not resist the urge to try it again. He allowed himself to be pulled, at first gently and then ever more forcefully towards the narrows. He got into a sitting position because it was really shallow just there, and the idea was that as you got to the turbulent part you pushed off into the swimming position. He was at this critical point when he felt a violent pain in his stomach, the effect of which was to double him up and bring his head down into the water just as he was taking a deep breath. The water got into his lungs and he began to retch and cough, but the pain pulled him down again. He knew it was the dreaded cramp so feared by swimmers, but he had never expected that it would be in the stomach, thus preventing you from straightening up. He was also now being tossed by the waves so did not know which way was up. Yet for a brief moment this worked in his favour because his head came out of the water when by chance he was trying to take a breath. As the pain pulled him down again, he shut his mouth. 'Jesus Christ, Son of the Living God, have mercy on me!' Then his feet touched the bottom, but not for long enough for him to take advantage of it. The relentless pain took his head down once more and he prayed, 'Jesus, Jesus, let me hit the bottom again,' and he did. Jimmy stretched backwards as hard as he could against the pull of the pain and his head came out of the water. He took a huge breath and felt that perhaps he might make it. The pain got him again, and he prayed, 'Jesus, Jesus, help me'. Immediately, something struck his hand and he realized that he had come to a stretch where a willow had toppled into the river and he grabbed at the branches so that the next time he was curled up in pain, he came partly out of the water. He was able to breathe... and then to relax. He had survived. Though he was still panting, he was struck by how happy he felt: he had reached his safe haven.

He clawed his way through the partly-fallen tree and got to the bank, where he lay panting for several minutes. He began to shiver, but the euphoria he had experienced the moment he knew he was safe was still with him, and he realized he was smiling. He made his way back along the bank to his clothes, picked up his towel and began to dry himself: that pleasant sensation that often comes over you as you remove the wet and feel instead the warmth of the sun came to him. He felt alive.

Yet the true significance of the incident occurred to him fully only in the middle of the night. He woke at about three o'clock and realized that he needed to go down the garden. He lay awake for a while, reluctant to leave his comfortable bed but, finally, urgency drove him to get up, go downstairs as quietly as possible and go out into the garden. As he made his way down the path towards the toilet he became aware of the brilliance of the pre-dawn sky: it ran from midnight blue in the west to a silvery azure in the east. Several stars were visible even in the palest part of the sky. Feeling wide awake, as he made his way back up the path, he decided to sit on Fred's bench at the top of the garden and savour this beauty.

At first his mind seemed to be overwhelmed by how almost imperceptibly the blue changed from dark to light. No one, he was sure, could paint the scene. But God could. He then remembered that he had once read that God was not only all-powerful but all-beautiful, and this led him to wonder how he could ever have doubted that God existed: what he was looking at could not have occurred randomly. It was paradoxically both utterly simple and yet wonderfully complex. He knew that the scientific explanations of what he was looking at were, at one and the same time, both elegant and sophisticated and this, it now dawned on him, fitted his developing notion of God. The economy of it all pointed towards Him, not because of some spurious notion of design, but because it made Jimmy aware of a creative thrust that could only have come from a being whose very nature was beautiful – and loving. Loving because this being knew Jimmy personally, and had either saved him that day or, at the very least, had been very close to him.

Jimmy thought of the two occasions he had come close to death: today in the river and so long ago in the tumbling pantry under the stairs in the air raid. Whether or not Christ had intervened directly did not matter. What did was that Jesus, the Son of God, had been with him on both occasions. He knew that he would be afraid again – it was part of life. However, fear would not rule his life ever again because, whatever happened, he now had a safe haven – indeed he always had, and that safe haven was Jesus.